Praise for *Cicada Summer*

"*Cicada Summer* is more than just a fantastic summer read. Maureen Leurck has written a captivating novel about the power of redemption and the benefit of never quitting. With characters who feel more like friends and situations that anyone would swear really happened, *Cicada Summer* perfectly blends enough drama, humor, and romance to satisfy in *every* season. Leurck's novel is everything I love about women's fiction."
—Jen Lancaster, *New York Times* bestselling author

"*Cicada Summer* is a compelling, heartfelt novel of perseverance and second chances. With a setting that is as winsome and real as the story's characters, readers will love this escape to Geneva Lake."
—Michelle Gable, *New York Times* bestselling author of *A Paris Apartment*

"Turns out renovating a heart is a lot like renovating a home: work from the inside out, expect disasters, and keep the faith. Maureen Leurck shows us just that in the touching and relatable *Cicada Summer,* her novel about starting over with tenacity, grace, and the inevitable yet necessary stumbles along the way."
—Zoe Fishman, author of *Inheriting Edith*

"In this uplifting story of hard-won second chances, Maureen Leurck skillfully reminds us that sometimes finding the way to a better future means first finding the courage to face the past. Absorbing and inspiring with well-drawn characters and a beautiful, vivid lake setting."
—Kristin Harmel, internationally bestselling author of *The Sweetness of Forgetting*

"A lovely summer read that weaves together two stories full of love, hope, and memories."
—Nan Rossiter, author of *Summer Dance*

Please turn the page for more praise for *Cicada Summer.*

CICADA
SUMMER

MAUREEN LEURCK

KENSINGTON BOOKS
www.kensingtonbooks.com

KENSINGTON BOOKS are published by

Kensington Publishing Corp.
119 West 40th Street
New York, NY 10018

All Kensington titles, imprints, and distributed lines are available at special quantity discounts for bulk purchases for sales promotion, premiums, fund-raising, educational, or institutional use.

Special book excerpts or customized printings can also be created to fit specific needs. For details, write or phone the office of the Kensington Sales Manager: Kensington Publishing Corp., 119 West 40th Street, New York, NY 10018. Attn. Sales Department. Phone: 1-800-221-2647.

Kensington and the K logo Reg. U.S. Pat. & TM Off.

eISBN-13: 978-1-4967-0653-9
eISBN-10: 1-4967-0653-6
First Kensington Electronic Edition: August 2017

ISBN-13: 978-1-4967-0652-2
ISBN-10: 1-4967-0652-8
First Kensington Trade Paperback Printing: August 2017

10 9 8 7 6 5 4 3 2 1

Printed in the United States of America

For Kevin, Ryan, Paige, and Jake

CHAPTER 1

If home is where the heart is, the house at 4723 Maple Street was in dire need of a cardiologist. The first time I saw the century-old four square, I wanted to reach out and give it a hug. The front porch sagged toward the walkway like a droopy sock, and the stucco on the second floor bubbled and pulled away from the frame like the entire structure was mid-crumble, a process hastened by the humidity from the lake a few blocks away.

Likely, the inside hadn't hosted a human being in years, and a variety of animals had ravaged everything from the wood floors to the electrical system. Yet, I could still see the beauty of what it once was and what it might become again.

I knew I could restore it and give it a second chance.

And so, on the April morning of the bank auction a week later, I stood in the spring rain in front of the Walworth County Courthouse in Elkhorn, Wisconsin, and hoped that the cashiers' checks in my purse would total enough to buy the house.

A familiar shape appeared next to me as I clutched the handle of my umbrella.

"Did they change the age requirements for bidding?" Jack Sullivan said as he smoothed back his prolific white hair.

"Funny. Shouldn't you be enjoying your old age with soft foods and game show reruns?" I turned my back slightly. Jack Sullivan was my father's high school classmate and, despite knowing that I was thirty-four, still found it hilarious to act as though I was fourteen.

He laughed, his tan, leathery skin nearly cracking off. "Probably. I couldn't pass up a chance to bid on this beauty, though."

"You seem to never miss a chance to destroy historic properties," I said. "How about you let me have this one?"

"Sorry, hon. Comps in the neighborhood are in the mid-five-hundreds. Vacation properties and new construction, of course."

I swallowed hard as I thought of his backhoe arriving at the house and turning the structure into a pile of rubble with one nudge of the machine. Likely, a two-story, four-bedroom house with brick facing and vinyl siding would be erected within six months. The bathrooms would house builder-grade vanities and ceramic tile that some buyers would mistake for travertine. The kitchen would have Corian countertops made to look like granite, and cabinets from one Swedish home furnishing store. All of it tailored to convenience, ease of upkeep, and neutrality.

The buyers wouldn't care about the house itself, only that it was five blocks from Lake Geneva, one of the most popular tourist destinations in the Midwest thanks to the size and beauty of the clean, spring-fed lake. Equidistant from both Milwaukee and Chicago, wealthy buyers from the cities would trample each other to use it for a vacation home or a rental property. The lakeshore was dotted with enormous summer estates that had been erected a hundred years ago by alliterative household last names like Walgreen, Wrigley, and Woolworth.

"Did you see the built-ins in the dining room?" he whispered. "Bet those have been around for decades." He sighed. "But soon, no more. My buyers want durable, not historic."

My face reddened as I thought of the quarter-sawn oak buffet in the dining room. It had leaded glass doors, etched in an argyle pattern. I couldn't get inside the house, but I'd seen it through the grimy windows. The wood was probably donated by one of the trees in the front yard and the leaded glass looked like it needed some repairs, but I could tell that it was able to be restored. I smiled as I thought of polishing it with lemon oil and running my fingertips over the worn, grooved wood.

"Over my dead body will you rip this house down and put up some vacation property, old man," I said.

He opened his mouth to retort, but the auctioneer thankfully silenced him.

"Bidding on the house at Maple Street, REO, will begin at $53,000," the auctioneer said.

Jack raised his paddle first, but a flurry of other paddles also were raised in the air. It started to rain harder, but no one moved.

"Do I have $175,000?" the auctioneer said, his lips moving quicker than the rest of his body.

I raised my paddle, and resisted the urge to look in my purse. My self-imposed limit for the house was $209,000. With the needed repairs, I couldn't afford to pay more.

"180,000? Do I have $180,000?" the auctioneer said.

Jack raised his bid again and turned to me. "Sorry, Alex. This one isn't in the cards for you."

My insides burned and I quickly raised my paddle again, bidding $200,000, even as the rational part of my brain begged me to stop, to give this one up. I had dreamed of restoring an old house near the lake for years, but all I had worked on were condos and easy, midcentury ranch houses that were on the outskirts of town in the squarely residential areas. But this was the one. The one that I had been waiting for.

It was the kind of house I had always imagined bringing back to life. It was the kind of house I had admired when I was young and would walk through town with my parents, staring up at the old mansions in town, wondering what kind of charmed secrets and luxuries were hidden inside. It was the kind of house that I imagined would bring happiness to the people who lived there simply by being so beautiful.

"$210,000," Jack said.

I slowly closed my eyes and bit down hard on my lip, trying to stifle my next bid. It didn't work.

"$220,000," I said, my voice barely above a whisper.

Jack gave a low whistle. "You're out of your league, Alex."

"Not the first time I've heard that, but thanks," I said. My eyes darted around wildly, half-hoping someone else would outbid me.

But the bid remained and the auctioneer said, "Sold! For $220,000 to Alex Proctor."

"Good luck, kiddo. You're going to need it," Jack said, giving me a conciliatory pat on the shoulder.

"Not a chance," I said, but the panic began to bubble in my stomach as I slowly walked over and handed over the funds in cashier's checks. I hoped we didn't find anything unusual in the house, or else my profit margin on the project would be nonexistent. A fruitless endeavor filled with dirt, sweat, and rodents.

"Here ya go. All yours," the clerk said as she unceremoniously pushed a key in my direction.

I held it in my hand and took a deep breath. *It will all be worth it,* I told myself. *This is something I've always wanted to do.* And when I was done, the house would host a family, through good times and bad. They would walk to the lake and appreciate the way it seemed crystal clear, even during the summer season, when boats churned through the water like a thousand duck feet.

The house would become a home again.

"Mom, does your new house have spiders in it?" My daughter Abby looked at me, her dark blue eyes narrowed in suspicion. She sucked a few macaroni noodles off her spoon and licked her lips.

I smiled. "I hope not. It's beautiful, Ab. I'll take you over there to see it once we get all of the junk cleared out."

She shrugged, but didn't look up from her bowl of macaroni and cheese. To a five-year-old, the fact that I renovated houses wasn't nearly as impressive as other parents who had jobs like doctors, truck drivers, or stay-at-home mothers. My houses were merely places to hide creepy, crawly insects, and maybe some ghosts and goblins.

"Guess how old the house is," I said as I leaned back from the kitchen table and opened a window. A cool, light breeze ran through the kitchen. It brushed our faces and lifted the sweat and stickiness off the countertops. Even though my ranch house was a couple of miles from Lake Geneva, in the less-desirable, year-round part of town, we still felt the crisp lake air.

She cocked her head to the side, her blond pigtails bobbling on either side of her head. "One hundred and five years old?"

"Older," I said. The breeze had stopped, so I picked up a stray piece of junk mail and fanned my face. I had spent the day surveying the Maple house, in the April rain, among windows that were either angry panes of broken glass or painted shut. When the occasional wind did blow through the house, it carried with it the grime and dirt of the front porch, like it had been waiting patiently all those years to get inside, and it wasn't going to miss an opportunity to infiltrate.

"One hundred and six?" she said.

"You're close. More like one hundred and fifteen. It was built in 1901," I said.

Her eyes widened. "Wow." She stirred her macaroni in thought. "Those spiders must be really old, then."

I laughed. "I told you, I didn't even see one spider today." Of course, not seeing was not the same as not existing.

She gave me a suspicious look. "Oh, you will," she said

knowingly. A fleck of cheese sauce landed on her white dress and she immediately dabbed it off with her napkin, a frown on her face. I glanced down at my own clothes—cargo pants stained with old primer, plaster dust, and wood stain, and a T-shirt I had owned since high school. Her fingertips sparkled with glittery nail polish as she folded her napkin, while my own fingers were rough and chapped from too much time spent pulling glaze off old windows and grouting subway tile.

I stood up and began to collect the plates from the table, stacking them haphazardly in the sink. My dishwasher had broken a month ago and I still hadn't found a replacement. With a stack of ever-growing bills on the entryway table, I needed to fix up the Maple Street house quickly, and get it on the market.

Buyers for vintage homes in the area were a special breed. I figured it might take some time to find the right fit—someone who not only wanted an older home, but who would take care of it and appreciate it rather than bringing in someone like Jack Sullivan to start ripping out what they didn't have the vision to understand. Most importantly, it had to be someone who lived here. Someone who *wanted* to live here, year-round. A truly elusive requirement: a resident.

I had lived in Geneva Lake my entire life, watching the ebb and flow of tourists during the summer season between Memorial Day and Labor Day. They packed the downtown area, spent tourist dollars on T-shirts and bumper stickers, seemed to forget all basic rules of the road when driving on Highway 50 into town, and crossed every street like they dared the residents to hit them. Honestly, I had been tempted more than once.

"Can we play outside?" Abby asked. She looked down at her white eyelet dress. "After I change."

I nodded and she scampered down the hallway to her bedroom, where I had set down her pink suitcase as I did each time she returned home from her father's house. Inside, her things were always neatly packed, thanks to my ex-husband Matt's slight OCD tendencies. Sometimes it felt like the joint custody arrangement was a barometer weighed to always point to some inadequacy of mine. When we were married, it was a quirk—maybe even something to be appreciated. Now that we were divorced, it was an annoyance at best, passive-aggressive at worst.

After Abby changed into a pair of jeans and a T-shirt, I drove to our favorite lakefront park. As she played on the slide and befriended another little girl with kindergarten ease, I sat on a bench, my fingers tingling with the anticipation of working on the house. I thought about refinishing the wood floors and seeing them come back to life after years of neglect; about removing all the dingy cream-colored paint from the woodwork, then sanding it down and staining it. I imagined there were more treasures buried deep in the house, just waiting to be discovered.

I sighed and looked out at the water. Only a few boats cruised around the bay, and the stillness of the lake reflected the sunset like a mirror, painting the surface with oranges and yellows. I breathed deeply, enjoying the way the lake air filled my lungs and throat. A certain part of me always settled when I was next to the water, like a tiny adjustment in my spine that radiated outward. The air smelled like wet rocks mixed with grass, and the gentle waves lapping against the retaining wall sounded like a mother shushing an infant. A quiet buzz of distant boats bounced off the trees that lined the lake and filtered out as a fluctuating white noise in the background.

Most of the piers weren't in the water until May, but I could still spot a few that were optimistically placed in the water already. The lake froze solid every winter and piers were removed quickly after the weather began to turn, a sure sign that the vacation season was over, like Mother Nature was ringing a bell and shouting for last call.

After Abby was tired and sweaty from the park, we drove home. As we got out of the car, I waved at the neighbors who watered their lawns and sat on their front porches. In our yard, Abby and I watched as lightning bugs began to fill the sky with their blinking bodies. I caught one in my hand.

"Look, Ab. Do you want to hold it?" I held my cupped hands out, but she shook her head.

"No." She shook her head and wrinkled her nose.

I sighed and opened my palms, releasing the insect back into the air. She was so different than I was as a child. In my childhood backyard, I loved lifting up all the flagstones and rocks to uncover wiggling insects, and I was always hanging from tree branches or exploring corners of the yard for buried treasure. I wasn't ever sure if I should encourage her to be more like me or if I should just go with what came naturally to her.

"Just wait. In a few weeks, the cicadas will be here."

Her eyes grew wide and she slowly shook her head. "I'm going to stay inside until they're gone."

I laughed. The insects woke every seventeen years, crawling out of the ground and covering the yard with their black bodies and orange eyes for six long weeks. I was seventeen the last summer they arrived, and I remembered that the noise from their humming and buzzing was almost deafening, blanketing the neighborhood in a loud white noise for weeks. Even a short trek outside to the mailbox turned into a battle as I had to swat them away again and again to stop them from landing all over my clothes. I couldn't imagine how Abby was going to react.

As I tucked her into bed that night, in her tiny room in our two-bedroom house, I kissed her forehead. Her breathing was already slowing as sleep began to cover her with a veil.

"I love you," I whispered into the darkness. I leaned closer and said, "I have a feeling about this one, Ab. This house is something special."

I closed the door to her room and tried to sleep until the birds outside my window began to chirp at 3 a.m., as though they couldn't wait any longer for me to work on the house.

CHAPTER 2

"I think this is the one. You were right about that." My contractor, Eddie, stood up from where he had lain on the ground outside the house. He dusted his muddy hands off on his jeans and glanced back at the cracked foundation, shaking his head.

"Meaning?" I said as I swatted away a bee. The outside of the house teemed with crawling creatures, the result of years' worth of overgrown rosebushes and hydrangeas that seemed determined to sprawl over every patch of unused grass, like they were mounting an offense.

"Meaning your foundation is shot. Not just shot, but crumbling away. Water damage, looks like." He motioned for me to crouch down and stuck his index finger right through the brick. "It's like whipped cream." He held it up in the air, the shortened stub of his ring finger framing the watered-down concrete. He'd lost half the finger in a tile saw accident years ago, a form of dues-paying to the construction gods.

"I figured as much when I bought it," I said. Many of the houses sold at auction had something structurally wrong with them, usually why they went for such cheap prices. The average person who buys a house is thinking more in terms of paint, carpeting, and maybe a kitchen remodel, not floor joists, support beams, and sinking foundations.

"Did you know that the rot goes all the way into the basement? And into the footings?" he said. He shook his head, his dreadlocked brown hair whipping against his face. Adjusting his bandanna, he gave me a serious look. "Worst I've seen. And you know what I've seen."

"You've got to be kidding," I said.

"I wish," he said and shook his head again.

I rubbed my forehead as I peered through the hole from his finger, straight into the basement. "So, what do you think we're talking about here?" My voice wavered and he glanced at me in surprise.

He took a few steps back, staring up at the stucco that peeled away from the frame like a bad sunburn. It begged for someone to bump against it so it could finally sigh and release dust that had been trapped for over a hundred years.

"Need to pour new footings, at least," he said.

"That isn't so bad. We've done that in almost every house," I said. We had worked together on five projects over the past four years. We poured concrete, stripped floors, and repaired windows side by side through divorce (mine), and the sleepless nights that come with having a newborn (his—Mia). Eddie had moved to the area five years ago from Milwaukee and, in addition to helping me with my projects, helped the summer residents keep up their vacation homes during the off-season. We met at the hardware store, of all places, in the pest control aisle. Fitting, since we would spend the next few years battling all sorts of different creatures in the houses.

"In the *basement*. We'd have to pour new footings in the basement, and even then I don't know if the house could withstand the necessary repairs and load-bearing to get it actually, you know, not condemned," he said.

"How in the hell would we get the concrete in the basement to . . ." I trailed off as he made a lifting motion to the foundation. "No. We can't." I took a step back and held my hands up.

"It's your only choice. You'd have to lift the whole foundation, and house, pour new footings, and leave it up there while they dry for a week or so," he said. "And then put it back down." He looked up and gave the hole another glance. "Assuming there will be anything left to put back."

I felt sweat start to trickle down my back. "And this is our only option?"

"Looks that way. Pour a whole new basement or . . ." He shrugged.

I managed a half smile. "Of course, this is the part when you tell me that you have a connection, and will find someone to do it for a couple thousand bucks?"

He laughed, showing the gold cap on his molar. "Not this time, boss." He held up a hand. "Five figures, easy."

I buried my face in my hands and took a deep breath. "I'm screwed. Why did I think I could take on an old house? Was this a huge mistake?"

"Nah. She's got good bones. We'll fix her up and make her so pretty that someone will pay top dollar," he said.

I slowly removed my hands and looked up at the house, allowing the first few feelings of anticipation to return. I crossed my arms over my chest. "Well, I don't have any other option right now. So let's lift the damn house up and fix it."

Eddie put his hands on his hips. "You got it, boss."

We walked inside, and a cloud of dust swirled thickly around us, spinning at the introduction of fresh air. I surveyed the piles of garbage in the living room—traces from whoever had lived there before—blankets, lumber, plates, a broken chair, books that were ripped in half. And cigarettes. Millions and millions of cigarette butts, some crushed into the wood floors, like the previous owners couldn't have been bothered to find an ashtray. The remnants of smoke caked the walls and left a film on every surface that we would have to eventually scrub off.

I stepped over about twenty crushed cans of Diet Coke (also likely filled with cigarette butts) as I made my way to the kitchen. It, unlike other parts of the house, had been renovated. Not well, and not for about thirty years, unfortunately. When the house was built, it likely had open wood shelving and a large, deep porcelain sink. Now it had cracked Formica countertops, wood veneer cabinets straight out of 1975, and broken ceramic tiles glued to the floor. All of it would have to go, and I would take particular pride in hauling out all the cheap material.

I surveyed the garbage on the floor of the kitchen—red Solo cups, dirty silverware, and pizza boxes—and shook my head. I had estimated that we would need two Dumpsters to clear out the house, but it likely would be many, many more.

Eddie handed me a shovel and we began to move the mess toward the front door so it could be tossed into the Dumpster later that afternoon. We didn't get three shovels full before the stench of a dead animal hit us at the same time.

"Ah, there it is. I was wondering how long it would take." Eddie moved the bandanna off his forehead and over his mouth and nose.

"Ten seconds. Has to be a new record," I said. The next shovel full came up with the offending odor—a flattened rat. "One of how many." I walked it outside and pitched it onto the lawn. When I returned, Eddie had cleared away a small path that was littered with more flattened rodents.

"Family reunion?" he said.

"Rodent apocalypse," I muttered as we began to scoop them up.

"I think this house wins the award for Most Disgusting Property Ever Purchased. I bet these rats killed themselves rather than stay here another night," Eddie said as he tried to pry one of the rats off the wood floor. He threw a shoulder into the shovel and finally the thing peeled off the floor in one piece.

I took a quick step backward over a pile of torn T-shirts and put my hand on the wood around the arched doorway. "Yes, but wait, there's more," I said in my best infomercial voice. I slowly pulled out a beautifully carved oak pocket door that separated the living room from the dining room. "It has a pocket door. That has to count for something, right?" Many older homes had pocket doors, and I was hoping mine would, too. They were used in the time before air-conditioning and reliable indoor heating to keep the heat from the kitchen out of the parlor during the summer and the warmth of the fire in the room during the winter.

Eddie grunted in reply, clearly not as impressed as me. I ran a hand along the beautifully preserved wood, kept so by the protection of the plaster door pocket. It hadn't been caked in years of cigarette smoke, or painted a faded cream like a lot of the other wood trim in the house. I tried to push it back into the pocket, but it slowed down and the metal hinges began to screech.

"Oops. Looks like we can add pocket door repair to the list," I said.

"You know, boss, look at it this way—you've always talked about how saving houses is your mission. If you can bring this one back to life, I think you can officially retire," he said.

"Never," I said. "If I can do this—if I can renovate this disaster—it's just the beginning."

"Just the beginning?" he said as he leaned on his shovel and surveyed the pile of dead animals. "Right now, that sounds more like a threat than a promise."

CHAPTER 3

I heard my cousin Traci before I saw her as I waited at the bar at Chuck's Lakeshore Tavern. Abby was back at Matt's, and I was left with an empty house again. Most nights when she was gone, I opted to leave the house rather than ruminate in her absence. Evenings were supposed to be spent with chaos and children, not silence and Lean Cuisines.

"Alex! Where the hell are you?" Traci shouted over the crowded bar, garnering more than a few looks of annoyance as people jumped aside as she barreled past them. Her diminutive figure finally appeared, and I waved her over. She threw herself into the bar stool that I had saved minus threats to life and limb, and sighed. "Sorry I'm late."

"No, no. It's fine. Thanks for coming all the way out here after work." I swirled a bottle of Spotted Cow beer as Traci signaled to the bartender and ordered their specialty—a Bloody Mary served with a pony can of Miller Lite on the side.

"No problem. It's not exactly a cross-country trip." Although she grew up in Geneva Lake, Traci had moved away after high school graduation. She lived twenty minutes away, in Richmond, Illinois, just across the state line. She took a long pull of her drink as soon as the bartender set it down, and half of it disappeared. She glanced around Chuck's. "Every time I come in here, it's like a time warp. I don't think it's changed in . . . ever."

I nodded and smiled. "Nope. Same beer. Same burgers. Same bartenders." I nodded at Tim, who lifted an eyebrow in recognition. That was the extent of the positive expression he gave out. The negative was usually reserved for the hotel visitors who wandered over from the nearby Abbey Resort excited to see a "real" Wisconsin bar and gorge on cheese curds. Chuck's wasn't in town proper; rather, it was across the lake in the town of Fontana, making it more of a locals' bar than a tourist attraction.

"Same great view. Man, I do miss living here," Traci said as she gazed over her shoulder out the big picture windows that lined the front of the bar. Arguably Chuck's best asset—Lord knows the sad pinball machine didn't keep us coming—the lake sparkled amidst the bobbing boats tethered to whitewashed piers in between white and orange buoys. To the left, I could faintly see the bend in the shoreline for the town of Williams Bay, and straight ahead was the downtown area.

"That's your own fault for moving away," I said. "So, how's work?" I said. Traci worked as a secretary for a high school in Richmond. She often said that a little-known secret was that it wasn't the principal who ran the school, but the secretaries and maintenance workers. If someone wanted something—anything—done, they had to go through one of those two groups.

She shrugged. "Fine. I spent part of today dealing with a teacher's soon-to-be ex-wife stalking him to gather dirt for a divorce. She keeps showing up at the office and delivering things like doughnuts and coffee. Probably poisoned." She toyed with the olive on a toothpick in her drink.

"Not all of us are crazy," I said with a rueful smile. *Most days, anyway,* I added silently.

She waved her drink around, sloshing red liquid out the

sides and onto the dark wood bar. "You, my dear, had a right to be crazy. He deserved to be punished for what he did. But for some reason, you chose sanity and maturity. Seems like a missed opportunity to me."

"Yes, well, I had Abby. I couldn't afford to go off the rails and burn his clothes on the front yard," I said. I didn't add that while I might outwardly project some form of normalcy, it was tempered by nights of tears, loneliness, and heartbreak. It was only because those nights purged me of the memories of what I had lost that I could maintain an emotional equilibrium.

"Well, just know if you ever want him to 'go away,' I'm sure I could find some guys who would be happy to help you with that." She winked and threw back the rest of her drink.

"Oh, don't tempt me," I said with a laugh. "Divorce is weird. It's like the death of something, even though at times it would be easier if the other person had died. There would be a reason for all the sadness and then you would move on. With divorce, it never ends. Or at least it feels that way. You never stop . . ." I shook my head before I could add *"missing the other person."*

She nodded sympathetically and exhaled, turning toward me on her bar stool. "So, the new house. A total money pit?"

"Remains to be seen. I finally have the first floor cleared of everything, and now we're about to start work upstairs. A roofer came out today and said the roof, thankfully, looks okay and just needs a few shingles replaced. So, nothing serious. But I did get the quote to stabilize the foundation and pour the footings in the basement."

"And?"

I laughed into my beer bottle as I took a long sip. "You don't want to know." I opened my purse and pulled out two small red lava rocks that I had found in the backyard. "Here. I thought Chris would like these."

She smiled. "He will. Thanks." She carefully put them in her purse. Her seventeen-year-old son, Chris, had Asperger's syndrome. He lived at home and worked as a bagger at the grocery store. His passion was collecting rocks, small treasures that he displayed proudly in his room like trophies.

"I'll keep my eyes open for any more. Lots more stuff to uncover at that house. Hopefully no more dead rats, though," I muttered.

She shook her head as another drink was placed in front of her. "You and your old house fantasy. Why couldn't you find something that's just kind of messed up, like usual? Like a nice ranch from the sixties, or a split level from the seventies? Those always have tons of problems for you to solve that don't require lifting the whole damn thing in the air. You always fix up and sell those to nice couples who are looking to start a family, no problem."

"Where's the fun in that?" I said quickly. "Anyone can do that. Besides, you know that I've always been obsessed with old houses. I've wanted to fix one up since I started down this road. My dad always said that there wasn't anything, or any house, that couldn't be saved."

She threw her hands in the air. "I knew you were going to say that."

"Then you didn't have to ask the question, right?"

"You're impossible," she said.

"Not the first time I've heard that. Just ask any contractor within a fifteen-mile radius," I said as I pulled my hair into a ponytail.

"Speaking of repelling men, when are you going to let me set you up with someone? There's a new teacher at my school who—"

I cut her off quickly as I tightened the hair at the back of my head. "Nope. Not interested."

She slapped the bar and turned to face me. "It's been four years. You've got to get out there and date someone. Please. Anyone."

I lifted my eyebrows. "*Any* one? Like a convicted felon or a serial killer?"

"Funny. No, I'm serious. It's time. And this teacher is really great. I think you two would get along. He's cute, smart, and likely not a serial killer or convicted felon," she said.

"As great of a sales pitch as that is—*likely* not a murderer—don't bother. I have too much going on with Abby and the new house," I said. In addition, the thought of going on dates and explaining my life history—and divorce journey—sounded like just about the worst thing I could imagine.

"Just do this as a favor to me. Like a gift," she said.

"No, thanks. Unwanted gift, like the stray cat that used to leave dead birds on the doorstep," I said.

She shook her head. "Did you just compare a cute guy to a dead bird? All that plaster and asbestos have really done a number on your brain."

"Probably. I repeat—talk to any contractor in a fifteen-mile radius."

She slapped her hand on the bar. "Well, fine. You can spend lonely nights at your newest dump—I mean, diamond in the rough—" she added when I quickly opened my mouth, "but what are you going to do when it's complete? Wouldn't it be nice to have someone to take you out to dinner, share a bottle of wine with, and talk to about something other than paint strippers?"

I shrugged. "In theory. But the answer is still no. I need to focus on the house."

"There'll always be another house, right? Didn't you say that this is just the beginning?" she said as she rolled her eyes.

"From your lips," I said with a smile, and she slumped her head on the bar.

CHAPTER 4

The day before the excavators were scheduled to come and raise the foundation of the house, I walked through the first floor, nodding at the original, wall-mounted porcelain sink with separate faucets for hot and cold water in the powder room. I again grimaced at the cheap, prefabricated kitchen cabinets that were made out of particleboard.

I admired the quarter-sawn oak built-in buffet with the leaded-glass doors, still just as impressive upon second viewing as the first time I saw them, as I again took inventory of the dining room. With all the debris cleared out of the house, I could see that while the floors were badly damaged due to water and unknown traumas, they could probably be saved with a good sanding, staining, and sealing.

The living room had an original, wood-burning fireplace that looked like it was still in working condition. The brick around the fireplace miraculously hadn't been painted or tiled over, but the bottom of the hearth was damaged. It was decorated with small stones sunk into the mortar and several were missing.

Moving through the house, I could see that much of the

plaster on the walls was cracked, but Eddie had definitely repaired much worse for me. If I was a different kind of flipper—like Jack Sullivan—I would rip all of it down and install drywall. With drywall there wouldn't be any patching, sanding, skimming, or cursing. It was easy, clean, and accessible. And also completely inauthentic.

I didn't dare try to flip a light switch, although a few of the original light fixtures were in place. I marveled over the pendant light in the kitchen, still fitted with a lightbulb from decades ago. Frank, my electrician, was due to come over after we lowered the house, and I knew he would be just as excited as me to see it. I guessed Frank might find a combination of old and new wiring, all far, far from up to code. There would definitely be some late nights together for the two of us. It could be kind of romantic, save for the fact that he was almost seventy and had been married for over fifty years.

I carefully sidestepped the splintered boards on the wood stairs as I walked upstairs. The four small bedrooms still had the faint odor of urine and garbage, even though they had been cleared out. Two of them didn't have closets.

I had read that back at the turn of the century, closets were considered rooms in a home and taxed accordingly, and people usually didn't have the clothing to necessitate a whole dedicated room. I smiled with appreciation. I barely needed a dresser for my things—my closet at home was stuffed with lamp bases, bookcases, and end tables, all things I had salvaged from my past projects to be used for staging in the future.

There were two bathrooms upstairs, an unusual feature for such an old home. One was the guest bathroom in the hallway, which held the crown jewel: an original cast-iron claw-foot tub. It was badly rusted and stained, but with some cleaning and patching it would look brand new. The other bathroom was off the master, a later addition that was complete with a 1970s powder-blue tub, sink, and particleboard vanity.

None of the bedrooms upstairs had the original doors, all replaced by fake wood hollow-core doors. "Why on earth would you take down a wood door and put this atrocity up?" I gave one door a light tap and it quickly shut, the flimsy material moving like leaves in the wind. I guessed it happened sometime during the eighties, when decorating seemed to move away from all natural materials and toward easy, manufactured, and convenient.

In the back corner of the smallest bedroom was a door. I gingerly stepped across the buckling wood floor, opened it, and went up the staircase leading to the attic.

"Please let there be nothing terrifying up here," I muttered as I carefully made my way through the doorway, ducking in case any wild animal decided to engage. I peeked my head up over the threshold, still holding my breath and expecting a family of raccoons to take issue with my presence. Or, worse, a squatter. I had found a squatter in a house last year, and he wasn't happy about leaving his cozy, illegal space.

Thankfully, I saw a nearly bare room. All that was left was a dresser that seemed to be missing all its drawers. No sign of any animals—or vagrants.

"Damn. It would have been great if the original doors were left up here," I said, my voice echoing against the wood beams as I climbed up. I was about to turn and walk downstairs when something behind the old dresser caught my eye. I tiptoed through the attic and discovered a small, rotting cardboard box tucked behind the dresser, against one of the eaves. If I hadn't looked at it just right, I would have missed it, as I guessed others had for years.

I carefully peeled back the old cardboard, the dust coming off in my fingers as it nearly crumbled after the weight of decades of immobility.

Inside was a stack of haphazardly stacked newspapers and some blank cards. The house had been abandoned for more than five years and, before that, had been bounced from owner to owner. Whoever left the boxes here was likely either dead or had stopped scrapbooking years before.

I was about to close the box up, when a glimpse of yellow caught my eye. I dug down and pulled out a small book. It had once been covered in what I guessed was a bright white material, but had faded into a dirty mustard color. As I carefully opened it, the binding cracking and groaning with age, I saw that it was a blank journal. As I turned the pages, two items slid out of the center and onto the floor: a photograph and a pressed flower.

I picked up the black-and-white photograph with two fingers. A handsome young man, in his twenties, I guessed, stood next to a vintage car. Although I supposed the car wasn't vintage to him since the back of the picture was dated May 15, 1947. The man smiled at the camera, leaning one elbow on the hood. His body might have looked casual and relaxed, but I could tell that he was proud of the car, that he was showing it off for the camera. His chin was square, like he came from good, hearty, rugged stock, but his hair was smoothed to the side, an effect that made him look like he belonged on a movie set. The way his mouth turned up at the corners and the sparkle in his eye made me wonder just who was behind the camera.

I shook my head slightly. Matt used to look at me like that, like he wasn't sure if I was real, but didn't want to look away long enough to find out. A deep, familiar sadness began to form in my stomach as I thought of the way he would always seem to study my face for a minute before he pulled me in for a hug. The way my body fit perfectly against his as he squeezed me tight. The way that he never was the first to let go.

"I hope your ending was happier than mine," I said to the photo before I carefully tucked it back into the book. I leaned over and gingerly picked up the pressed flower. It looked to be a pink rose, cut many years ago. Just the act of moving it through the air made some of the petals scatter onto the attic floor.

I placed the flower back with the photo and closed the book, setting it back in the box. A truck rumbling outside brought me back to the present. I glanced out the window and saw that Eddie had arrived with a crew to start prepping the basement.

I tried to brush off the invisible spiderweb of shared experience that had grown around me and the keepsakes. Yet, before I was halfway out of the room, I turned and picked up the box, carrying it downstairs and setting it in a safe place on the front porch.

CHAPTER 5

I took a long, deep breath as I drove my car through the Geneva National subdivision and onto Palmer Drive. The manicured lawns of the gated golf course community boasted perfectly striped lawns and brilliantly colored tulips, and Palmer Drive was the most spectacular street of them all. It had the biggest homes, with the best landscaping and the brightest flowers. Each bud was carefully tended to weekly by a landscaper to ensure that nothing was out of place. Except for me, as I drove to pick up Abby from her dad's house.

Matt had moved from a rented town house by the lake to the house in Geneva National a few weeks prior, but it was my first time there. As I drove up to the entrance gate, the guard made me endure the humiliation of calling the house to ask for permission to let me in, and he gave my rusted Ford truck a suspicious look as I pulled through the iron gates. I had a feeling he would also glance in the bed of the truck before he let me leave, to ensure I didn't take anything that didn't belong to me.

I fidgeted as I rang the doorbell, trying not to stare up at the giant tan craftsman-style house that was built last year, but made to look like it had been around for decades. It irritated me that my heart beat faster while I waited for Matt to answer. After four years of this, I had hoped that I could handle the situation. To see his house, and his new life—without me—was another painful step among millions of others.

I relaxed when I saw a short, round figure open the door.

"Alex! Come on in!" My former mother-in-law, Susan, stepped aside and held her arms out to give me a quick hug as I entered the foyer. She wore a sleeveless, collared shirt and Bermuda shorts, her feet bare. She smelled like cinnamon and vanilla, a favorite perfume that she had been wearing since the dawn of time. "It's so good to see you," she said as she released me.

"Thanks. I didn't realize you would be here," I said. I glanced up in awe at the two-story foyer adorned with a crystal chandelier that likely cost more than my house.

Susan followed my gaze. "Atrocious, isn't it?" She waved an arm around in exasperation. "The previous owners were very flashy."

I smiled, pressing my mouth together to suppress a laugh. "I've never seen the house."

She made a motion for me to follow her. "C'mon. I can show it to you." She pointed to the living room, with its leather couch, chair, and the television hung on the mantle of the fireplace. The throw pillows were shades of brown, decorated in a geometric pattern, and I could tell that they were the ones provided by the furniture store. As though Matt had walked in, pointed at one of the first displays he saw, and bought the whole thing.

I noticed that the throw pillows on the couch were stacked on top of each other, like pancakes. He used to do the same thing when we were together and it drove me crazy. Throw pillows were supposed to be stood up, not stacked, I told him over and over again. After a while, it became one of those Things in our marriage that added to the resentment, like how he always forgot to put his dishes in the dishwasher instead of the sink. A silent war, albeit mostly being fought on my side.

"I'm sorry. What's the big deal?" he used to say, bewildered, when I would call him out on it.

It wasn't a big deal, something that only infuriated me more when I tried to explain it was a part of a bigger picture. It was what the dishes and the pillows *represented*. And there was no way to do that without sounding like a lunatic.

Yet, as I looked at the pillows in that moment, it both irritated me (hadn't he learned?) and made me wonder why it was such a battle line in the first place. If it had been reversed, would I have listened to him yell on about pillows? Probably not. When we were together, why did everything have to represent something?

I started to step forward, but stopped. "No, thanks. I probably should just grab Abby." The thought of walking around Matt's house when he wasn't there made me feel like I was snooping, which, of course, I would have been, albeit sanctioned by his mother.

She nodded sympathetically before she craned her head upward and called for Abby to come downstairs.

"Coming," Abby called from somewhere upstairs. "I'm just hanging up my swimsuit."

"Swimsuit?" I asked with my eyebrows raised.

Susan nodded. "There's a pool and a hot tub in the backyard."

Of course there was. Everything that a little girl could dream of. Abby had a pool at my house, too: an inflatable pink one that half-sagged when it was filled with too much freezing water from the hose.

"I told him he'll have to hire someone to take care of it. To take care of this whole house. Why does one person need such a big house?" she grumbled. "If it wasn't just him and—" She stopped when she saw my face. "Oh. I'm sorry. I didn't mean . . ." She shook her head in embarrassment.

"No, it's all right. I know what you meant." I shifted on the marble floor, shoving my hands in my pockets. Although I had known Susan for years, there was now this divide between us, this silence. Before the divorce, we were close. She stayed with us after Abby was born, taking turns with my mom to help during the first few weeks. Abby was her only grandchild, and she would often bring over small presents that she said she had simply stumbled across, but I knew it was just an excuse to come over and hold the baby. I didn't mind, because it meant that I could sneak in a nap or take a shower while she rocked Abby. She always patted me on the back and told me I was doing a great job, even though I often felt just the opposite.

When the divorce happened, people had to choose sides, even though neither of us ever asked anyone to do so. It just came naturally, and friends and family were split. *Choose a team,* a divorce demands. *Root for someone,* even though no one ever wins. By virtue of blood relations, Susan was on Matt's team and neither of us could ever seem to get over it.

We were saved from more uncomfortable conversation by the *thump* of Abby running downstairs.

"Mommy!" Abby threw her arms around me. As she always did, she seemed bigger than when I'd dropped her off just two days before.

Susan bent down on one knee and held her arms out. "I'll miss you, sweetheart. I love you."

"Okay. Love you, too," Abby said.

I smiled, grateful for their closeness. My parents had retired to Fort Lauderdale a year earlier, so Matt's parents were Abby's only local grandparents. I said good-bye to Susan as I grabbed Abby's hand to leave. I felt her watch me as we walked to the car and I started it up.

"Did you have fun?" I asked Abby as we pulled down the driveway.

She nodded. "Yes! Daddy and I went swimming in the back-yard and then watched a movie together." She sighed. "His new house is so fun. Julia showed me how to do a handstand under-water."

"Oh." I swallowed hard. "That's great." Julia and Matt had been dating for six months, from what I understood. She was a pretty, petite blonde in her early thirties who worked as a dental hygienist in a nearby town. I imagined her to be the human version of a Jack Sullivan flip house: convenient, pretty, shiny, and uncomplicated. Matt had asked a month ago if she could meet Abby, and it wasn't as though I could say no. I hadn't realized, though, that meeting her had evolved into spending time together. I exhaled slowly before I continued. "Do you want to go get some ice cream?"

She nodded quickly as we left the gated subdivision, drove away from the perfectly cloistered life that seemed so easy for her to fall into, and pulled onto Highway 50 to drive back toward our house, past the horse farms and cornfields that separated their gated community from my street. Back to where I belonged.

At one point, Matt belonged there, too. He grew up in town, just as I did. He was three years older, so it was more that we knew *of* each other than anything. I knew that when he was home from college, he worked summers on the docks at Gordy's Boats in Fontana, helping people with their rented Cobalt speedboats by tying endless inner tubes and lines off the back well and reminding them to observe the No Wake Zone buoys. When the boaters were finished and heading back in, he would politely shout an offer to drive the dinghy out to the boat and drive it back into the marina instead of watching the driver struggle and sweat through all the channel traffic.

I watched him as I doled out hot dogs and ice cream from the snack shop at the beginning of the docks, admiring the way his skin tanned after all those long afternoons in the sun while I remained pasty white in the shop. I watched him as he returned home from college, worked that last summer, and then got a job at Gordy's in boat sales. And I watched the way his eyes lit up when we ran into each other a few summers later at a party after too many keg beers.

Five years later, we were married. I worked in marketing for the Grand Geneva Resort, and he worked his way through law school. Then came the surprise of Abby, a few years too early, and we bought a fixer-upper near town, several blocks from the lake. We planned to slowly bring it back to life and create a beautiful home for our little family. I believed that things were just beginning, that our lives had reached a wonderful new place.

The opposite all happened so fast after that. The divorce, selling the fixer-upper that would never be fixed, the monetary settlement that eventually allowed me to buy my first renovation property.

The money came from when his law firm brokered a deal for a lakefront condo developer. The grand opening ceremony of the development was in the spring that Abby turned one, and by the end of that summer, the divorce papers were signed.

And in the four years since, there hadn't been one summer that didn't remind me of him.

CHAPTER 6

Two small, mustached men were waiting for me the next day as I pulled into the cracked driveway of the Maple house after I dropped Abby off at school. Despite the fact that it was only 9 a.m., they shot me impatient looks as I climbed out of my truck.

"Are you the metal scrappers?" I asked as I noticed the pile of copper pipes in the bed of their truck. They nodded. "Great. Follow me." I led them around back of the house and opened the door to the cellar. At some point in time, the house had been renovated to enclose the cellar so that the occupants could walk into the basement without having to walk inside, but the stairs were steep, and the enclosure was far from insect- or rodent-proof.

"Have at it," I said as I pointed to the copper pipes that ran the length of the dirt-covered basement.

Their eyes widened as they took in the long, thin metal that crisscrossed underneath the floors. I had told Eddie to call anyone who would be willing to come into the house to remove all the pipes, something the excavators told me would need to be done before we could jack up the house. Eddie said the scrappers would cut all the pipes out, including the water heater, for free and then sell it for the value at a scrapyard.

"Just be careful of the walls," I said. I walked over to one and gave it a quick tap with my foot, and decades of old dirt and dust fell to the ground.

As they got to work in the basement, I walked outside to wait for the foundation support crew to arrive. They were supposed to, essentially, impale the house with giant metal posts before they lifted it up that afternoon.

I stood on the driveway and craned my neck down the street but didn't see signs of the crew. The house was on a picturesque, tree-lined street, with the oaks looking like they predated everything. Most of the other houses were either tear-downs or Frankenstein amalgamations of old houses that had been partially ripped apart and added on to. When I squinted, I could see what the block might have looked like a hundred years ago, when tourists were just beginning to discover Lake Geneva as a destination.

Movement next door caught my eye, and I turned my head to see a lace curtain being pulled back from the window. A small, gray face peered out at me. I gave a quick nod, but the woman didn't look away. She continued to stare at me, sizing me up. I waved this time, smiling to acknowledge her gaze. That finally did it; she shut the curtain and disappeared.

I figured she was doing something else, but then she appeared on the porch of her house, beckoning me with a long, thin hand. As I walked closer, I could see that she was almost as old as her house. She wore a bright pink pantsuit and a face full of makeup. Her hair was white and teased out like a mushroom on top of her head.

"You bought the Moore place?" she said.

I nodded. "It isn't in the best of shape, as you can see. Were the Moores the last family to live there?"

She shook her head. "No. That was years ago." She slowly

sat down on one of her bright yellow wicker porch chairs, her eyes wide. "I thought they were going to tear the house down."

"They were going to. And another buyer probably would have. But I've always wanted to restore a house like this. Save it," I said.

"Why? Everyone said that it would be worth more to the neighborhood if it was just torn down," she said.

"Because I think it deserves another chance, another family," I said with a smile.

Her hand shook as she brought it up to her face, wiping at her clear-framed glasses. "It did use to be a beautiful house."

I shifted, shoving my hands into my cargo pants, and studied her. "In what way?"

"It was once a bright white, before . . ." She moved a shaking hand toward the peeling blue stucco and shook her head. Her face darkened, and she looked away, down at her own baby blue–painted front porch.

"Before someone ruined it," I said with a frown.

She nodded, and her eyes grew bright again. "You should have seen it during Christmastime. Mrs. Moore would hang evergreen garlands along the porch and put candles in all of the front windows. Mr. Moore would light luminaries along the front walkway on Christmas Eve, and it made the whole house look like it was glowing." She paused and smiled, looking at her lap. "They always had the biggest tree, too, right in the front window where everyone could see."

I glanced back at the house and, despite its deterioration, I could see what she saw. I could see the strings of bulbs on the tree in the big picture window, and the luminaries glowing along the walkway, bookended by sugary white snow.

"It sounds beautiful," I said.

"It was. At the neighborhood party, Mrs. Moore always wore a beautiful red Christmas dress with a full skirt, and Mr. Moore wore a spotless black suit. And she made David wear a tie. I can still see it, clear as day." She paused and wiped her eyes before she laughed. "Some days, things feel like they happened yesterday, and what did happen yesterday seems like it happened years ago." She shook her head, her thin white hair floating in the air. "I know that doesn't make any sense."

"It does, actually." There were days when Abby's first birthday seemed closer than her fifth, that the passage of time wasn't a linear one, but one that swerved back and forth, coming closer at some points, touching the present in ways that didn't seem possible. It couldn't possibly have been four years since I was married, since Matt was my husband. Yet it felt like a lifetime ago that he was my partner.

"Are you going to live there when it's all fixed up?" she said.

I shook my head. "No. I'm just going to restore it and sell it. Hopefully a nice family will buy it and appreciate all the history inside."

"Oh. That's too bad. You seem to really love the house." After a pause, she said, "I'm Elsie Burke, by the way."

"Alex Proctor. How long have you lived here?" I said.

"Forever. Too long. Long enough that they should have taken me away in a body bag years ago," she said. After a sigh, she added, "Seventy years. I grew up in this house and never left."

I smiled. "Most people move from house to house like locusts, looking for bigger and better. I really admire that you've stayed here for so long. I can't imagine how the town has changed since you first moved in."

She smiled. "Some good, some bad." She leaned forward. "I was around for the bunnies, you know." Her tone lowered to a whisper. "In fact, I was one." She put a finger to her lips, her eyes sparkling.

I laughed. "Playboy? You were a bunny at the old Playboy Resort?" In the mid-sixties, Hugh Hefner had opened a Playboy Resort at what was now the Grand Geneva Resort, complete with bunny waitresses and smoking jackets.

She nodded and waved a wrinkled hand in the air. "Oh, yes. I was thirty-eight, but of course I lied and told them that I was much younger. It sure was fun. The stories I could tell . . ."

I laughed. "Well, I'd love to hear them sometime."

She put a hand to her mouth. "Remind me to tell you the story about Frank Sinatra and the Labor Day party of 1969."

"Oh, I will. That sounds wonderfully scandalous," I said. My head turned as I heard a truck pull into the driveway with the letters BOB'S EXCAVATING stenciled on the side. "Definitely save that story for me. I need to run back next door. I have a basement to reinforce and about a hundred and fifteen years of old concrete and junk to haul away," I said. "If you get bored, come on over and give us a hand."

She looked like she wanted to say more, but she relaxed and gave me a wave good-bye.

I was halfway down the steps when I stopped and turned, pulling a piece of paper and a small golf pencil out of my back pocket. I scrawled my phone number on it and held it out to Elsie.

"Just in case there are any emergencies with the house. Don't hesitate to contact me after hours if you see anything worth noting," I said.

She took it from me and slowly nodded. "I'll make sure it stays safe. I'm looking forward to seeing it pretty again."

I smiled. "Me too."

CHAPTER 7

The crane pulled back like a snake ready to strike as the crew stood by, ready to roll the sixty-foot steel beams under the house. When they finished, the house would hover five feet in the air. I stood on the sidewalk and waited, my heart pounding. If, for some reason, everyone had miscalculated the weight of the house or the condition of the joists, it could all crumble into dust. And it would happen in front of the small crowd that had gathered on the sidewalk. Elsie, as promised, remained on her front porch, watching.

"Last chance! Anything else you want to get out of the house before we filet it like a fish?" Bob, the crane operator, called down to me from the manning station, where he held the controls.

I shook my head and watched as the posts ran through the house with a sickening crunch and the screech of metal. I covered my mouth while the posts were secured and the house began to rise into the air. The hydraulics puffed and sputtered, until finally, the house was lifted five feet off the foundation, high enough for the excavating crew to maneuver a backhoe into the basement to pull out all the old stone and concrete.

With a *thump*, the lift turned off. The crowd didn't move or speak, stunned at the sight of the house in the air.

"Show's over, folks," I said with a clap, when it became apparent it wasn't going to crumble to the ground. I bent forward and put my hands on my knees in relief.

I picked up Abby at her after-school program later that day. She greeted me with a weary smile. Her two pigtails were askew on the back of her head and her face was flushed.

"We played Capture the Flag," she said as she buckled herself into her booster seat. "It was so much fun."

"Oh good! Was your friend Lucy there today?" I said.

She shook her head. "Her mom picked her up from school today." She paused and then opened her eyes wide. "Could you pick me up next time?"

I swallowed hard and gave her a small smile. "Maybe. If I can swing it and get Eddie to cover for me at the house, I would love to. But After School is fun, too, right?" My tone was light, encouraging.

She nodded. "Yeah, but sometimes it's nice to just go home. Like when I go to Daddy's house."

My hands gripped the steering wheel. "Of course. Let me see if I can come pick you up next time."

She chattered on, peppering the conversation with staccato, bubbly words. I listened, but my mind was far away, back to when I'd planned to work part-time and be there every day for pickup.

In that alternate life, I volunteered in Abby's classroom and went on her field trips. I knew all the kids in her class and grabbed coffee with the other mothers during my free time. I had seen them before—all the normal, typical moms—standing around at drop-off. They all dressed the same: stretchy black capri pants, tank tops, and zip-up hoodies with running shoes and aviator sunglasses. In one hand was a coffee mug and in the other rested the handle of a jogging stroller that held a cooing baby. I didn't know many of them; they were women who had moved to the town, rather than grown up here. I guessed that some of them decided to relocate up north after spending summers at the lake, with the idea that living in Lake Geneva would be like a year-round vacation.

I could always pick out the first-time residents around January each year. They would go through the summer with delight, in disbelief that they lived somewhere so beautiful and relaxing. Fall would come, and they would enjoy the leisurely days in town without the thousands of extra bodies, checking out at the grocery store in under thirty minutes. The holidays would sneak up, and the town would come alive with Christmas lights, cider, and a glorious patch of ice on the lake. But once all of that was over, all we were left with in January was a frozen lake, unplowed roads, and football.

They always stared out at the lake, squinting at the groups of ice fishermen driving big pickup trucks that towed wooden huts. The cars stopped near the center of the lake, and the fishermen, dressed in head-to-toe snowsuits, cut holes in the ice, dropped a fishing line into the freezing water, and cracked open a beer. The new residents would shake their heads and assume the lake would swallow all the cars and huts, even though it never did. Well, almost never.

They would wonder why, when they only moved an hour north, it was so much colder, so much snowier. And why didn't any of us seem bothered by it enough to plow the streets several times a day? After a couple of years, they would start to adjust and shrug when anything less than a foot of snow fell, and possibly even root for the Packers over the Bears.

Yet, even though they were year-round residents, I could feel their eyes on me when I dropped Abby off at school, maybe wondering whether I was the mom or the babysitter. Wondering why I wasn't there each morning, why I wasn't volunteering to be a room mother.

In my former life, I didn't even *want* to be a room mother

and probably would have faked every possible illness to get out of the job, but now that the choice had been taken away from me, the grass was verdant green.

At home, Abby and I ate a gourmet dinner of grilled cheese and tomato soup, then I tucked her into bed. I collapsed on the couch and took a sip of the warm beer on my thrift store end table. I winced at the skunked liquid and my eyes shifted to the crumbling cardboard box in the foyer. I had dropped it on the tile, my arms cramped from pulling boulders of concrete out of the basement. Upon impact, it had released more dust on the tile floor in protest.

I closed my eyes and again pictured the house as Elsie had described it, during the holidays. The neighbors filled the house like packing peanuts, drinking hotty toddies and gossiping about each other. Maybe the men, after too many drinks, sang a rousing chorus of "We Wish You a Merry Christmas" while the women laughed and rolled their eyes. The children ran underfoot, the girls with big white bows in their hair and the boys with uncomfortable suit jackets. Maybe the husband and wife stole a tipsy kiss in front of their friends by the tree. I could smell the cider, feel the warmth of the wood-burning fire, and hear the roar of the increasingly boisterous crowd. Things were perfect, at least for a night.

When I opened my eyes, the silence and emptiness of my own house settled onto my shoulders. When we were married, Matt and I would always watch the news together, even if one of us was nodding off. After four years, I still missed that nightly ritual.

I paced back and forth in my bedroom, straightening up the laundry pile and scrubbing old primer stains off my shirt. Finally, I went into Abby's room and curled up next to her in the twin bed, my arm tucked around her waist.

CHAPTER 8

The backhoe expertly maneuvered around the driveway and toward the house, until it disappeared into the hole that the crew had made in the foundation. It returned, its shovel full of concrete and material from the basement, dumping it unceremoniously in a pile on the driveway. Then, back around it went for another trip.

"So, that's it? Somehow I thought it would be more dramatic. What do you think?" I said to Abby. She stood at my side, eyes following the backhoe. It was Saturday, and she'd begged me to come to the house to watch the excavators work. After we had raised it in the air, the house had transitioned from "spider lair" to "magical floating castle" in her mind.

"Looks pretty cool to me," she said.

Eddie stood to my left and nodded, his arms crossed over his stained white T-shirt. "Yeah. And your house is still five feet in the air." He pointed to the hydraulics, which remained in place, and would do so until new concrete had been poured and allowed to set. The entire process was supposed to take a week, and we were on day two.

"True." I watched as another load of foundation was deposited outside. A couple walking their dog across the street slowed to almost a stop as they stared at the lifted house and construction materials scattering the yard. I waved and they hurried along, eyes cast down. "I don't get it," I said as I watched them leave. "Do I look that scary?"

Eddie opened his mouth before quickly shutting it again, a smile teasing at the corners of his lips as he looked down at Abby. "I'm not sure how to answer that."

"Funny. No, really. You'd think that people would be happy that I'm restoring this house, bringing back a bit of history." I shook my head.

He shrugged. "Maybe they think it would raise property values more if you just ripped it down and built something new. Vacationers pay top dollar to stay around here."

"It probably would," I said. "Sure as hell would be a lot easier to sell." I stopped as the beeping from the backhoe grew louder as it reversed through the basement. "Wouldn't that be nice? I wouldn't have to worry about who was going to buy it, if they were going to rip everything out that I killed myself to save."

"You wouldn't scare off the buyers by insisting you meet them first before you go under contract...." he added under his breath.

I turned to face him. "And what's wrong with that? I'm going to put so much into this house. Shouldn't I do due diligence to make sure the buyer won't just rip it down?"

"There's some saying about beggars and choosers that would be appropriate to mention right now," he said.

"Who asked you?" I muttered.

"You did, actually. When you asked me what would be the reason—"

I cut him off with a swipe of my hand. "Enough. Back to work."

"You're the boss." He turned and headed toward the foundation, disappearing into the hole after the backhoe.

I shook off his words. If I let anyone come into the house, they might not appreciate it and give it the treatment it deserved. Abuse it, even, and then it would be right back to where it was—neglected, run-down, an empty shell of what it used to be.

I exhaled and pulled sheathed pruning shears out of my pocket. I pointed them toward the overgrown rosebushes that lined the property. "Want to pick out some flowers now?" I said to Abby. The last time she saw the house, she commented on the pink roses, and I wanted to collect a bouquet for her bedroom.

She nodded and we had started toward the flowers when she suddenly stopped. I followed her gaze to the house next door, where Elsie sat on her porch watching us with a faint smile. "Who's that lady?"

Before I could answer, Elsie waved us over. There was a pitcher of cold lemonade sweating on a white wicker table and two plates of tea cookies. She wore a bright purple pantsuit and heels.

"Expecting company?" I said, my hand on Abby's shoulder.

She shook her head, and a look of embarrassment flashed across her face. I realized that she had been hoping the company would be me.

"Mom, can I have one of those?" Abby pointed to the pink frosted tea cookies sprinkled with rainbow nonpareils.

"If Mrs. Burke says it's okay," I said, and she nodded.

She pointed to the yellow wicker chair next to her, and Abby sat down, perched on the edge with her spindly legs crossed at the ankles, and nibbled the cookie.

"How old are you?" Elsie asked her.

"Five," Abby said proudly.

"Five. A very special age. Yes, special." Her milky eyes clouded further with some distant memory before she smiled, brushing away the thoughts with a few blinks of her thin eyelashes.

Abby looked up at her house, staring at the leaded-glass windows above the doorway. "I like your house. It's really pretty."

Elsie smiled broadly, her tiny teeth dwarfed in her mouth. She patted her knee. "Thank you. I've lived here for a very long time." She leaned forward. "If your mom says it is all right, you may go inside and get the candy dish from the living room. It's a special dish that's pink with a bluebird on it."

Abby looked at me, and I nodded my permission. She disappeared inside, walking with her back straight and her feet flexing in front of her, knowing she was being watched.

"If you have things to do at that house, she can stay here with me," Elsie said. "It's nice to have someone to talk to."

I hesitated, looking back the house, and then to Elsie's porch, where Abby reappeared, proudly holding a candy dish full of individually wrapped chocolates.

"Would you like to stay here with me, Abby, and talk?" Elsie asked. "Afterward, I have a pond in my backyard if you would like to feed my koi."

When Abby nodded her agreement, digging into the chocolates, I slowly walked off the porch. I would only be ten feet away, I reasoned.

"Maybe save that Frank Sinatra story for another time," I called to Elsie.

She winked at me and then turned to my daughter. I lingered around the edge of the lawn, listening, as Abby bubbled over with talking about her friends at school and her favorite subjects. She was happy to have a captive audience, and Elsie, to have chatter to fill the silence.

I picked up the hedge trimmers and began to work on the

hawthorn bushes, stopping mid-clip every few minutes as I listened to their conversation.

"... and then every summer, the roses would be in full bloom and Mrs. Moore would be out there for hours, tending to her garden. ..."

I smiled as I attacked the thickest of the bushes, imagining the roses restored and the brilliant flowers exploding with color all over the side of the house.

After the bushes were trimmed back and the outside of the house had begun to appear less like something out of a horror movie, I walked back over to Elsie's house to retrieve Abby. The crew had left for the day, leaving piles of broken concrete stacked in the Dumpsters lining the driveway. The sun was beginning to set, and chickadees chirped in the birch trees flanking the front porch, like a factory whistle sounding at the end of a long workday.

"Ready to go?" Abby's eyes had begun to droop, the candy dish in front of them had long been emptied, and the lemonade drained. Elsie, on the other hand, looked energized, her eyes bright and her cheeks flushed.

Abby nodded and stood up, wiping her hands on her yellow romper. "Well, bye. Thanks," she said casually as she walked toward me.

"No, thank you," Elsie said quietly with a smile. She watched as Abby climbed down the front steps and headed toward my car. She turned to me. "Your daughter is quite the little lady."

I smiled and was about to turn around and head to the car to join Abby, but she continued.

"You know, I don't have many visitors to my house anymore. I used to, back when the block was young and there were mothers pushing carriages up and down the street, trying to get their babies to sleep." Her hands twisted in her lap. "But now, everyone is indoors."

I swallowed. "Do you have any children?"

She slowly turned to look at me, her thin lips pressed together. "No. It was just Harold and me. Until five years ago. Cancer."

"I'm so sorry," I said.

An embarrassed look flashed across her face as she wiped at her eyes. "Ah, too many memories."

I shifted. "Speaking of memories, I found a box of things that might have been from the Moore family. I'd love to give it back to them. Would you happen to know a forwarding address?" I said.

"Oh. No, I don't," she said quickly. Her mouth twisted into a frown. "What kind of things?"

I went and retrieved the attic box from my car and set it on the porch. I carefully lifted the book and handed her the photograph of the young man standing next to the car.

She stared at it for a long time, slowly bringing one shaking hand to her mouth. She blinked rapidly, like she was sure the photo would disappear.

"Who is that?" I asked.

"David Moore," she said quietly. She turned the photo over and saw the date, then nodded slightly. "Just as I thought. He would have been nineteen here."

"Were you friends?" I glanced back toward Abby and saw that she was picking the dandelions that had sprouted in the yard.

Elsie didn't say anything and handed the picture back to me. "That was the summer of the cicadas."

"Like this year," I said as I tucked the picture back into the book.

"I remember it, because David had just gotten that car, the one you see in the picture. He was so proud of that car. He saved up all year to buy it, and drove it around the block for hours after he bought it. His parents thought it was frivolous, getting a convertible, but he loved it."

"I can tell from the picture," I said.

She looked down at her hands briefly, before she looked back up and smiled. "The cicadas that year were late, supposed to come out in early May, but they didn't. We all waited on the block, expecting to wake up and find them clinging to the bushes and the trees. David bought that convertible in June, and the next morning, the cicadas showed up."

I laughed. "I can imagine it wasn't as much fun to drive a convertible with those insects flying around." Out of the corner of my eye, I saw Abby slowly begin to walk toward me, her shoulders slumped with frustration. I took a quick step toward her, to let her know that I was coming.

Her thin lips twisted into a smile. "No, it wasn't."

"So, what happened to him?" I took another step toward Abby, who whimpered with exhaustion as she walked back up on the porch. I put my arm around her and drew her toward me, smoothing her sweaty hair across her forehead and kissing the top of her head. I thought of David's expression in the picture and knew there was more to the story.

"He died," she said quickly. Her hands folded in her lap in a precise, matter-of-fact way, and she glanced at Abby. "Later that summer. In a car accident."

After a pause I exhaled. "I'm so sorry. That's awful."

"When someone is taken so quickly like that, it never quite feels real. You never come to terms with all the . . ." She trailed off and looked down.

"Regrets," I finished before I could stop myself.

"Yes," she said quietly, giving me a knowing look.

"Mom, I'm so tired," Abby said as she hugged me tighter, her body limp against mine.

"It's getting late," Elsie said with a nod to Abby.

"Yes," I said slowly, hoping she would continue about David, but her face was blank.

Her gaze was focused on the backyard of the Moores' house, her mind lost in some moment from the past, but I stopped mine from wandering back to those first sun-kissed summers on the pier with Matt.

CHAPTER 9

Six days after we lifted the house, a bearded crew member checked the support posts on the house before giving the thumbs-up. The hydraulics operator, perched in the seat of a crane, nodded, and then slowly moved one of the control handles forward. With a loud creak, my 275,000-pound house began to lower.

I twisted the gold band I wore on my right hand—a present from Matt after Abby was born—nervously as the house moved. Abby was at my side, holding her breath. Crew members stood on the perimeter, leaning forward in tension, ready to give the Stop signal to the operator should something begin to go off-kilter.

"This is so exciting," a neighbor behind me whispered. A crowd had gathered on the sidewalk in front of the house. Word had gotten out that we would be lowering the structure today. It had become something of a neighborhood spectacle—floating in the air like Dorothy's house in *The Wizard of Oz*. It had once been an eyesore, a silent neighborhood pest that everyone either ignored or hoped would be swept away in a summer storm, but now, it seemed, it had become something of an under-dog to root for.

My shoulders tensed as the house dropped six inches quickly, and the crowd behind me sucked in a breath. I gripped Abby's shoulder and she yelped in surprise.

"What if it falls?" I heard someone say.

"Then I'm screwed," I muttered under my breath. I released Abby's shoulder and twisted my ring faster and faster until finally, a puff of dust and debris emerged as the house once again met the foundation. There was a pause before the operator shouted, "All clear!"

I collapsed forward, hands on my knees as relief flooded through my bones. The neighbors behind me clapped and cheered. Abby threw her arms around me, and I gave her a crushing hug.

"Mom! Ow!" she shrieked.

The house was ready. I was ready.

At the end of the day, a black Yukon with a Salty Dog Café license plate frame pulled into the driveway. Abby had forced us to buy it when we were on vacation—our last vacation—on Hilton Head Island. She loved the black Labrador puppy wearing a yellow hat that decorated the frame, especially since it was during her phase of wanting a puppy. She stomped her foot and clutched the frame in protest until we finally acquiesced. It was a leftover from a previous life, an unexpected reminder that had the power to knock the wind out of me when I least expected it.

Matt got out of the car with an uneasy smile. He wore a white button-down with the sleeves rolled up to his elbows and dark jeans with tan loafers. His sandy blond hair looked lighter, as though he had been outside in his pool. Both he and Abby had the kind of hair that turned sun-streaked in a matter of hours in the sunlight, the kind of highlights worth a fortune in a salon.

My pulse quickened when I saw him. Each time I saw him, I still saw the man whom I had married and the boy who had first kissed me over Labor Day weekend a million years ago. It was still strange to see his hands by his sides, not reaching for me, not pulling me toward him. Many times, a flash from an alternate universe would occur, and I could see myself running toward him, feeling his arms wrap around me as he pulled me close. Telling me we could start over, that he was sorry for everything he had done. That he still loved me. That he wouldn't stop until he found a way for me to forgive him.

Yet I also saw the man who stood in front of me as everything I had imagined and planned for the future had changed. I also saw the man who easily signed off on the divorce papers without so much as a protest.

I saw the man who became close with someone else, who gave his attention to another woman at a time when I so desperately needed him. I saw the man who had had an affair. Or, at least who'd been planning to have one when I caught him with incriminating text messages.

He loved me, once. We were in love, once. We had a good marriage, once. In the past, I never thought any of those things would have caveats attached, yet there we were. Everything, it seemed, had changed. Except for me and all those memories of him.

He was the light and the dark, monster and hero, all wrapped into one. My past, present, and broken future, all in the same person.

Abby flew toward him on the driveway. "Hi, Daddy," she said into his shirt. He hugged her and kissed the top of her head.

"We just had dinner—chicken tenders—so she shouldn't be hungry. And I put a paper in the bag from her teacher. It has the schedule for the kindergarten graduation next month," I said quickly.

"Great, thanks." He nodded. I held out her bag and I saw

his hand shake as he took it. He slung the bag over his shoulder and shifted, looking around me like a flower aching to reach the sun around a pesky, overgrown bush. "House coming along?"

I glanced back at the house and nodded. "So far, so good." My mouth twisted. "Doesn't have a crystal chandelier, though."

He rolled his eyes slightly. "My mother won't let up about that."

"As she shouldn't," I said lightly.

"Very funny. She keeps getting on me to get up on a ladder and clean it, but I don't have a death wish." He smiled at me, and my shoulders relaxed with our banter. It was familiar, comforting.

He quickly shifted toward his car, moment over. "So, Abby said she's been helping to fix things up in there. I'm not trying to be a jerk, but are you sure it's safe for her?"

The smile vanished from my face, and I felt my cheeks redden in anger, but before I could answer, Eddie spoke from behind me.

"No, we're not. Wanna come and test some things out for us? There's a pile of electrical cords in a puddle of water and we need someone to dry them off." Eddie made a motion for Matt to follow him. "Your hair is made of rubber, so that'll ground the shock."

"Funny," Matt said. "Always nice to see you, Eddie."

"Likewise," Eddie called across the yard, his voice booming against the Yukon.

Matt watched as Eddie went inside the house before he turned back to me. "I was wondering if I could ask you something. Just a quick question."

I kept a hand on Abby's shoulder, although I considered asking her to go inside if his request should be anything but quick. "Okay."

His eyes shifted down as he surveyed the long crack on the driveway that appeared as though it had been seal-coated many times, but kept returning. We'd had flooding rains two years ago, and I suspected that the water had swelled the asphalt to the point of no return.

Usually it didn't happen like that. Usually the rain collected over time, widened the cracks, until one day, they were impossible to ignore.

"I was hoping you would agree to my mom and me taking her on a vacation. It would be to Disney World, maybe sometime in the fall." His words tumbled out, and he almost seemed surprised by them. I still knew him well enough to suspect that he had practiced that speech on the car ride over, thought about the exact best way to phrase it, and yet it had all come out in a messy tangle.

"Disney World?" I said as I crossed my arms over my chest.

"Yes. She kept asking me if we could go after I told her about it, and I know she'll be in school in the fall, but it's really the best time with work." His words grew smaller as he spoke, almost dimming down to a whisper.

I opened my mouth to protest, but Abby spoke first. "Please, Mom?"

"Of course. Sounds fun," I said tightly, forcing myself to half-smile. I looked back at Matt. "We'll have to discuss the details as you know more." My chest grew tight as I thought of him taking her on the vacation, giving her all the experiences that we had once talked about doing together. I so clearly remembered having a teasing conversation about all of the trips we would have to do once she was born, and a trip to Disney World was high on that list.

Matt shifted his weight and shoved his hands in his pockets. "You're welcome to come, if you want." He shook his head. "My mom was the one who suggested it. Pushed for it, in fact."

I didn't know if he meant that she had pushed for the trip, or to invite me, so I didn't say anything. I just shook my head slightly, immediately pushing any consideration of the proposal out of my head. It wouldn't make sense for me to go. I would have been an add-on, an afterthought.

"Okay. Well, thanks," he said again before he turned to get Abby in the car.

I said good-bye and watched him drive off with our daughter in the car he had bought right before we separated, with the license plate frame from our last vacation together.

All of those memories seemed to exist in another time and place, an alternate universe where I had no place living. A time when my life was secretly being defined by one decision at a time, making it impossible to see what the sum total of everything might turn out to be—choosing work over a date night, one more episode of *Law & Order* over getting into bed at a reasonable time when we still might have had the energy to be intimate, simply asking him to put his dishes in the dishwasher, again, rather than doing it out of frustration that had built so high it would never be hacked down.

Barely acknowledging our anniversary, never buying each other Christmas gifts, forgetting to kiss each other good night. It all seemed so normal, the typical result of the sediment of our relationship settling into predictability. Certainly nothing to worry about. Until one day, we were different people from the ones who got married.

At least, it seemed that way. Sometimes I wondered if the divorce made us even more different. If we could have found our way back to the middle had he tried. Had he not entertained the idea of an affair or had he begged for forgiveness. Shouted it from the middle of the lake, or done some grand gesture worthy of a movie. Had he refused to sign the papers, saying he couldn't live without me. But he did, he didn't, and then he did.

And four years later, I stood on my cracked driveway and watched him drive away in the same car that had taken him away when he first left, when I had no idea that he would never come back.

CHAPTER 10

"Look, it all has to be taken out and replaced," Thad, the plumber, said. He knocked a gnarled knuckle against the connected metal flues. "Unless you don't want to sell." He laughed, the tufts of hair in his ears wrinkling.

I stared up at the pipes that ran through the wall in the first floor, and Eddie shook his head.

"Well, obviously, that isn't the case," I said. "So, *all* of it has asbestos in it?" I already knew the answer, but asking prolonged the reality. All of the pipes would have to be replaced or else it would never pass inspection. If we weren't going to renovate anything, we could leave the pipes in the walls, and there wouldn't be any risk of exposure. But now, we would also have to jackhammer all of the cement outside to replace the piping to the street.

Renovating old houses was often a game of playing catch-up. Any changes meant bringing a house up to the innovations and improvements, not just from the past ten or twenty years, but the past century.

"You got it," Thad said. "We can have it all done within three days."

"I'd like to see two days," Eddie said, craning his neck into the hole of the bathroom, following the piping up until it disappeared into the plaster.

Thad shook his head. "I don't think I can have my guys here 'round the clock to get that done. Three days would—"

"Would be too long," I finished. "We need to get this done immediately. Every day wastes more money." And I was beginning to need all the help I could get, budget-wise. I had knocked on all the bathroom walls and they all sounded like they were filled with plumbing, which meant pulling out the plaster in the whole room. Then, everything would need to be replastered.

"Fine, fine. We'll do our best," he said.

"Better get started, then," Eddie said, eyebrows raised.

Thad walked off, muttering to himself about how he was never working with us again. It was a speech we had heard many times before, with almost every worker we had hired. Too fast, not enough money, too demanding, we didn't understand the scope of the work. What we definitely did understand was that there were many people out there looking for work, and that someone who could bring in quality work on a timeline within our budget was the most important component to my renovations.

As Thad left, he passed Frank, the electrician, in the driveway. They shared a look of warning as they swapped out. Frank had told me that most of the electrical system also needed to be replaced, which I had figured. Almost all of my houses required some kind of electrical work, but it was usually minor. But I knew that back when houses were built decades ago, knot-and-tube wiring was used. It ran on fuses instead of circuit breakers, with no grounding or high-capacity. The Maple house had it, and it all had to be ripped out or else insurance companies wouldn't insure the house. Not to mention, it was a serious fire hazard.

Frank had said he was surprised the electrical system had

survived as long as it had, since it was installed back in the days before modern appliances, computers, and electronics. As time marched on and the owners required more and more electricity, the fuses would have blown on a regular basis, nearly every time anyone turned on a hair dryer or started the microwave.

He, too, had walked off just as Thad had, muttering about unrealistic expectations after our conversation.

"Do you ever wonder if all these guys have a special bottle of bourbon at home just marked 'Alex'?" Eddie said as we watched Thad pull out of the driveway.

"That's pretty likely. Maybe I'll buy them each a bottle when this is all finished," I said. I clapped my hands and rubbed them together. "Anyway, I'm going to start on attacking those awful kitchen cabinets." I shuddered. "I can't wait to see those things cracked in half." I lifted the sledgehammer that rested against the exterior wall.

"Right on. I'm going to take a look at some of those front picture windows to see what they need," Eddie said. "Want me to save any glass shards for Matt?" I had told him about the Disney World trip and how Abby had talked of little else since the conversation.

"Don't tempt me," I said. I slung the sledgehammer over my shoulder. "But before I start in the kitchen, I want you to show me what you're doing to those windows, too."

I followed him up the porch to the four-over-one windows that lined the living room wall. They were huge by modern standards, both at least six feet tall and three feet wide. Four smaller panes of glass were on the top part of the window, and the bottom part was one single piece. Or, it should have been. Two of the four windows had broken or missing bottom panes, and most of the small top panes were missing, as well.

"So, what's the plan here?" I said.

"Well, my guys are going to pry the whole thing out with this guy." He lifted a five-in-one tool in the air. "Don't worry, it was meant to be taken out," he added when he saw my mouth open immediately. "Then we can take a look at the frame and see what might need to be repaired, or if the weights on the sash need to be replaced. We'll clean it up, replace the glass, paint the exterior facings, make sure it's all working right, then pop it back in." He cleared his throat. " 'Course they're likely full of lead paint, so we'll need to be careful when we sand them."

"Lead paint. The bane of my existence." I rolled my eyes. Nearly every house built before 1980 had lead paint in it, a fact that made most people freak out. But it could all be contained in the right way, if someone knew what they were doing. "And you can really do it for all these guys?" I said as I leaned forward and stared critically at the badly painted, dirty, splintering window frames. I knew sash windows were built to last, but the picture windows looked like they needed to have their last rites read to them.

"Do I have a choice?" he said.

"Good point." As I went inside to begin demo on the kitchen, I glanced back at the picture windows. I smiled as I thought of the sunlight streaming into the living room on a warm spring day, the breeze lightly brushing against the curtains before sweeping through the whole house, touching every surface. The breeze would bring the scent of the roses and lilacs that lined the front porch into the living room.

I lifted my sledgehammer, and with a satisfying swing, drove it straight into a wood veneer cabinet. It immediately collapsed onto the floor with a *thud*, like it was happy to be put out of its misery. I lifted the hammer again, ready to take down the next cabinet.

"Alex? My crew found something you might want to see." Eddie's voice called from outside.

I walked down the cracked front steps, following Eddie's voice into the backyard strangled by long, prickly vines. Piles of them sat to the side, as though pouting from being stopped in their rampage to overtake the property.

"For one, we found that." He pointed to an arched wooden

structure on the ground. A crew member held it upright, and I realized it was one side of a garden arbor. The white paint had bubbled and peeled away from most of the wood. "They know not to throw anything away for scrap, so we'll set it aside if you want to restore it."

I nodded as I took in what looked to be hand-carved arches on the top and the crisscross of the wood on the sides. "It's beautiful. Well, it once was."

"And then I just saw this." He pointed to one of the maple trees in the backyard. He walked around to the side of it, the side that pointed toward Elsie's house. He brushed back more ivy that had grown up the tree like fingers inching toward the sky, and showed me a carved circle.

I leaned in and squinted, pulling more vines off the tree trunk. It was only about six inches tall, and had faded so much into the wood that it was almost undetectable. Inside the circle read: *D.M. + E.S.*

"David Moore plus . . . someone. Elsie? I wonder if her maiden name starts with *S*." I glanced toward her house.

"The old lady next door? Could be. We wouldn't have found it at all, except one of my guys was back here, trying to trace the old sewer line and came across it," he said as he wiped his forehead on his arm.

I traced my finger on the grooves of the letters and around the circle. "How sweet."

"Sweet? Yeah, right. He was probably just trying to get into her pants," Eddie said with a laugh.

I thought of the photograph, and David's expression as he looked at the camera. "No. He loved her."

CHAPTER 11

I collapsed on my couch after a long day at the house. Thad had begun cutting all of the asbestos plumbing out of the walls, ripping out the old metal, and tenting off the area so none of the dangerous material would be inhaled.

I had finished the kitchen cabinets and moved on to the upstairs master bathroom, pulling out the rotted, builder-grade vanity, mirror, and light fixture. There hadn't been anything worth salvaging in that room. If there had been any period pieces—a pedestal sink with legs or a claw-foot tub—I would have restored and saved them, but the pieces I pulled out were circa 1995 and already deteriorating.

I rubbed the back of my sore neck. I had strained it while lifting up the vanity. Even with the help of one of Eddie's guys, it still didn't want to let go of the wall. Usually those pieces would crumble like dust, as though they were the ones who had been around for centuries, but that bugger clung on like an insect to an oak tree branch during a storm.

I picked up the pile of mail on the couch next to me. I swiped through coupon books, junk mail fliers, and the water bill—after last month's running toilet, I would save opening that for after I'd had a beer—before I pushed the whole thing on the floor. I checked my voice mail, and listened to a message from Traci.

"Look, I know you said you didn't want to meet anyone, but it's been forever since you've dated someone. That new history teacher at school—hello, *history,* he likes old things— wants to meet you. You guys are going out to dinner next weekend. His name is Gavin Magnesen. I'll text you his number. He's expecting your call. Don't kill me."

I collapsed against the back of the couch, my pulse quickening at the thought of a first date. I hadn't been on a proper date in over a year, since a minor flirtation with a guy I'd met at Home Depot. And even that couldn't really have been considered a date. The idea of having to present some alternate, perfect version of myself and make funny, light conversation made me want to sleep through the summer.

I lay back and closed my eyes, allowing my thoughts to drift to the past, to the time when David had carved his initials in the tree.

I could see the pink rosebushes exploding with blooms along the side of the house, and the white arched arbor off to the side, ivy growing across it. David's new convertible was parked in the driveway, and he and Elsie sat in the backyard by the maple tree. They kissed behind it, just out of view of the neighbors, but not hidden enough to make it seem as though they were doing anything wrong.

He showed her the initials carved in the tree, and even though she thought it was a little corny, she smiled and kissed him again. She asked him to pose by his new car for a photo, one that she kept in a journal, along with a pink rose from the garden.

I slowly opened my eyes and stared at a ticking clock on the wall, thinking about how when people moved out of a house, it began to die. The foundation seemed to crumble faster, the paint peeled quicker, and the wood floors warped in just a couple of seasons. People kept a house alive, not the other way around. And when the Moores moved out after David died, they took a piece of the house's soul with them.

The familiar feeling of loneliness began to settle down on my head as I wondered if my life would hold any more of those kind of romantic moments or if that part was over. I wondered if I had already used up all my credit in the love department and now would spend the rest of my life paying off the balance. Was I like the Maple house after everyone moved out?

I felt the sadness begin to move down my body, to my shoulders and down my arms like a shadow. One more minute and it would have me. It was as though I was standing on the edge of a cliff, peering over, and a thorny vine was slowly encircling my ankle, threatening to bring me over the edge.

Instead of letting it pull me over the edge, like I had so many times before, I stepped back.

I stood up, and walked out the door.

I made my way through the crowd in Harpoon Willie's, a dark-paneled watering hole in Williams Bay decorated with various sports memorabilia. Despite it being a Wednesday night, the place was packed shoulder to shoulder with the after-work crowd. I lifted a hand to a couple of Eddie's crew members clustered together in the corner before I reached the bar.

I surveyed the crowd of half-drunk men who glanced my way through a haze of cheap draft beer. Most of them I recognized as locals, but there were a few tourist types. They would increase in number as the summer marched on, especially the bikers who stopped in for a drink while they cruised around the lake.

I signaled to the bartender for a beer and relaxed against the bar. I was almost in a good mood when a petite, pretty blonde perched on a bar stool against the window made my stomach drop. Julia, Matt's girlfriend. She was with two other women dressed in scrubs, out after a day at the dental office, with glasses of white wine on the table. She didn't see me, but that was due to the fact that I quickly hid behind a large, sweaty man near the bar.

"Have a seat," a voice next to me said.

I shook my head even before I saw who spoke. When the voice's owner registered, I shook my head even harder.

"Sullivan. What are you doing here? Following me now?" I frowned, and grabbed my beer, and took a sip.

"Nope. I live just around the corner. I was going to ask you the same thing," he said. He was relaxed, his forearms on the bar in front of him. He cracked a wide smile, flashing the hole in the back of his mouth where he was missing a tooth. He glanced at the stool next to him. "Sit. I'll let you buy me a drink."

I opened my mouth to protest again, but I glanced over at Julia and her friends, one of whom started walking toward the bar. Suddenly, sitting next to Jack seemed like the safer option.

"So," I said as I settled into the stool, "find any beautiful houses to destroy lately?"

He smirked. "None as beautiful as the one I lost to you at the auction. That house doesn't even have a garage, Alex. Think about that for a minute. We live in Wisconsin. Where it snows."

"Really? I wasn't aware." I shook my head slightly, frowning. The lack of a garage was something I hadn't considered much. If there wasn't anything structurally wrong with the house, I probably could have chosen to build one. But as it was, there wasn't any money left in the contingency fund for extras.

"And tell me, how much did you have to spend to fix that crumbling foundation? Twenty, thirty thousand?"

I avoided his gaze and slowly closed my eyes. "Don't worry about it. It was worth it. And I'd do it all over again."

"I'm sure you would. Do you know how much I spend to build a whole new foundation on my houses? It's—" He stopped and laughed. "Never mind. You look depressed enough already." He signaled to the bartender, who refilled his drink without a word.

"Easy, Jack. Maybe try to make it to dinnertime before you fall flat on your face," I said. "Although, on second thought, keep going. You, facedown in the dirt, is something that would brighten my day."

Ignoring me, he continued, "That house should have been stripped for parts and then torn down. Sure, you could save some of those things you people like, like the tub or the fixtures, or whatever, but that whole house isn't worth saving. It's well past its prime, and it's time to move on." He took a slug of his drink. "I could put up two houses for the amount you're going to spend in throwing some Band-Aids over that money pit."

"Quantity over quality, Jack. You give flippers a bad name," I muttered.

"Why? Because I treat it like a business? Because I go after what makes the most profit?" he said.

I cleared my throat. "No. Because you treat it *only* like a business—fast and cheap. Flippers like you come into a house and rip out damaged hardwoods to put down laminate flooring, demo brick fireplaces in favor of marble surrounds, knock down plaster walls to put up drywall, and take a sledgehammer to claw-foot tubs." I paused and adjusted my legs on the stool. "You don't have any respect for the fact that almost everything in an old house was meant to be there—made to be there, made for the house—and not mass-produced in a factory somewhere. The type of work that makes people run away when they hear a house was a flip because they figure the work was half-assed."

A bemused look crossed his face. "I think my sales record would disagree with you."

"Well, let me ask you something: What do you have against old houses? What do you have against restoring homes for the people who actually live here, year-round?" I said as the bartender slid me another drink. My shoulders relaxed even more, and a light, airy feeling of a cheap beer buzz filled my head.

"Don't have anything against them. Just can't make money off of them. And you won't, either." He turned toward me. "Let me ask you something—you've heard of the Waterview Group, haven't you?"

I narrowed my eyes. They were one of the biggest real estate developers in the area, and also the deep-pockets client that Matt had represented right before our divorce. The hefty fee they paid him trickled down to me in our settlement, giving me enough to buy my first renovation property. "Of course," I said slowly.

He leaned forward. "Did you know that they're looking to build another resort? One closer to town? One close to . . ." He trailed off, leaning back for effect.

I frowned and shook my head. "The rumor of a resort near downtown has been around forever. Try again."

He laughed. "Only this time, it's true. They've quietly bought some properties in the area, trying to carve out space. To bulldoze." He made a clearing motion with his hand.

I shrugged. "Okay. That doesn't matter, because I'll never sell to them."

He leaned forward on the bar and slumped his shoulders. He lifted a finger to the bartender, who shook his head. Studying him, I didn't realize just how intoxicated he was when I'd first sat down. He slowly stood up, hanging on to the bar for support, and leaned toward me.

"Everyone has a price, Alex. Just wait—you'll get some tax lien or permit issue and you'll sell. Mark my words," he slurred. "And when that happens, call me first. I might let you save a few things before I rip it down. Can't say the same for Waterview."

"Go home and wait out the hangover," I said as I waved away his liquor-soaked breath.

He turned and slowly made his way to the door. When he

was outside, I exhaled and put my forehead against my arms on the bar. Waterview was a notoriously high-pressure developer, with a lot of cash and little ethics. If they put their crosshairs on my house, I wouldn't even qualify as the mouse in the Goliath story. And Matt might be the one to sign off on their purchase strong arm.

My face started to flush, and the room quickly became much smaller as my pulse quickened. I downed my beer and glanced over my shoulder at Julia. She and her friends stood, gathering their things. I settled back in my stool and trained my eyes on the baseball game on the television above the bar.

"Here. From the table in the back." The bartender placed a shot of something clear in front of me. I followed his pointed finger toward Eddie's crew members. They raised similar shot glasses in the air. Typically, I would have said no, but before I could stop myself, I grabbed it, lifted it in the air, and drank.

The liquid burned my throat, and I took another sip of my beer to extinguish the flames. The room began to take on a light, fuzzy appearance, and I felt my face flush from the alcohol. I quickly became overheated, and stood to go outside, my legs slightly wobbling.

The cool spring air washed over my face outside, and I took a deep breath. My lungs immediately filled with the cigar smoke of a middle-aged man standing in the parking lot. I started to cough, bending over and sputtering. As I did so, the cough turned violent and I nearly threw up all over the gravel.

I heard someone say, "Isn't that Matt's ex-wife?" My head whirled, and I saw Julia and her two friends staring at me as they stood next to their cars in the parking lot.

Shit.

"Hi there," I said. I took a step backward, and my foot went into a small divot in the parking lot and I wobbled.

"Alex, are you all right?" Julia called, her tiny, pointed nose wrinkling. "Do you need a ride home?" She smiled, but I could see behind her eyes that she couldn't wait to tell Matt that she'd seen his ex-wife nearly throwing up outside a bar. I doubted she would be voting for me as Mother of the Year anytime soon.

"No, thanks," I called to Julia as brightly as possible.

She nodded and waved before she got into her car and pulled out of the lot. I ignored the judgmental looks of her friends as they paused for a moment before doing the same.

I didn't want to be the pathetic ex-wife, drinking at a bar by herself. I didn't want to be rattled by Jack Sullivan and his doomsday predictions. I didn't want to be alone, at home, listening to my clock tick and missing my daughter. And I certainly didn't want to be on the receiving end of pity from Julia and her perky friends.

I took a deep breath and texted Traci: *A date sounds good. Looking forward to meeting him.*

CHAPTER 12

I woke the next morning with a terrible headache. As I sat up in bed, I put my head in my hands and took a long, ragged breath as I fought the urge to text Traci again and tell her the whole thing was a joke.

Without stopping to shower, I got into my car and drove straight to the Maple house. The house would distract me from the fact that I still seemed to care what Matt thought of me.

Frank, the electrician, was already waiting for me in the driveway in his beat-up white Astro van. The look on his face when he got out of the car told me he wasn't exactly looking forward to working on the house.

"Ready to get started?" I didn't stop as I headed toward the house. I heard him sigh wearily and then follow me up the cracked concrete porch steps.

I turned and faced him in the foyer. "Now, I'm sure you can guess what I'm going to say: Never drill or cut into anything without asking twice. Three times, to be safe."

"Got it." He took a step toward me. "I'm going to get started in the basement and—"

I held up a hand. "We. We are going to get started, but first we're going to do a walk-through and discuss the rewiring plan. Again."

He sighed, but followed me through the house. I explained that we had to wire the first floor from below, through the basement, and the second floor from above, through the attic, to minimize damage to the walls. I reminded him that no one was to hammer holes in the walls, that a hole saw could be used if necessary, but that was it. I pointed out all of the decorative moldings on the first floor and reminded him to be careful around all of the plaster corners and archways. We ended back in the basement, in front of the old fuse box.

I put my hands on my hips and stared at it. "How many amps would you say this carries?"

He squinted and leaned forward. "Probably sixty or so. Barely enough to run all the appliances in the kitchen. Most houses need about two hundred amps these days."

"Well, back in the day, no one had hair dryers, flatirons, and wine fridges, et cetera." I gave the fuse box a pat. "Time for the old girl to enter this century."

"Yo, Alex, come on up to the kitchen when you get a chance," Eddie called from upstairs.

"Have fun," I said to Frank, who grunted in reply.

In the kitchen, Eddie stood on the perimeter, pointing to a section of the flooring that he had begun to pry up. I knelt down, and saw all of the layers of flooring underneath the existing cracked ceramic tile. The ceramic tile was glued to an underlayment of plywood, which in turn was installed over two more layers of linoleum, each glued directly onto one another. Thankfully, an underlayment was between the linoleum and the original wood floor.

"Wow, so that's what's under there." I reached a finger forward to stroke the beautiful wood floor exposed through the layers of hideous linoleum and tile.

"Nope. Stay back. I'm pretty sure that some of that linoleum was glued down with asbestos adhesive," Eddie said.

I dropped my head forward and slowly stood up, my hands on my thighs. "Of course it was. *Of course.* So now we . . ."

"You know the drill. Protective gear, wet down the floor, take it up, dispose of it properly." He shook his head as he stared down at the exposed corner of hardwood. "Man, does everything in this house have to be toxic?"

"Watch it," I said. "I already have a pounding headache."

He eyed me critically. "You look terrible. Late night last night?"

"I ran into Jack Sullivan, who was as charming as ever," I said. I thought of his doom-and-gloom predictions about Waterview Developers and a wave of nausea washed over my flushed face. "Listen, I'm going to work outside. I need some fresh air."

I stood in front of the house, hands on hips, shielding my eyes from the sun, as I contemplated where to start. Some of Eddie's crew members were working on the window sashes, adding an epoxy to the cracked and missing wood around the frames, and brushing on a liquid to strengthen any weak or rotting spots.

The dilapidated wooden fence bordering the property caught my eye. It had passed its expiration date long ago, and it was now precariously braced with a few two-by-fours until we built a new one. But one strong wind and the whole thing would fall over.

I spotted a pair of work gloves sitting on the front steps, slipped them on, and marched toward the fence. Already sweating out the liquor from the night before, I pulled at the two-by-four and the fence moved to closer to the ground, at a forty-five-degree angle. I gave it a good push, ready for the satisfying *crack* when it would fall to the ground. But . . . nothing. It swayed, but remained in place. I pushed it again, but it did the same thing.

Gathering up all my strength, I threw my weight into it, grunting and pushing, until I couldn't keep myself upright, and the fence collapsed with me on top of it, lying on it like it was a surfboard.

My already aching body didn't appreciate the extra trauma, and I lay on the splintery wood panel, trying to decide what throbbed the most.

"Are you hurt?" a voice said in the distance.

I raised a finger in acknowledgment as I slowly lifted my head off the wood. Elsie stood at the property line, dressed in a pair of knit pants and a turtleneck despite the weather, and she eyed me with concern.

"Did you mean to do that?" she said.

I shook my head as I slowly got up off the ground, inch by inch, groaning muscle by creaking bone. Once upright, my head started to spin, and I took a quick step backward along with a deep breath.

"You don't look so good. You're white as a ghost. Come, sit. Have some water," she said.

My hands shaking, I agreed, and sat on her front steps as she poured me a drink from a frosted pitcher. I took a long gulp and felt my pulse return and my sense of equilibrium coming back.

"Are you sick?" she said.

"Not exactly." Sick to my stomach from the drinks and what I had done last night, yes. The embarrassment of seeing Julia and my conversation with Jack began to wash over me, and I closed my eyes, trying to push it out of my head.

"How's the house coming?" she said. "All day long there's people coming and going, and they all seem to be afraid of you."

"Oh, they're not afraid of me. If they were, they wouldn't complain half as much as they do," I said.

"Well, they all seem to run around, scurrying like mice when you pull into the driveway each day," she said.

"Good. We have a lot of work to do. Plumbing is happening,

electrical is in the process of being done," I said as I pressed the cold glass to my cheek. "Then it will be bathrooms, the kitchen, flooring . . . landscaping." I glanced at my flattened fence. "Who knows what else we'll find."

I remembered the initials.

"Actually, we found something in the backyard, carved on one of the maple trees." I pulled out my phone and swiped to a picture of the carvings. I held it out. "I'm assuming *D.M.* is for *David Moore*, and the *E.S.* is . . ."

Her eyes grew wide as she slowly took the phone from my hand. She held it close to her face, studying the picture. "Yes. It's me. My maiden name was Slattery." She shook her head slightly in disbelief before she exhaled.

"I thought so," I said gently. I took another sip of my water.

Her eyes were watering, but her mouth twisted in a small smile as she handed my phone back to me. "You know, he was so handsome and charming, he was such a catch. He could have had any girlfriend he wanted in town, but . . ." She looked down at her hands. "I was two years younger, and never thought he would look at me as anything more than a kid, like a little sister. As we grew older, I became more bashful around him. It wasn't easy to watch my playmate from childhood grow into this man while I remained awkward and quiet with my nose buried in books."

She glanced at the backyard, studying the tree where they had carved their initials. "We kissed for the first time at the Christmas party, when I was sixteen and he was eighteen. A group of us had snuck outside, behind the old arbor, with a bottle of Scotch. Everyone else had gone inside from the cold, but David and I remained. I remember my cheeks were flushed from the weather, and I started to shiver, and he put an arm around me and drew me near to warm me up."

I smiled and nodded, the sounds of the Maple house grow-ing further away as I pictured Elsie and David in the backyard, huddled against the arbor, with sparkling snow lightly falling around them.

"I lifted my head and his face found mine, and we kissed." She blushed slightly as she adjusted her glasses. "I was already warm on the inside from the Scotch, but it was nothing compared to how I felt then. It was like . . ." She trailed off, her eyes searching the porch for the right description.

"Summer," I said. I adjusted myself quickly, crossing my legs. "Like the first days of summer, when you almost can't believe it's here, and don't want to think about it too much, or enjoy it, because you're afraid it'll be taken away."

Before I could stop myself, the memory of the first time Matt kissed me flashed before my eyes. It was Labor Day, and he was home from college. A group of us were out on a boat at sunset, going for a late cruise, and since the weather was starting to grow colder, I threw a hoodie over my short sleeves to warm up. Matt and I were at the bow of the boat, legs stretched out, while everyone else was on the back, sitting around the cooler.

I can't remember what we talked about, but it was something that made me laugh. I remembered the feelings rather than the details. He teased me about being younger, and I leaned forward to slap his leg. His hand lightly caught my wrist, in a way that made both of us stop. There was a pause, and the lake air crackled around us, and before I could stop myself, I leaned forward and kissed him.

In that moment, I could feel everything change. Everything grew quieter and louder at the same time. The cheers of our friends on the boat muted in the distance, but the lake water lapping against the boat became louder. It was just one kiss, and when we pulled apart, my face flushed as our friends clapped.

"Sorry," I remember saying. I could barely look over at him, but when I did, one corner of his mouth was twisted up in a smile.

He leaned forward and put a hand next to me on the white leather seat. I held my breath as he put his cheek next to mine and whispered, "Don't be."

It was all so surreal that I almost didn't believe it had happened when I woke up the next morning. I didn't want to think about it too much, or else I might wake up and realize it was all some ridiculously good dream, that I'd had a small sample of such an amazing thing, but that it wasn't real.

Years later, it occurred to me that maybe it wasn't. Maybe it *was* a dream, the memory a ghost itself, trapped between reality and fantasy, reliving a day over and over again because it refused to be exorcised.

Elsie shifted in her yellow wicker porch chair, and it brought me out of the past. "So what happened then?" I said quickly as I brushed my hair from my sweaty forehead.

She frowned and sighed heavily. "By the summer, he was gone. He bought the car that you saw in the picture. Oh, his parents hated that car. They wanted him to get something more practical, but he had his heart set on a convertible." She shook her head. "And one morning in August, he and I got into a terrible fight, and he drove off." She pressed her lips together, unable to continue.

"I'm so sorry," I said after a moment. "That must have been so difficult."

"Thank you." She nodded. "It was all so long ago, and I haven't thought about any of it in years." She smiled. "I suppose you fixing up that house stirred up a lot of old porch dust."

"Yes, it has." I didn't tell her that it had begun to stir up dust in not just her life, but mine, as well.

The heartbreak that I had been able to compartmentalize for over four years was seeping back into my life like blood through a gauze pad, bringing back everything I had tried to bury.

* * *

Later that night, after Abby came home from Matt's house and I had tucked her into bed, I turned on my computer. I checked my e-mail and a few house renovation Web sites before I typed the name *Gavin Magnesen* into Google. We were meeting for dinner the following weekend, but I hadn't yet built up the nerve to search his name.

I clicked on the first result, the high school's Web site. His classroom page popped up, complete with a picture of him. When I saw his photo, I sat back quickly. He looked younger than I expected. Late twenties, I guessed. He had short dark hair and an adorable five o'clock shadow on his cheeks and chin. He looked like he could be a professional soccer player, not a high school history teacher.

I glanced in the mirror at my disheveled appearance, but quickly looked away. I was potentially out of my league with Gavin and would need to step up my game. Flat-iron my hair, wear a dress, paint my nails. All things that never happened anymore.

I stood up and went to my closet, looking for appropriate date attire, when my phone buzzed. I reached across my desk and checked the number on the display, but I didn't recognize it.

"Alex Proctor? It's Elsie Burke again." Elsie's voice was small, barely above a gravelly whisper. "Did I catch you at a bad time?"

"Did something happen at the house?" I said automatically. I began to walk to my desk and search for my car keys.

"No, nothing like that. The house is just as you left it: torn apart." She thinly laughed.

"Good. So what can I help you with?" There was a long pause, and the phone crackled. "Hello?" I said.

"I'm here," she said. I heard her sigh, a long, whistling sound that echoed through the phone. "Thank you for speaking to me earlier. It's been so long since I talked about those things—about David—that it's almost like I forgot that they happened."

"Of course," I said. When she didn't continue, I said again, "Is there something that you need?"

"Well, yes. You see, I didn't quite finish the story." She cleared her throat. "You see, the day before David died, I found out I was pregnant."

I sat back quickly in my desk chair and brought my knees to my chest. "Oh, wow."

"I was planning to tell him the next day, but we got into that fight about something silly, and he drove off. I figured I would tell him after we both calmed down, but of course, I never got that chance," she whispered.

"That's terrible," I said.

"After he died, I was in such shock that I didn't tell my parents, or anyone, for months. I didn't eat much during that time, so no one could tell I was carrying a child. By the time I told my mother, I was nearly six months along. She didn't handle the news well, nor did my father, and so we made the decision to give the baby up for adoption," she said. "Give *her* up for adoption. It was a little girl."

I tightened my arms around my knees and nodded, even though I knew she couldn't see me.

"I only held her once before the nurses came and took her. They said it would be better if I didn't get attached. But, of course, I already was," she said. "That was just how it was done back then, I suppose. My parents handled the whole process. I never even met the adoptive parents, or knew their names." She cleared her throat again. "But I always wanted to know that she was all right, that she was able to grow up with a good family." Her voice grew quiet. "It's silly, but she had a wing-shaped birthmark on her right shoulder, and I remember thinking that it was a sign that the angels would watch over her, and make sure she was happy."

"I don't think that's silly at all," I said. My voice caught in my throat.

"I never looked for her, and had somewhat convinced my-self to forget about it, but seeing your daughter . . ." Her voice broke and she paused. "Well, I think I might want to. Find her, I mean," she said. "If she would want to see me. I have felt as though she might not want to meet me, or she might be angry that I gave her away."

"I get that. But it's been so long, and if it were me, I would want to meet my birth mother," I said.

"If I find her, then I won't have to wonder anymore. I had been able to forget about it, but now that all those memories have come back, it's been hard for me to let go again. I can't go back in time and tell David, but maybe I could forgive myself if I meet her. Would you help me?"

I frowned. "I'd love to help, but I'm not sure what I could do. I don't know anything about finding adoption records."

"Maybe not, but I don't, either. But I know that you're strong, and you understand loss. I've seen you at that house, and I know you don't give up," she said firmly.

Immediately, I wanted to protest: *Yes, I do. I give up all the time.*

"Please help me," she added.

I again hesitated, not wanting to promise anything that I wasn't sure I could deliver.

"Mom?" said a voice from the hall.

I turned my head to Abby, who stood in the doorway. Her long hair was tangled around her shoulders and her eyes squinted in the light. "I can't sleep. Can I come in your bed?"

"Hold on just one minute, Elsie," I said, and cradled the phone on my shoulder. I turned to Abby and nodded. "Of course."

She padded over and climbed into my bed, the teddy bear that I bought for her when I was pregnant tucked under her arm. "Love you, Mommy."

"Love you, too," I whispered to her. She fell asleep almost instantly, safely tucked underneath the comforter. I thought of how I nearly died each time I had to say good-bye to her, and couldn't imagine if I had lived my whole life without her.

I exhaled and adjusted the phone on my chin. "Elsie?" I pressed my hand against my chest. "Yes. I will do everything I can to help you find your daughter."

CHAPTER 13

I had a nightmare about the house that night. In my dream, I stood on the sidewalk, screaming, as Jack Sullivan drove a bulldozer straight into the front porch. It was decorated for Christmas, as Elsie had explained, with evergreen garlands and a tree in the front window. Mrs. Moore was inside, hanging ornaments with her husband while David strung the lights.

Jack drove the bulldozer into the porch, and the house began to collapse, the Moore family screaming and trying to claw their way out of the rubble as the house fell around them. At the last moment, before they disappeared under the concrete, I saw that Abby was in the debris, too.

I woke up, both sweating and freezing, and glanced at the clock: 5:32 a.m. Abby was still asleep in bed next to me, so I carefully stood up and walked to the kitchen. The sunlight was just beginning to peek through the horizon, and I could hear the birds chirping around the feeder in the backyard that Abby had brought home from school last year. I took a long, slow breath as I brewed a cup of coffee. I pushed open a window, and the spring air rushed over my skin, bringing me back to reality and safety.

Taking my cup of coffee, I went out on the deck and wrapped a blanket around my shoulders to ward off any last bit of early morning chill. I sipped the cup, enjoying the silence for a few minutes, before the screen door opened and Abby padded out.

"Mom, why are you up so early?" she said. Her eyes were half-open and her hair stuck up in all directions.

"I was thinking about my house and couldn't sleep. Do you want to snuggle with me?" I held open my arms and she climbed into my lap. I wrapped the blanket around both of us, and she closed her eyes.

I kissed the top of her head and inhaled, taking in the soapy smell of her hair. In that minute, at least, all was well.

My mind wandered back to my promise to Elsie to help her find her lost daughter. To the house, which had first lost the Moore family, and then lost its beauty due to years of neglect. To the Moores, who had lost their son and a grandchild they never knew existed. And then I considered myself, who had lost a marriage, a family, and my trust in everything I thought was true.

We each had lost so much. Yet it seemed as though there was something changing in the air, a whisper of second chances, for all of us. In that moment on the deck, I watched the sun rise high and illuminate my neighborhood, and I realized that restoring the Maple house was no longer just a renovation, but an opportunity for renewal. Maybe in putting it back together, I would be complete again. In clearing the cobwebs from the house and unsticking all the old windows, I could move forward along with it.

Maybe I, too, could be restored and be even better than before.

CHAPTER 14

Finding Elsie's daughter was at the top of mind as I worked on the house the next day. A part of me whispered that I shouldn't take this on. That it was really none of my business. I could simply fix the house up, sell it, and move on. But after seeing her with Abby, and knowing that I might be able to help her heal in some way, I knew I couldn't walk away.

And so I thought of her as I worked in the upstairs hallway, ripping off yellowed wallpaper that was faded and stained by years of cigarette smoke.

"What did they use on this? Superglue?" I muttered as I grabbed a corner and gave a hard tug. A tiny corner of the paper came off in my hand, but the majority of the piece remained. It mocked me on the wall, whispering, *Nice try, but I've been here longer than you.*

I grabbed another corner and gave the blue-and-yellow-flowered print a pull, but again, only a tiny shred of paper came off, curling like a ribbon on a birthday party gift. I sighed and looked around the hallway, where every inch was covered in the ugly print. I estimated that the paper was put up some time in the eighties, or maybe the seventies, when wallpaper was all the rage.

Trends in houses come and go. In the 1950s, everyone ripped claw-foot tubs and Victorian details out of their houses, in favor of vinyl and man-made materials. Thankfully, this house had been spared some of that, since we still had a claw-foot tub in the bathroom, but the room hadn't completely escaped the eighties. It was covered in a horrible blue and white—well, what used to be white—butterfly wallpaper pattern with flecks of metallic silver in it. If it wasn't so faded and stained, it might have been considered a unique design feature, but it hung on the walls like a dirty blanket.

I grabbed my scoring tool and started moving it in a circular motion, making tiny perforations in the paper. Then I sprayed it with a gel that would break down the glue underneath. I stared at the wall, trying to will the enzyme to soak into the paper. After a moment, I lifted my putty knife and started scraping.

"Finally," I said as I was able to wedge the tool under the paper and lift some of it off. "Victory is mine." But as I carefully tore away the piece, I stopped in surprise.

"No." Instead of bare wall under the paper, there was another layer of wallpaper, this time black and gold swirls, likely from the late 1960s. "Great." I slumped my shoulders forward before taking the edge of the scraper and working a tiny hole in the new layer of paper. From what I could tell, there was at least one more layer underneath, so faded that I couldn't tell the color. Three full layers of wallpaper to scrape and pull from the plaster.

I had encountered multiple layers of wallpaper before—notably, in the 1960s bungalow I did the year before—and it was one of the most frustrating and mind-numbing of all renovation tasks. I knew flippers who had pulled the face off the wallpaper, and then painted the backing after sanding the walls.

They looked fine enough for the sale, but if the home owners ever wanted to change the paint color, they might curse the day when they bought the house from a flipper who wanted a quick sale. Not to mention, if water ever got into the walls, the glue could reactivate and create a giant disaster, with the paint bubbling and sliding off, and mold growing in between the paper and the wallboard.

I scraped until my shoulders burned and my hands were nearly crippled into a half-open fist, but I had only removed one tiny section of the wall. It was the worst kind of grunt work, and I estimated it would take days, and a lot of Tylenol, to take it all down.

Sweat poured from my forehead, and as I stopped to wipe it I heard my phone ringing from downstairs. I walked down and saw that I had a voice mail. It was from Gavin.

"Hi, Alex. Thanks so much for calling me. I was hoping that you would. Dinner or drinks sound great. I'd love to come up there and meet you somewhere by the lake. What about on Wednesday night after work? Just text me a time and location, and I'll be there. Talk to you soon."

His voice was warm, friendly, and I could tell that he was smiling as he left me the message. I wiped my dusty forehead on my forearm and shrugged, not wanting to overreact, but I couldn't stop the smile from moving across my face. My shoulders suddenly didn't ache as much, and I jogged back upstairs, sprayed down another section of wallpaper, and got back to work.

Two days later, I pushed open the door to Pier 290, my stomach in knots. As I stepped onto the restaurant's wide pine floor, my ankles wobbled slightly in the three-inch wedge heels that I had found lurking in the back of my closet. I carefully moved across the entryway's uneven floorboards that were salvaged from one of the old historic estates around the lake, praying that I didn't literally stumble through my first date in six months. In the hallway leading to the main restaurant area, I passed by vintage black-and-white photographs from the lake's history and plaques indicating which pieces of wood were salvaged from various historical estates.

I spotted Gavin sitting at the bar, a tall pilsner glass in front of him. He wore a crisp white shirt with the sleeves rolled up to the elbows, tan shorts, and boating shoes. His tan belied the fact that he spent every afternoon inside, teaching. I could immediately guess that probably half of the girls in his class had a crush on him.

I slowly walked forward, my hands shaking, wishing I had thought to get a manicure, or a pedicure, or a haircut. I wore a denim shirtdress, purchased from Target. It was the first outfit I had seen when I went in the day before to buy some new shoes for Abby. The model in the poster board above the display was resting against a brick wall, one hand casually tucked into a pocket. That was what sold me on the dress: pockets. They were a place to thrust my hands when I was nervous, and they could help me achieve a relaxed yet attentive stance when I would really just want to melt into the floor like butter.

"Gavin?" I said as I rested my hand on the bar.

He flashed a brilliant smile, the corners of his eyes crinkling with warmth and thankfully making him look older. "Thanks for coming," he said.

"Of course. Thanks for making the trek up here," I said.

He gestured toward an empty seat next to him, but I shook my head and pointed outside. "Why don't we sit down out there? There's a great sandy beach area down by the lake."

We settled into two Adirondack chairs on the sandy beach between the restaurant and the docks. Fire pits lined the beach area, with chairs set around them so people could enjoy a cocktail by the water. Where the inside was more formal and proper, out in the sand I could safely kick off the terribly uncomfortable wedges and exhale. *Better he sees me like this now,* I thought.

"So, house flipping, huh?" Gavin said as he leaned back into the whitewashed chair. As he settled backward, he looked like he fit perfectly into the surroundings. He could have been a vacationer enjoying a midweek dinner out, or a local exhaling after a long workday. "Like the people on television?"

"I prefer to call it 'renovating,' but sure," I said. "Except HGTV isn't exactly breaking down my door to come and film. They only seem to be interested in people who renovate houses in places like California, where the market is insanely expensive. And, of course, there's little reality to anything that happens on those shows."

He laughed. "Ah, too bad. But seriously, Traci said you're working on some historical property right now?"

I raised my eyebrows, wondering just how much my cousin had told him. I had the feeling that he knew volumes more about me than I did about him. "One hundred and fifteen years old, actually. The foundation was a disaster, the roof has some leaks, the plumbing was a nightmare, and the electrical system was a serious fire hazard. But it's . . . beautiful."

He cocked his head to one side and gave me a small smile. "That's great. I'm a history teacher, as I'm sure Traci told you, and I'm kind of mildly obsessed with preservation. I grew up in one of those old, rickety houses with noises and quirks and secret passageways."

I leaned forward, forgetting to sit perfectly or tuck my hair behind my ears. "Really? I love that. Any buried treasures?"

He laughed. "Not at all. We did have this one door that never seemed to want to stay shut, though, and we were convinced that we had a ghost living with us."

I nodded. "You probably did. I totally think houses collect all kind of energies from the people who used to live there."

"Any ghosts in your current property?" he asked.

I thought of Elsie, and shook my head. "Maybe skeletons in the closet, but nothing ghostlike."

"Well, I'd love to see it sometime. I'm sure you're doing

right by it," he said. He glanced over his shoulder at the waitress. "Should we order some food? More drinks?" He leaned forward and lowered his voice. "This is your out, you know. If you think I'm a troll, just slowly get up and leave. No hard feelings."

I smiled before I looked up at the waitress. "We'd like to see some menus, please."

"Ah, good. I haven't scared you off yet," he said as she left.

"Night's still early, though," I said as I tucked my bare feet underneath my skirt.

"True. I won't get too confident," he said. The waitress brought more drinks, and we settled back into our chairs. He looked out onto the water. "What a great spot."

The water was calm, only dotted with one boat in Williams Bay that bobbed on the surface. I could see the boaters sitting up front, feet up, drinks in hand, heads turned toward the brilliant sunset.

The warmth of the sunset moved over my shoulders, and I inhaled deeply, taking in the scent of the lake water. "It's perfect," I said.

Halfway through dinner, he leaned back and smiled. "So, how did you get involved in all of this house restoration stuff? Was your dad a contractor or something?"

I shook my head. "Not at all. He was an engineer before he retired a few years ago. But he always loved to fix things up around the house. Probably because he loved figuring out how everything worked. He always had me watch him while he would tinker with the kitchen sink, or made sure I knew the exact place to spread joint compound on drywall. One time, he quizzed me on the difference between various paint strippers before I could go outside and play with my friends. You know, your basic schoolgirl knowledge."

He laughed. "That's great, though. Clearly it all paid off."

"And what about you? Why did you want to become a history teacher?" I said.

"I told you I was always kind of mildly obsessed with preservation, and so I started off as a history major at the University of Illinois. But, as you might imagine, that doesn't really leave too many options for careers, so I switched to education with a history minor. I figured if I couldn't do, I would teach," he said.

"And now you teach world history in high school," I finished.

He nodded. "Yes, and I'm kept on my toes every single day. The amount of times I have had to defend and explain nearly every single historical event would leave your head spinning." He took a sip of his beer and shook his head. "But I love it. Great school, great kids. I've been teaching for six years now and no burnout in sight."

I easily did the math, confirming his age to be twenty-eight, but before I could get nervous about our age difference, he said, "Traci said you've been flipping houses for only a few years now. Why didn't you start sooner?"

My smile faded slightly. "Oh. I started after my divorce. It was something I had always planned to do, and suddenly I found myself at a time in my life when . . ." I trailed off as I swallowed hard. "I had to." The words popped out quickly, before I could stop them, and I felt my face flush slightly. I grabbed for my glass of water, taking a long, slow gulp to steady my nerves. Talking about Matt on a first date definitely wasn't on the agenda.

He nodded quickly, and changed the subject by telling me more about his childhood home. He told me how it was filled with strange nooks and crannies, and how, when he was twelve, he and a friend tried to talk to the ghost with a Ouija board during a sleepover, but a thunderstorm knocked out the power and they were too terrified to go through with it in the dark.

After dinner, we left the restaurant and walked to our cars. Now for the uncomfortable part, I thought. The part where he would try to kiss me, or run away, or awkwardly ask for another date. The time when the last couple of hours could be summed up with a few words or a gesture.

"I'll walk you," he said. As we reached my car, he said, "Well, Alex, it was great to meet you. I had a really nice time." His eyes flickered back to the restaurant, and I noticed they had flecks of green in the center.

I nodded, my throat growing dry in anticipation. "I did, too."

He opened his mouth to say something else, but I surprised myself by talking over him. "Dinner again sometime?" I said. I nervously laughed as he lifted his eyebrows in surprise.

"I was just going to say the same thing. Of course. Why don't you check your schedule, and we'll come up with another time?" he said.

I nodded quickly and rubbed my sweaty palms on my skirt. He leaned forward and gave me a kiss on the cheek, soft and sweet, before flashing me another smile.

CHAPTER 15

The day after my date with Gavin, I was still on a high when I left the Maple house during lunch and headed down to the local courthouse to see if they had any birth records for Elsie's baby. I had searched on my computer earlier that morning, and found the blog of someone searching for a child given up for adoption. I quickly read a few entries and learned that the author had gone to the local courthouse to pull records for her child's birth certificate. I had a starting point, a beginning of the breadcrumb trail.

It might have been midweek, but the town was still nearly as crowded as the weekends since the summer season was in full steam. When I'd first arrived at the house that morning, I had to kick out a visitor who tried to park in the driveway. Street spaces were scarce, leaving tourists to circle around the neighborhoods, but the weather was perfect—blue skies, bright sun—so not many people were leaving the beach.

I turned down Broad Street, heading toward the county clerk's office, when my eye was caught by a redbrick building with the words *Lake Geneva Historical Society*. I had planned to go there at some point during the renovations to see if they had any information on the Maple house. I hesitated at the stoplight. I could see an employee, with her back to me, sitting at a desk. Meanwhile, up ahead, toward the clerk's office, a sea of people walked down the sidewalk.

Once inside the historical society, I was greeted by a familiar face.

"Alex! Alex Proctor, it's so good to see you!" Shannon Stone, an old classmate from high school, beamed at me. Her bangs were short and straw-like, just as she wore them in high school. She bragged about cutting her own hair, although it really wasn't something to boast about. She also seemed to know everything about everyone, as though she was cataloguing everyone's secrets and storing them up for winter like a gossip chipmunk. "It's been what? Twenty years?" She looked me up and down slowly.

I nodded. "Something like that." I hadn't attended any of my high school reunions. It wasn't as though I was making a statement by not attending. It just felt like the people whom I wanted to still see, I did, and the people whom I didn't . . . well, I wasn't going to go out of my way to force the interactions.

"That's just too long for old classmates to go without seeing each other!" she exclaimed, her bangs floating upward, then settling back down on her forehead.

"I suppose." I hooked a thumb into my jean shorts and swayed a little in my beat-up running shoes.

"Well, you look the exact same," she said. The corners of her mouth turned down at the lie.

"Thanks. So do you. Listen, I was—"

She kept talking, cutting me off with a smile. "And Matt? How's he doing? Gosh, he was just so handsome back in high school. I'm sure he looks the same, too."

My hand fell to my side. "Oh. He's fine," I said quickly. "I'm just—"

"Any kids?" she said.

I sighed. "One. She's five."

"Ah, a little girl. Matt must be beside himself with love for her, I'm sure. I haven't seen him in forever, either. How's he doing?" she asked.

"We're divorced, Shannon," I finally said.

She put a hand to her mouth. "I'm so sorry. I hadn't heard." She frowned and wrinkled her nose, yet her eyes twinkled and I could tell that she very much had heard. Of course she had.

"Well, it happens. Anyway, I'm here to look up some information about a house I recently purchased over on Maple Street. The address is 4723 Maple," I said quickly. I glanced down at the nameplate on the desk and saw that Shannon was the director of the historical society. No way to get around her, so I figured I might as well steam right through her.

"Sure," she said with a smile as the delight left her eyes. "That house doesn't have historical status, does it? It doesn't sound familiar."

I shook my head. The house was too far in disrepair to have ever been considered a historical icon, and from what I had heard, one had to go through a lengthy process to prove the house was significant enough to be preserved. My affection for it and the claw-foot tub upstairs wouldn't exactly pass for "significant."

Shannon turned and bent down to her computer, typing in the address. "Oh, I think I remember that house. It was practically falling over last time I saw it."

I couldn't argue with that.

She squinted at the computer. "Ah. Yes. We actually have two documents on file."

She walked over to a row of filing cabinets, and selected one that read 1947 and another from 1901. "We just started electronically cataloguing all of our materials, and it's been a pain, but it makes things so much easier." She brought the files to me.

The first, from 1901, was the original plat of survey from the house. The footprint of the house looked the same, which I had figured, since it didn't seem to have had an addition over the years like most of the other older homes in the neighborhood. Yet the property was much larger in the original survey, encompassing a structure behind it.

"What's that?" I pointed to a small rectangle behind the house.

"Let me see." Shannon leaned forward and studied the drawing. "I think that was the original carriage house, for probably horses and then automobiles later on. It isn't there anymore?"

I shook my head. "No. The backyard is much smaller now." I pointed to the rectangle. "I think that's the house behind it, actually. The owners must have sold it off at some point."

She nodded. "That's likely what happened."

She handed me the other file on the house. Inside was a newspaper article dated December 15, 1947, and titled "Christmas Season Is Here" with a black-and-white photo of the Maple house.

"Oh, wow," I whispered as a tingle ran down my spine. Here it was, in front of me, a photograph of the house just as Elsie had described it. I lightly traced the outside of the house, my finger swooping across the evergreen garlands and red velvet bows adorning the front porch. It was before the time of disrepair for the house, and even though the picture was in black and white, I could tell that the paint on the porch was fresh, the concrete steps were newly poured, and the stucco carefully maintained.

I stared at it, blinking rapidly, as I thought of making it look that way again. It felt like a sign, like a hand had reached out across time to pat me on the back and tell me I was on the right path.

"You know, 1947 was another cicada year," I said, my voice just above a whisper.

"Oh, yes. Of course," she said quickly.

She waited for me to say more, but I just glanced down at the photograph again. "Could I get a copy of this?"

She shrugged and took it from me. "Sure." She brought the photo to the copier and tapped her fingernails against it as it whirred to life. "So, what happened between you guys? You were such a great couple."

I stared at her, waiting to see if she was joking, but she just kept tapping her fingers. "Honestly, it's none of your business," I finally said.

Her eyebrows fell, and she twisted her mouth to the side in annoyance. "You know, I think I heard he had a new girlfriend. Someone young, pretty."

"He does," I said with a nod.

When I didn't say more, or react, she frowned again and slid the photograph's copy toward me on the countertop. "I didn't mean to pry. I've had troubles in relationships, too." She wiggled a bare left ring finger at me. "Twice."

I ignored her invitation to commiserate and glanced down at the photo before picking it up. "Thanks."

"You really think you can make that hunk of junk look good again? It doesn't look anything like that photo anymore," she said.

I shook my head. "No. But it will."

I bid Shannon good-bye and headed down to the Walworth County clerk's office. I glanced at my watch as I waited in line. Twelve thirty. I shifted my weight and sighed heavily, swaying back and forth impatiently. I had only a half hour left of my lunch break before I had to meet Eddie back at the house to go over the condition of the flooring.

We were hoping to patch the upstairs flooring and save most of the original wood, but we wouldn't know how much until we started pulling up boards. If the subflooring was damaged beneath the warped wood, it would all have to come out and we'd have to start from scratch. I could use an engineered hardwood to replace it, but, of course, it wouldn't look the same. Ideally, I would find some salvaged wood to patch in, but I didn't have the weeks required to search for that kind of material.

After ten long minutes, I reached the front of the line. A woman with shoulder-length gray hair motioned me forward.

"How can I help you?" she said. Her name tag read *Karen*, and her eyes had a weary look that I guessed was from dealing with paperwork and cranky customers all day, every day.

"Yes, hi." I pulled a piece of paper out of my back pocket, my hands shaking. I was surprised that I was nervous, like I was prying into something that I shouldn't, or that she would turn me away for being some kind of inappropriate snoop.

I pointed to my house's address. "I just bought a house on Maple Street, and I'm doing some research on some of the old occupants. I was wondering if you had any information on death records, or marriage records . . . or birth records." The words tumbled out quickly, running together like melted ice cream and chocolate syrup.

Karen gave me a suspicious look. "For whom?"

"For a child who was born in the 1940s who might have lived in the house." A lie, but a small one.

She glanced down at the names and then looked back up. She folded her arms over her chest. "Is it a relative?"

My face flushed. "Well, not exactly. I—I was asked to possibly find a baby who was put up for adoption."

"And they were born here, in this county?" she said, her gray hair at a standstill around her shoulders.

I nodded. "Yes, the baby was. I read that you could check for any records on them, so I could find out what happened to the baby."

She gave me one more measured look, seemingly certain that I was a serial killer stalking my next victim, as she slid a form across the counter. "Fill this out, and I'll see what I can do." She went to turn and then stopped. "And there's a fee." She waited to see if that would stop my murderous intentions, but I just nodded.

When I was done filling it out with the baby's birthday and

county of origin, she came back. She put reading glasses on the tip of her nose and read the form. "I'll go check and see what we have for you," she finally said, turning with the form in her hand.

I exhaled when she disappeared behind the door marked *Archival Files,* rubbing my forehead. I had a long date with the wallpaper ahead of me, and I'd hoped that I could make easy headway on Elsie's project before starting.

Karen reappeared, with handwritten notes on a Post-it. "Okay," she said. "So, those records are sealed due to Wisconsin law. If you had a Social Security number, I could give you more information."

I sighed. "No, I don't have anything like that."

She shook her head. "I didn't think so. Social Security numbers weren't issued in that time until a person was a teenager, usually around age fourteen. Sorry." She frowned and shrugged her shoulders.

"Well, thank you for looking," I said.

She leaned forward and put her forearms on the ledge. "You know, you might try to find the name of the adoption agency and start there."

I nodded. I didn't think Elsie knew that information, but I would see what I could find out. "Thanks," I said as I left, my shoulders slumped in disappointment.

That evening, I went home and searched online for any adoption agencies that had been around in the 1940s in the area. As I scanned the Google search results, I rubbed my neck. The wallpaper upstairs was finally all scraped off, but I suspected that I might have permanently damaged my upper body in pulling down all that hideous print. I silently cursed—again—at whoever had decided to take the easy route with the house and glue layers upon layers of wallpaper to the walls.

Of course, I had seen the result of a few other questionable decisions in houses, like the time someone had used industrial staples and roofing nails to hang their family photos, just ripping them clean off the walls when they moved out, leaving huge gashes in almost every room. Or, in the bungalow, the former owners had flushed kitty litter down the toilet before they left, which solidified in the pipes when it hit the water and clogged up the entire sewer line.

I popped a few ibuprofen as I clicked around on the Internet, but I was soon distracted by the buzz of my phone. When I saw it was Matt, my stomach dropped slightly.

"What's wrong? Is Abby okay?" I said immediately.

"She's fine," he said. "She just has a cough and can't sleep. She lay down in bed over an hour ago, but can't get settled. I was sitting with her, but she asked to talk to you before she falls asleep."

"Put her on," I said quickly. There was rustling as he handed her the phone.

"Hi, Mom." Abby's voice was hoarse and scratchy with a tinge of sadness, and my heart nearly broke.

I stood up, ready to grab my keys and run out the door to go pick her up. "What's wrong, Ab? Your dad said your throat hurts. How does it feel?"

"Bad. My throat feels fuzzy, and it hurts to drink," she said.

I started to slip my feet into my moccasins and tucked my wallet into my pocket. "Do you know if you have a fever? Did your dad take your temperature?"

"Uh-huh. Dad said it's . . ." I heard her ask Matt. "A hundred," she finished.

"Okay, honey. That's not too bad. I bet you'll feel better by tomorrow. Just rest right now. Let me talk to your dad, and I'll come and get you and bring you home, okay?" I said quickly.

There was rustling, and then Matt got on the phone. "I just gave her some Children's Motrin, so her fever should come down. I can take her to urgent care if it gets any worse."

I shook my head. "No. I'm coming to get her now." I walked outside and reached for the garage door to pull it open.

He paused. "Alex, she's fine. I'm on top of it." His tone was even, level. Calm.

"She needs me," I said as my hand dropped to my side. My voice shook, even though I had willed it not to.

"Look, I'll keep a close eye on her. I think it's just a virus. If she's not better in the morning, I will call you," he said.

"But . . ." I couldn't insist that I come and get her. It was his—court-enforced—time with her. I knew he would take care of her, and I knew he would stay on top of it, as much as it killed me to admit it. I would have to stand by and let him handle it.

"Alex, she'll be fine by tomorrow. I just wanted her to talk to you and let you know what's going on. Don't worry."

I swallowed hard and forced the words out. "Thanks for that. I really appreciate it. Let me talk to her one more time."

"Mom, I'm going to sleep with Daddy tonight. He'll protect me," she said when she got back on the phone.

I smiled, my eyes closing. "Of course."

"I know," she said. "I'm going to go rest now, Mom."

I hung up, went back inside, and sank back down on my couch, slipping off my shoes again. I had never felt more extraneous in Abby's life than in that moment. She had been sick when she was with Matt before, but her sickness had started with me and I knew she was on the mend. I had never sent her there healthy and gotten a call from him that she was suddenly ill.

Of course, I should have expected there would be many more things like that—maybe middle-of-the-night calls if she had a bad dream. I swallowed hard as I realized that was better than the alternative: What if I never got a call? What if there came a time when she was perfectly content with being consoled by Matt?

He was a good dad, no question. I couldn't fault him on that for a moment. And he had been a good husband, before. As much as I tried to push it away, a small part of me whispered that I had chosen to file for divorce. Of course, it wasn't that simple, nor did the blame rest completely on my shoulders. It was all the result of a million tiny choices. He chose someone else. It was also a glaring reality that neither of us would have chosen where we were.

As I fell asleep, I dreamed of a time when Abby was small, and all our problems were, too.

CHAPTER 16

For the first six weeks of her life, I was sure that Abby wouldn't sleep anywhere except snuggled underneath my chin with my arm resting on her back. She would fall asleep while nursing, and I would hold my breath and slowly inch her up my body, until we found the sweet spot between my chest and neck, with her bookended by my breasts. A few times, I made the mistake of trying to gently place her in the crib, but she would wake before her body even hit the mattress and start screaming like she was being electrocuted. Since I was averaging about five hours of sleep on a good day, it didn't seem worth it, and I sacrificed physical comfort for a few guaranteed moments of rest. Oftentimes, it felt like that—one decision over another. Showering or napping or eating. There was never any option to request All of the Above. Things that I had considered basic necessities to function were suddenly stripped away, and I didn't have any road map to figure out how to get them back.

My mother and Matt's mother helped periodically, but after about a month they visited less and less, as did other friends who had offered to cook a meal or watch her while I napped.

The newness and excitement of an infant had expired, just at the time when I most needed help.

When I looked back at that time when she turned a year old, I often thought about how each phase seemed so hard, so never-ending. But end, they always did. Yet when I was in the middle of some transition—teething, colic, a sleep regression—it felt interminable. It felt like that was the new way my life would be forever, and things would never be any easier.

They always did improve, of course, only to be quickly followed by some new curveball, some new challenge to my sanity. I made it through, though, in the hurtling way that the first year happens. It often felt like each day was a week long, and each week happened in the moment of a day.

And when she was eleven months old, she came down with an awful case of croup. Her cough sounded like a barking seal, and I felt so helpless as I watched her struggle for breath, her face red and her eyes watery. She was old enough to understand that she was sick, but not old enough to know that she needed to rest. So she would cruise around, holding on to the furniture, wheezing and coughing, frustrated that she couldn't do the things that she always did, like push her walker around on the wood floor and hide underneath the kitchen table.

"Is the monitor turned all the way up?" I said to Matt that Saturday morning as we sat on the couch, cups of coffee and folded newspapers between us. Abby was down for her morning nap, something that she was slowly transitioning out of, but for that morning, we had an hour of quiet.

He didn't look up from the paper. "Yes, Alex. Just relax. Our house isn't that big; we can hear her down the hallway."

I sat up straighter on the couch, my skin pricking with anger. "I can't relax. Do you think we should have given her another dose of her antibiotic before we put her down? She'll be due about halfway through the nap. I don't want her to get worse.

Her cough finally sounded better this morning." I twisted the gold band on my right hand, a present from Matt after Abby was born, in worry.

"She'll be fine," he volleyed back. He took a sip of his coffee and set it back down on the end table as he looked at me. "Everything will be okay, I promise."

It was something he said to me often, when I was worried about something and allowing it to consume me. When I was upset when the church for our wedding was booked on the date we wanted, he'd said it. When the sellers of our house didn't accept our initial offer, he'd said it. And when I found out I was pregnant with Abby, far before either of us were ready, he'd written a letter to me and left it on the kitchen island. It ended with those words: *Everything will be okay. I promise.* I saved the letter in an old shoe box in my closet, and pulled it out throughout my pregnancy whenever I started to feel stressed or anxious.

Yet, after Abby was born, the words didn't have the same impact on me anymore. I had ignored them and glanced out the window at the backyard. The spring weather was just beginning to turn warm, and I could see tulip shoots and other greenery emerging from the perennial beds in the back. We'd bought the house in the middle of winter, when the backyard was covered in snow, so when it all melted in the spring, I was surprised to discover the backyard wasn't the expanse of green grass like I'd thought. Rather, it was separated by giant perennial beds that required more weeding and attention than I was prepared to give them.

I had wanted to rip them out and plant grass, so we could eventually get a swing set for Abby, but I didn't have the energy when I was pregnant. And I never could find the time after she was born, despite spending many hours sitting on the couch nursing her, staring at those awful, weed-filled flower beds. Matt, of course, didn't have the time or the desire to work on them. "Just hire someone," he told me. Even that seemed monumental, so the weeds and flowers remained, with more weeds overtaking the beauty each year, until that year, when it was just a mess of undesirable plants fighting with each other and choking off sunlight and oxygen to everything else.

I sighed deeply, craning my head into the kitchen to glance at the time and calculate when I could give her the medicine. He looked up and put a hand on my foot, lightly pressing down. "I promise." He smiled, that same big smile that I'd fallen in love with so long ago. "You worry too much. About everything. Just relax." He traced a finger on my foot, tickling it.

I jerked my foot back reflexively. "I'll try."

"I bet I can help," he said. He put the newspaper down and leaned forward toward me on the couch, putting a hand on either side of my waist. He kissed my neck and I flinched.

"No, we can't." I glanced at the monitor, squinting to make sure that the green light that flickered when she cried was shining steadily. Even though the monitor picked up every sound, even movement at times, I was always afraid it would malfunction and she would be crying hysterically in her bed while I sat downstairs.

He sat back and ran a hand through his hair, his mouth turned down in disappointment. "She's asleep."

"Yeah, but her nap might be short," I said. "She's sick, we should think of her. If she woke up in the middle of it, I would be scarred for life."

I backed away, perfectly aware of how ridiculous, lame, and manipulative my reasons were, when I was really thinking of how I still needed to lose five pounds around my mushy stomach from the pregnancy, how my legs weren't shaved, how I was wearing old underwear and an unflattering bra. And how it all seemed like an intrusion. Unplanned. Sex and intimacy in those days felt like one more thing I would have to do, Matt just one more person to make happy. Sex, one more item to check off the to-do list of things I was supposed to accomplish each day.

He laughed, still undeterred. "All we do is think of her. I want to think of you for a while. Or not think at all."

I shook my head, and he began to slowly back away. I saw the rejection in his eyes, and I immediately felt guilty. We were married. We were supposed to be intimate, be close. But then I became annoyed that I felt guilty—didn't I do enough for everyone already? It was an awful, self-perpetuating cycle of negativity that I couldn't figure out how to stop. The worst part of it was that I was aware of all of it—that I was being ridiculous, insensitive, distant, angry.

"Later tonight. After she's in bed," I promised him with an encouraging smile and a quick nod.

He forced a smile, moving his eyes back to the newspaper. "Okay. Later, then."

But, of course, there was no later. Abby wouldn't go to bed easily, and it was after eleven when she finally fell asleep and I closed the door to her bedroom for good. By that time, Matt was asleep on the couch, his laptop on his lap and his fingers still poised on the keyboard. I woke him, but all he did was grunt, close the computer, and curl up on the couch with a blanket. I slept alone in our bed that night, as I had been doing more and more often. He would work late and I would go to bed right after Abby. He would fall asleep on the couch and not wake up until morning. I began to enjoy having the queen-sized bed to myself, so that when he did come in, it felt unwelcome. I didn't sleep well when he was next to me, and I would wake up those mornings crabby and exhausted. He would be tired, too, from me elbowing him all night to stop snoring, turn over, move back. Sharing a bed became something that we did because it was what we were supposed to do, but it got to a point where it was easier for him to sleep on the couch most nights.

And then, of course, a year later, I never had to share a bed with him again.

CHAPTER 17

"Let's do this. One . . . two . . ." I didn't finish before the crew lifted their sledgehammers and began hitting the steel bathtub in the upstairs master bathroom. I quickly stepped back as they pounded away at the old tub, breaking it into small pieces so that they could haul it away to the Dumpster outside. Pieces of porcelain sprayed through the air, until finally the tub was completely broken apart on the cracked porcelain tile, ready for the trash.

The tub was powder blue, installed back in the 1970s, when colored fixtures were all the rage, and it hadn't ever been reglazed or, it appeared, recaulked. A black line of mold and mildew ringed the tub where the faux marble walls met the edge. The drain on the bottom was covered in rust and grime, not having seen a sponge or cleaning product in years. There was no saving the hideous fixture, so it had to go.

I stepped back to let Eddie's crew begin to haul away the tub remnants, but as they worked, I caught a glimpse of the floor underneath. I asked the crew to brush aside some of the pieces and stared at the floor. It was soft and black, rotting away from what appeared to be years of moisture.

"What the . . ." I grabbed a sledgehammer, turned it around, and poked the end of the handle at the soft wood. My stomach dropped as the end of it easily sank into the floor.

"It must have been leaking for years," I muttered as I lightly tapped around the floor, feeling the handle sink in the same soft wood. I stood and slowly backed away from the exposed flooring. "Everybody, out of the bathroom," I said before I ran downstairs.

I found Eddie in the kitchen, breaking down what was left of the kitchen cabinets. He dropped a piece of painted plastic wood when he saw my face.

"What now?"

"Floor under the upstairs tub is rotted through. Like, whipped-cream-foundation rotted through," I said.

His face took on what I imagined to be an equally nauseated look, and we went to the dining room to locate the spot in the ceiling under the bathroom. He paused and looked at me.

"We have to. Go for it," I said before he grabbed a ladder and cut into the ceiling.

Bits of plaster and dust rained down into the dining room as Eddie carefully tore away at the ceiling. He stopped suddenly and whistled before he grabbed a penlight out of his pocket and shone the light upward.

"Oh, no. What?" I said. I tried to peer up the ladder, but the ceiling was a black hole and I couldn't see anything.

He looked at me, his face pale. "The water rotted through the floor joist. Like, completely." He pulled a penknife out of his belt and poked upward. He shook his head. "Yup. It's almost completely gone." He cupped a hand around his mouth. "Everyone better be out of that bathroom, unless they have a death wish."

"So, what do we need to do? Brace the beam?" I said when he climbed down.

He shook his head. "It's too far gone. We have to replace the whole floor joist."

"Which means opening up this whole ceiling, bracing the floor from underneath, and installing new supports." I swallowed hard as I looked up at the ceiling, realizing that would set us back another day . . . and more dollars. I took a deep breath. "Okay. At least we discovered the problem."

"You're not kidding. That wood has only a couple of inches of support left. If you had left the tub, and just reglazed it or tried to cut corners, it would have fallen through to right here." He pointed to a corner of the room. "Hopefully without someone in it."

I thought of how many times Abby had been upstairs, wandering around in the rooms, imagining she was a ballerina twirling around on the wood floors. If she had set one foot in that tub, it might have fallen through the floor. I again wondered how one house could have so many dangers. "Are all the other joists sound?" I asked.

"As far as I can tell," he said. He looked upward again, and shook his head, before he clapped a hand on my back. "And the fun continues."

"Lo mein or fried rice?" Traci asked with a sweep of her hand across the white Chinese take-out containers spread out on her kitchen counter.

"Both. Why choose?" I said as I heaped my plate full of MSG and sodium. I stopped and stretched a hand in front of me. "My fingers are already swollen from sanding down the walls, why not make it worse?"

She grabbed two beers from the fridge and carefully balanced them in one hand and a plate full of food in the other, as we walked into her family room and settled on the couch. Her family room was comfortable, covered in dark wood paneling left over from the 1970s, and brown and cream plaid couches that swallowed whoever dared to sit down. The carpeting was a light tan shag that looked like the strings of a mop.

"Sorry the place is a mess. Jason isn't the greatest about having Chris clean up after himself, and I was too exhausted after work on Friday to put everything away," she said as she surveyed the books, papers, various electronic devices, and maps that were scattered all over the family room. Traci's husband, Jason, was a police officer, and he often took the overnight shift while Traci worked during the day so someone could always be around for Chris. She said that most days they were like ships passing in the morning, tagging each other in the endless rotation of looking after Chris and working.

"This is nothing. Come to my house, and then an apology will really be called for." I laughed, although it wasn't true at that moment. I had spent the night furiously cleaning the house in an effort to dull the ache of not being able to comfort Abby while she was sick. According to a text I got from Matt that morning, Abby was doing better, but I still felt like a failure for not realizing that she was getting sick when I'd dropped her off. That, coupled with the unknown bathtub safety issue, made me feel like the worst mother in the world.

"So. Gavin?" Traci said as she bit into an egg roll and wiped the grease from it off her chin.

I twirled a lo mein noodle around my fork. "He's nice. Really sweet, and we had a good time. We're going to have dinner again soon, I think."

She dropped her egg roll on her plate. "What? I didn't realize you guys had already met. Why didn't you tell me?"

"Because I knew you would be really excited, and would make me more nervous about the whole thing. I figured I would scope out the situation first for myself and then let you know how it went," I said before I stuffed a pile of noodles into my mouth.

"What's there to be nervous about? He's a cutie, and you deserve to have some fun. Finally. For the love of God, have some fun," she said.

"True, but for starters, he's almost too cute. Like, out-of-my-league cute," I said. "And young. And nice. And I'm painfully rusty at all of this."

"No, you—" she began to say when her son's voice came down the hall.

"Hey, Mom," Chris said. "I can have dinner?" Chris appeared in the family room, and I was once again struck at how handsome he was, and how typical he seemed at first glance. A blessing and a curse, Traci often said. He was an eighteen-year-old boy, with broad shoulders and long limbs and hair that flopped over the center of his forehead. After the first few moments of seeing him, however, a person might notice that he stood with a somewhat awkward stance and that his face rarely changed expression.

She nodded. "Sure. It's in the kitchen. I got you plain white rice and sweet and sour chicken." He opened his mouth, and she quickly added, "Without any pineapple or green peppers."

He turned to leave, without looking in my direction, and she said, "Did you say hi to Alex?"

His eyes flickered toward me, and he gave me a wave. "Hi, Alex." His voice was even-toned, and without inflection—like always—and he looked at his mom for dismissal.

"Hey, Chris! I love your shirt," I said, pointing to the Chicago Blackhawks logo.

"They won last week," he said. "How many goals did Jonathan Toews score?"

"Oh, I'm not sure. I didn't watch the—" I started to say when Traci interrupted me.

"You know, Chris," she said. "Just tell her."

"Three! He scored three goals!" His eyes grew wide, alive, and twinkled with excitement as he hopped up and down. "Do you like the Blackhawks?"

I laughed. "I do. They're a great team."

He took a step toward me, engaged. Wanting to engage. "Do you live on Lawn Avenue?"

Traci held up three fingers. "Three questions, like we talked about," she said to Chris, and then gave me an apologetic smile.

"He can ask me whatever he wants," I said. "Yes, I do," I said to Chris.

He jumped up and down again, before he stopped and pointed his finger at me. "How many televisions do you have?"

I cocked my head to the side. "Two, I think."

"One more question," Traci said.

His eyes shifted around the room as he rocked back and forth on his toes. "Okay. Are you fixing up a house that is old?"

I answered yes, and he hopped up and down again.

"Is it really, really old and have a lot of things that are broken? Maybe I should come see it sometime," he said.

"I'd love that." I smiled. "If you want some work to do, there's plenty of it at the house."

He opened his mouth to ask more questions, but then looked at Traci, who shook her head.

"Go grab some dinner," she said.

He turned and walked out of the room, toward the kitchen, on his toes. "I'm gonna grab some dinner now," he whispered to himself as he left. "And then I'm gonna go back to my room."

"Like I said, I would be happy to talk to him," I whispered.

Traci smiled as she stared at her plate of food. "Yes, but it can get intense. We're working on the three-question rule. At least he's happy today."

I nodded. "He *seems* happy. I don't think I've ever seen him so excited." There had been more than one time when I'd gone over to Traci's house when Chris was having a tougher time. I had seen him drop to the floor and cry, whine and hop up and down, and shake in frustration. All, typically, over things such as running out of orange juice, not being able to find one of his rocks in his room, or having difficulty tying his shoes.

"Today is a good day. Who knows what tomorrow will be like?" she said. "Or next week." She cocked her head to the side and set down her food. "Speaking of which, can you believe he'll be eighteen next week?"

"No. How is that even possible?" I shook my head.

She stood up and walked into the kitchen, reappearing with a stack of papers. She held them in front of me and sighed. The top read *Application for Guardianship*.

"I get to go to court next week and submit this application to basically take away all of his adult rights." The papers in her hand twitched.

"Meaning, what?" I frowned.

"Meaning he will stay a child legally. Jason and I will be responsible for, and in charge of, all of his legal, financial, and medical decisions. We already are now, really, so that will just continue," she said. She walked back to the couch and sat down, placing the papers carefully on the end table. "I love how there's a section for 'standby guardian'—someone who gets to take over in case Jason or I kick the bucket." She took a long sip of her beer before she smiled. "Sorry. Didn't mean to be such a Debbie Downer."

"No, you're not at all. It's a lot to deal with," I said. "Let me know if I can help in any way," I added.

"Well, maybe. Obviously, he's been really interested in your house, asking lots of questions. Is it really okay if I bring him by some time to see it? He keeps asking me the layout of the floor plan, and I can't answer. Which, as you might imagine, makes him more than a little agitated," she said.

"Of course. Anytime. I would be happy to regale him with the tales of the shellacked woodwork and the hideous wallpaper," I said.

"Thanks," she said. "And since you seem to be in the business of saving everyone these days, how's the hunt for the neighbor's daughter?"

"I didn't get anywhere with the county clerk, but it was suggested I try to find the name of the adoption agency," I said.

"How would you find that?" she said.

"I'm not sure. Unless Elsie remembers or knows it, we could be in for an uphill climb."

She looked down at her plate. "And if you find the baby?"

"Well, I suppose I would try to contact her, let her know that Elsie is looking for her," I said quickly, tucking my legs underneath me on the couch.

"And then what?"

"And then . . ." I shrugged. "I'm not sure. It would really depend on what she wanted to do. How she felt about being given up for adoption, I suppose."

She looked up. "And what if she doesn't want to meet with Elsie? How are you going to break it to that poor, sweet old woman that her daughter doesn't want to meet her?"

I sighed. "I'm hoping it won't come to that. I'm hoping that she won't have any grudges, that she'll understand why it all happened."

Traci shook her head. "Decisions like that are never understood, even by the people who make them. You're already messing in these people's lives—you need to be careful."

I held up my hands. "I'm not trying to meddle. I'm just trying to help her out."

She sighed. "Sorry." She glanced toward Chris's room. "That wasn't about you. There's just a lot of emotion around here, with the guardianship hearing. A lot of justification. Regret. A dash of self-pity."

I nodded. "Of course."

We sat silently, considering our lo mein, before Chris came back in the room and sat down closely next to me. He smiled and handed me a book.

"Look." He pointed to a picture of a black cicada, its red and yellow eyes bulging out of its head, looking otherworldly. "That's what they look like."

"He means the cicadas coming next month," Traci said.

I moved my head back an inch to focus on the book. "They do look like that. I remember from last time they were here."

"Space," Traci said gently, and Chris moved back to a comfortable distance.

"They're gonna be everywhere. Millions and millions," he said, his eyes bright.

I laughed. "Probably. Are you excited?"

He nodded and looked down at the book again, humming softly. He smiled before looking back at me, his eyes so wide that the whites surrounded the irises. "The last time they were here, I was already born. And now they're coming again."

"They are," I confirmed.

"And then they'll all die and come back again in seventeen years. And I will be thirty-four." His eyes flickered to me. "The same age as you." He looked at Traci. "And I will have a girl named Abby and my own house and a job, just like you."

Traci's eyes cast down, and her mouth twisted to the side. "We'll see, buddy." She didn't look at me, but instead stared at her food, unable to say anything else.

Later that night, I woke up to my windows rattling and the sound of rain driving against my roof. A flash of lightning illuminated the bedroom, and a *crack* of thunder shook the house. I sat up and glanced at the clock: 3:20 a.m. I started to sink back down against my pillow, when another, angrier *crack* was followed by a brighter flash of lightning. Early summer storms were fairly common in the area, as though Mother Nature had to have one last tantrum before she acquiesced and blessed us with the short summer months.

I grabbed my phone and looked up the weather radar as I

tried to push images of horror movies out of my head. I had always frozen when I was alone in thunderstorms. Which, thankfully, wasn't that often. When I was growing up, my parents were always downstairs. In college, I always had a roommate. After college, Matt. But now, nothing. There were nights when it was supposed to storm when I had proactively asked Abby to sleep in my bed, comforted by her presence. But, of course, she was still at Matt's house this night.

My fears weren't without founding. When I was seven, I woke up to a storm beating down on the house. I ran into my parents' bedroom, certain that the boogeyman was going to grab my ankle as I stepped down from my bed. I nestled safely between them, my mother's arm around my body as I curled next to her. Their bed smelled like laundry detergent, the product of my mother's meticulous, weekly washing of all the beds. My dad was lightly snoring, the rhythmic sounds pulling me back to sleep. Protected by them, the storm became a thing of wonder rather than terror. Everything was safe again; the world was a kind place. I had just about drifted back off to sleep, when we heard a loud *pop* and the sound of glass shattering.

My dad sprang up out of bed, yelling that my mother and I should stay back. We didn't listen and crept behind him, following the sound to my bedroom. There, on my bed, were a thousand pieces of shattered glass where the window had blown in. Large shards rested on my pillow instead of what had almost been my face. With a margin of ten minutes, everything would have changed. Ever since that night, thunderstorms had inspired a Pavlovian fight-or-flight, hide-or-be-hurt reaction.

Sweating, I saw that the weather radar showed an angry swath of red and orange storms nearly on top of our town, with a red scroll of a tornado watch moving across the top of the screen. It warned that anyone in the path of the storms should take cover in a basement or the lowest point in the house.

My hand shaking, I breathed heavily before I quickly ran to the light switch and flipped it on, my lungs easing a bit in the light. I grabbed my phone and my charger and went downstairs, turning lights on as I went, before the flashes of lightning could startle me in the darkness. I again thought of getting a dog as I walked down to the basement, because at least then there would be another living thing in the house that would be more freaked out than me.

I curled up on the thrift store couch in the basement, and pulled an old crocheted blanket from my grandmother around my shoulders. I wished I had a television in the basement, but I settled for listening to music on my phone. As the Rolling Stones' "Satisfaction" came on, my blood froze as I heard the wail of tornado sirens outside. I hoisted myself up to one of the small well windows and tried to peer outside, but I couldn't see anything with the rain driving against the glass.

Remembering the warning, I moved away from the window and curled up in a corner of the couch, my back slick with sweat. *Abby*. I checked the radar again, and exhaled when I saw that Matt's house was farther north than the line of storms about to hit.

The power flickered, and I wrapped my arms around my knees and shut my eyes tight.

Please don't let the windows break.

I wished I had the old weather radio that Matt had bought for me. At first he'd thought I was joking when I told him I was afraid of storms, but the first time he saw me freak out and run down to the basement after the first rumble of thunder, he stopped laughing. The weather radio was my gift for our first anniversary. It ran on batteries, so I could use it if the power went out. We had smartphones, but there was still something comforting about a classic weather radio.

It was the most romantic present he had ever bought me. Unfortunately, I threw it in the trash along with most of his other gifts after we split up, a case of throwing the baby out with the bathwater.

As I listened to the wind push against the upstairs windows, my biceps started to shake from holding on to my legs. After a few minutes, the storm began to die. The sirens faded into the darkness, and the thunder and lightning softened and grew further apart—until all that was left was the rhythmic tapping of the rain.

CHAPTER 18

The rain had stopped by morning, and, after unkinking my neck from the hours of sleeplessness, I headed to work. I was just about to turn onto Maple Street when my phone buzzed with a call from Eddie. I ignored it, pulling into the driveway moments later. I wasn't yet out of my car before he came running out of the house, waving his hands in the air.

"It's flooded! It's all messed up!" he shouted. I saw that his cargo shorts were soaked, and he carried a squeegee in his hand.

"What?" I said as I ran toward the house.

He stopped and took a breath, panting. "The roof. Remember those loose shingles that the roofer was supposed to fix next week? They collapsed and pretty much disintegrated. The upstairs is almost totally flooded."

"What? How is that possible? The roofer said it wasn't that big of a problem," I said.

"Maybe it wasn't . . . before we got all that rain. It must have been the final straw," he said.

I pushed him aside and ran up the cracked concrete steps. I didn't get halfway up the stairs to the second floor before my foot hit water. I stopped and slowly finished the staircase.

"Oh, shit." On the second-floor landing, water swirled around my ankles, soaking my old shoes. The water seemed to be coming from the upstairs corner bedroom. I waded through the water and looked up into the bedroom. I could see where water had poured down the wall, leaving a stream of rainwater against the plaster. It flowed across the wood floors, and toward the rest of the house, thanks to the pitch in the floors.

" 'Oh, shit' is right," Eddie said. He put his hands on his hips and shook his head. "I had a bad feeling with all that rain last night, so I wanted to drive by and make sure everything was fine." He paused and shook his head. "I have a wet vac so we can get started."

"Are any of your guys free?" I said. It was Sunday, and they weren't supposed to be here at all. I didn't even want to calculate the time-and-a-half pay I'd have to shell out if they were even available.

"Couldn't reach anyone," he said. He looked down at the wood floors. "Water's been here all night. It's probably soaked down to the subfloor by now." He twisted his mouth into a frown and looked at me. "We'll try to save it, but . . ."

But I knew that the longer the water sat on the wood, the longer it would expand into the grain, warping and pulling at the old material until it was too badly damaged to sand or repair. As we had seen in the rotted floor joist beneath the upstairs bathroom, water was an old house's worst enemy, capable of crumbling foundations, destroying floors, and decimating plaster.

"We need a pump or a—" I stopped as I thought of Elsie next door. I remembered the koi pond in her backyard. I sprinted over and banged on her door.

She came to the door wearing a silky black two-piece pajama set. She looked me up and down and clutched the top of her pajamas.

"Hi! Sorry to bug you, but do you have an extra pump for your pond? We have some water issues next door and need to get it out pronto." My words rushed together, and she arched a penciled-in eyebrow. Even early on a Sunday morning, her makeup was perfectly done. She nodded and pointed me to the shed in the back.

Armed with the pump, Eddie and I floated it in the bedroom, snaking the discharge tube out the second-floor window. The pump whirred to life, and the water started swirling, moving toward the pump and out of the house. I breathed a sigh of relief as it started disappearing, praying that the wood floors were still strong enough to withstand the rainwater.

I watched the pump while Eddie went into the other bedrooms to start squeegeeing water toward the foyer, closer to the pump.

"This would be easier if these floors were even somewhat level," he called from the tiny bedroom next door.

"They probably were . . . fifty years ago," I said. I poked my head out of the doorjamb and peered into the bedroom, where Eddie was shoving water from one corner to another, gaining momentum to flush it out of the room. "C'mon. It's the smallest room in the house. You got this," I said.

He stopped and shook his head, his dreadlocks giving off a small spray of water. "Does this even qualify as a bedroom?"

"Don't stop," I said quickly. "And yeah, I figure it must have been used for a nursery or a baby's room at one point." The room was just ten by nine, small enough that a man could stretch out his arms and touch each side.

I wondered if the Moores had planned to use it for another child. I wondered if Elsie and David's baby might have stayed in this room if she had kept the child. My shoulders sagged with the weight of what could have happened in this room, had times and people been different. The hushed whispers, quiet cuddles, and rhythmic rocking of baby soothing inside the nursery had the adoption never happened, and I felt as though the room knew what it had missed.

"It's working," I said as the water finally pushed out of the bedroom. I grabbed a broom and started sweeping it toward the pond pump, which sucked it up and dumped it out the window.

We had most of the standing water cleared from the second floor, and I had stopped to shake out my cramped, waterlogged fingers, when I heard a distant rumble.

"No." I turned to Eddie, my eyes wide. "I thought the forecast was clear."

He cocked his mouth into a half frown and stuck his head through the window in the tiny room, looking up at the sky. "I hate to tell you this, but there's a nice dark cloud moving slowly from the west."

I closed my eyes and shook my head. "But we haven't even tarped the roof. It's all going to come in again."

"I would get up there and lay down the plastic myself, but that cloud looks nasty. Don't want to be stuck up there if a bad storm hits," he said.

"Maybe we could lay the plastic down on the floors now, to prevent any more water getting on them," I said. I was about to run out and grab the sheeting, when I heard the unmistakable sound of rain hitting the roof.

"Too late," he said. Within seconds, water started leaking from the roof again, coming down in cold droplets and landing on the wood floor, thanks to the wind bringing in the standing water on the roof.

"Keep moving," I said. I kept the pump running and pushed water toward it as it came in from above. My pants were soaked from my feet to my knees, and my face was slick with rainwater. It was already wet, so I allowed the tears that had been building in my eyes to spill over. I knew we were going to lose several days to clean up this mess, which would mean more money hemorrhaged from my already pitiful contingency fund.

When the storm finally stopped, Eddie and I stood in the upstairs hallway, watching as the ankle-deep water was sucked in toward the pump.

"Water's been up here for"—he checked his watch—"about six hours."

"Enough for it to have soaked all the way through."

"We'll be lucky if we can save any of the floor," he said. When he saw my face, he wrapped a wet arm around my shoulders and gave me a squeeze. "I'll do what I can. Dry it out as much as possible."

I shook my head and closed my eyes. Replacing the flooring would run well into the thousands of dollars. If only I had had Eddie look at the roof first, fix that. It had passed inspection and looked to be safe. Yet I knew that one of the first rules of an older house was that a lot of problems can be lurking under something that appeared to be structurally sound. I knew better. And now I was going to literally pay the price for being an idiot.

As we worked to pull the water out of the house a second time, I watched as some of my faith in and hope for the house got carried away along with the rain. I went back out to my car to grab a towel and dry off, when I saw a familiar figure drive by. I leaned forward and squinted, my hand in a half wave of bewilderment.

"Gavin?" I whispered.

Even through his car window, his embarrassment was palpable as he stopped and waved back. I could see he wore a white Richmond Burton High School T-shirt that stretched across his broad chest, and a blue Cubs ball cap was pulled down across his forehead. The effect made him look even younger—and thus, much, much younger than me.

"What are you doing here?" I said as I tried to dry my hands off on my thighs.

"Oh. Well, I was in the area, and thought I could drive by

your house. I remembered you said it was on Maple, and . . ." He shrugged, his face growing a deeper shade of red.

"So you're stalking me?" I said with a smile.

He lifted his palms in the air. "What can I say? The way you talked about the house intrigued me. I had to see it for myself. Of course, I didn't think you'd actually be here and I'd look like a creeper."

"It was a gamble." I looked back at the house, and Eddie came outside, waving me back in.

"You leaving this to me now?" he called, holding a push broom in the air.

"I need to get back inside," I said. "We had a roof leak last night, and it's kind of a total nightmare."

"Need any help? I can run to the hardware store, or anything you need. Those rains last night were incredible," he said.

"Sure," I said after a moment. "Come grab a broom."

Eddie unceremoniously tossed a broom at Gavin when we walked into the dining room. "Start sweeping. Fast. These floors will soak up all this water like a sponge."

Gavin nodded and started working. Eddie shot me a look, his eyebrows raised, but I rolled my eyes in return. I mouthed *work* to him, and he turned and grabbed a mop, while I turned on the shop vac and started sucking up the water that they pooled.

Two hours later, the rain had finally stopped and we were able to assess the damage. The floors on the first floor were able to be saved. The water hadn't rested on them for as long. We tarped off the stairs and were able to pump out the moisture before it soaked into the oak floors.

Upstairs was another story. The smallest bedroom had sustained the most damage. The water had poured in from the roof for too long, and the wood had already started to warp. We knew we were going to have to cut out at least part of the floor. I hoped that was all, and that we could patch the wood, but we couldn't be certain until we went in and started to cut away the rotting wood. If the damage went all the way to the subfloor, we'd have to pull everything out and start over.

"We did the best we could, boss. Not bad for how much water was in here," Eddie said as he wiped his forehead with his arm.

I shook my head, my eyes still wide as I surveyed the floors. I couldn't begin to estimate how much the damage would cost. We would have to redo half of what we had already done.

"We screwed up. We should have started outside first," I said, my voice barely above a whisper.

Eddie remained silent in agreement, shaking his head as he looked at the floors. It was a basic rule, a tenet, of house repair. Fix the outside first—the roof, the foundation, the siding—to protect what was inside before moving on. I thought we had done that with fixing the foundation, but I had never imagined that the roof was in as bad of a shape as it was.

"It's all my fault," I said.

"Nah. I could have tried to talk you out of it," Eddie said. "We'll get it all fixed up."

Gavin crossed the room and rested the broom against the wall. "What else can I do? What about coffee? I can run out and grab some in town."

Before I could answer, Eddie nodded enthusiastically. "Yes. Thanks," he said. As Gavin left, I held my breath and waited for the inquisition. But Eddie just clapped a hand on my back and said, "Good work."

CHAPTER 19

The first step in repairing the damage from the water leak was to patch the hole in the roof, and, thankfully, the forecast cut us a break and gave us a few clear, warm days without any rain. The shingles were just being nailed into place as the crew got started on the inside. Eddie was barking orders inside, hustling the work along so we could stay on schedule, and they were quickly repairing the damage. I was just walking outside onto the porch, feeling as though we were back on track, when Matt returned Abby.

"How's the inside?" Matt asked as he looked up at the roofers hammering away.

"Coming along," I said automatically. Of course, I wasn't going to tell him that we were worried about mold growing in the walls from the moisture, the floors rotting and warping, or the electrical system sparking.

"That's good." He opened his mouth to say more, but then closed it, nervously glancing at the house.

"Eddie's inside, if that's what you're worried about," I said. I cocked one eyebrow at him. "He's not around to harass you."

He shook his head. "No, no. I'm not . . . worried." He glanced down at his phone. "I need to run. Good luck with the house." He turned to leave. "Oh, and by the way, I saw you at Pier 290 the other night," he said quickly. His eyes darted around like he wished he could take the words back.

"Really?" I cocked my head to the side as I thought of my date with Gavin. Suddenly, I was doubly happy that I had taken the time to flat-iron my hair. I reached up and touched the wavy, unruly mess that was gathered into a bun at the back of my head.

"I was there to grab a carryout order, and waved, but you didn't see me," he said.

"Sorry," I said. "I was on a date." I couldn't help the small smile that spread across my face. A very tiny emotional victory, but one nonetheless.

He nodded. "It looked like that. You looked . . . happy."

For a moment, I saw a strange expression flash across his face, as his eyebrows pulled down and he frowned. But he quickly relaxed and turned toward his car. "Well, see you later."

I watched as his car pulled down the driveway and then realized just what that expression was. It was one I hadn't seen for a long time: jealousy. It was both a gratifying and unmerited emotion. He didn't get to be jealous of my relationships—not anymore. Not after what he had done. But the fact that he could still feel that, even in some small, insignificant, fleeting moment, felt satisfying in the most unsettling way.

I turned back toward the house, where Abby was sitting on the steps, drawing an elaborate picture of a sand crab with pink chalk. "We'll leave in a minute, Ab," I called to her as I turned toward next door.

Elsie opened the door before I knocked. She emerged onto her porch wearing a hot pink pantsuit, gold earrings, and bright red lipstick. "There you are. I was starting to worry." She flashed a smile before she hurried past me and walked down her front steps with surprising ease, stopping to turn at the sidewalk and impatiently put her hands on her hips.

"Library closes in four hours. We need to hurry," she said.

After Elsie had told me that she didn't know the name of the adoption agency that had placed her child, I'd suggested we head to the library as the next step.

Abby, Elsie, and I walked into the library, an A-frame building, reminiscent of Frank Lloyd Wright's work, with the back of the structure all encased in glass, showcasing spectacular lake views. Impeccably-cared-for gardens in the front boasted huge impatiens and roses in hot pink and velvet red. In the distance, I could see a sailboat regatta, the boats resting like butterflies on the water's surface.

It was a perfect location for a sprawling estate, or maybe a waterfront restaurant—prime real estate—but the land had been bequeathed to the town back in 1894 by socialite Mary Sturges for use as a library. After the Great Chicago Fire, she and her family had moved to Lake Geneva while their home was being rebuilt. Once their house was complete, they donated the lake house to the town, with the stipulation that the land be used for a library and a public park. I loved that Mary had done that, and I liked to think that if we were contemporaries, we might be friends. Of course, in this alternate universe, I would also have to move in the same aristocratic social circles as her, but still.

"Hi, ladies," Georgia, a librarian with short dark hair and purple cat's-eye glasses, said as Elsie, Abby, and I walked inside. She smiled down at Abby. "We just got a new Angelina Ballerina book."

Abby looked up at me and I nodded. She scampered off to the children's area to plunder the newest arrivals, shrieking in delight when she saw the display.

"Anything I can help you two find?" Georgia asked as she adjusted the glasses on her face.

I glanced at Elsie, but her face remained drawn. "Well, we are doing some research on . . ." I glanced at her again, but she didn't meet my gaze. "On a family member of mine. Specifically, on adoption agencies back in 1947. I'm looking for a list of agencies in the area during that time."

Georgia's brow furrowed as she slowly looked from Elsie to me, before she nodded. "Well, I do have a business registrar from that time period. It's in the historical section in the back, by the reference desk. It's been a while since anyone has asked for anything of the sort, though, so I can't promise what kind of condition it's in. Would you like me to find it for you?"

"No, thank you." Elsie nodded and folded her hands in front of her. I noticed they were shaking. "We can find it ourselves."

The historical section of the library was a glass case filled with volumes of old newspaper clippings, genealogy research, and various oral histories of the lake. I stopped on one volume of the history of the *Golden Age of Lake Geneva during Victorian Times*. There were descriptions of lavish lakefront parties on the estates of the various wealthy families, and illustrations of the steamers and yachts that took people around the lake during the lazy summer days.

Elsie's hand went to a volume titled *Newspaper Clippings, 1968–1969*. I told her I didn't think that was what we wanted, but she waved me off. She opened it to May 10, 1968, and smiled.

"Look." It was an article on the opening of the Playboy Club. The accompanying photo was of a row of bunny waitresses, hair perfectly coiffed, in their uniforms with their long legs in front of them, brilliant smiles on their faces.

Elsie's finger tapped at a blonde on the end, the most stunning of all the women.

"Is that you?" I leaned forward, and recognized the familiar almond-shaped eyes and wide smile. "Wow."

She smiled the same smile at me before she turned back to the photo. "So long ago. I know that, and yet every time I look in the mirror, it's a surprise. I always expect to see this girl looking back at me. Instead, I see . . ." She trailed off and sighed. She held a wrinkled, age-spotted hand in front of her. "I certainly don't feel this age."

"Well, I don't feel my age, either," I said with a laugh. "I feel much, much older."

"You, dear, are still young enough to do anything you want. Travel the world, have more children, find a handsome lover," she said.

"Well, not exactly true, but I like your optimism." I thought of Gavin and smiled. *Maybe one out of the three,* I thought.

"It's never too late for a second chance," she added as she patted my arm.

"Oh, you haven't found it yet? Let me help." Georgia reappeared and stared at the glass cabinet. Elsie frowned, but didn't say anything. "Here we go," she said as she plucked out and opened a large volume with crackling, yellowed pages. A well-manicured, blue-painted fingernail ran down the table of contents before she turned to *F.* "Aha. 'Family services.'" She whispered to me, "That's what they were called back then." She again glanced at Elsie, who didn't look up from the list of names.

I pulled out my phone and took a picture of the list of three names: Children's Society of Southeast Wisconsin, Kenosha Children's Services, and Walworth County Children's Home. "I wonder how many of these places are still in business," I said with a sigh.

Georgia pointed to a computer against the wall. "Feel free to use the computers for research."

"Mommy, I need to go potty." Abby appeared, clutching a messy pile of books that was rapidly slipping out of her hands.

"Would you like me to log you in to a computer?" Georgia pressed.

Elsie held up a hand, and I noticed for the first time that she had a sparkling diamond tennis bracelet on her hand. "No, thank you. You've been more than enough help." She stared at her until Georgia turned and left, glancing back over her shoulder before shrugging and returning to the circulation desk.

I opened my mouth to tell Abby to wait, but Elsie shook her head slightly. "Too many eyes here. Too many questions. Too many curiosities."

"I don't think anyone is watching us," I said. But Elsie had made up her mind, and so I took Abby to the bathroom, checked out two books for her, and then we walked out of the library.

Back at Elsie's house, Abby settled on the porch with her books and Elsie put two plates on the table and then opened a box of cookies. "Bakery?"

"No, thank you." I quickly eyed the contents of her countertops and determined she must exist solely on sugar and air, for I didn't see anything that didn't have a fat content high enough to terrify a cardiologist.

She ignored me and placed three tea cookies on a plate and shoved it in my direction. I accepted it with a sigh. Abby spotted the treats and grabbed the cookies before returning to her cozy spot on the porch.

Elsie waited until Abby was outside before turning and tapping a pink kitchen phone. I lifted it, marveling at the cotton candy color, before I started calling the three agencies we'd found at the library. I was able to locate their numbers after a quick search on my phone.

The first was no longer in service, having been absorbed by a larger agency. I called that one first, and got a recording to leave a message.

I shook my head at Elsie, who sat at her kitchen table, a cup of tea in front of her. She nodded, but her face fell. I dialed the second number, and the woman who answered the phone told me that they had no record of a baby born on that day in this area.

"Final call," I muttered as I slowly wound the dial around. I was quickly transferred to the records department. When someone answered, I explained what we were looking for.

"Let me check and see," a woman on the line said. "Most of our records were moved electronically, but some of them are still in paper files, locked away in our storage unit. What did you say the DOB and county was again?"

"December 25, 1947, in Walworth County."

"C'mon. C'mon," she muttered. I heard a *slurp,* and I pictured her drinking from a coffee mug as she sat in an office overflowing with papers and file folders. "Ah. You're in luck."

"You found a match?" I looked at Elsie, and she gripped the mug in front of her.

"Looks like it. Similar time period, same area," she said.

"So, what's the information?" I signaled for a pen and paper, and Elsie began to rifle through her cabinets.

"Well, I can't give it to you, of course. If you're interested in the biographical details, you can make a formal request, and then we contact the adoptee. If he or she agrees and allows us to release the information, only then will we be able to release it."

"Really?" I said, my hand still poised over a piece of paper.

"Really. I'm sorry. It's the state law. Wisconsin has sealed adoption records, to protect all parties involved."

"I keep hearing that, but can you tell me exactly what that means?" I said with my eyes closed.

"It means the birth parents can't receive identifying information on the adoption. However, they can sign an affidavit that states their willingness to have contact with their birth child, and file it with the state."

"And that's it?" I said. I couldn't imagine that there wasn't any other option.

"For the most part." She sighed wearily. "On the other end, when a child is a legal adult at eighteen, they can request nonidentifying information about their birth parents like age, medical history, things like that. They can also ask for an original birth certificate if the birth parents signed that affidavit of consent I mentioned before."

"And if they didn't sign that affidavit, or even know it was an option, and the child had tried to search for them in the meantime?"

"Then . . . I'm sorry. I would suggest filing one immediately and waiting. In the meantime, I can do some digging on this possible match and let you know if I can exclude the child for you," she said.

"Oh." My shoulders slumped forward, and I shook my head slightly when Elsie offered me more paper. "Okay. Well, I guess we'll do that, then."

"I don't know why you have such a long face. This is wonderful news," Elsie said after I hung up.

"I was just hoping to get the information today. I'm sure they'll call back soon, though." Despite what I said, I wasn't so sure. We had no idea what Elsie's daughter thought of her adoption, if meeting her birth mother was something she was open to doing. A brief, horrifying thought crossed my mind that it was possible she didn't even know she was adopted, and we would never find her.

Elsie toyed with the diamond tennis bracelet around her wrist that I had noticed in the library. "I think all the time now about what she might look like, where she lives, if she hates olives as much as I do." She quietly laughed. "If she thinks about me. If she will ever understand why I did what I did." She looked down at the bracelet again. "If she will understand that things and decisions are never as simple as they appear from a distance."

I put my hand over hers and squeezed. "She will," I said.

She gave me a grateful smile and paused, head cocked to the side for a moment. "The day I had her, there was a snowstorm. The weatherman had predicted a dry Christmas, but when we woke up on Christmas Day, a light snow had already begun to fall. I remember I went to my window to watch the snow, and that's when I felt the first pain."

I sat back in my chair and tucked my legs under me as I nibbled on a cookie and listened.

"I was so naïve, so uneducated, that I thought she would be coming soon, so I frantically woke my parents and told them we had to hurry to the hospital." She smiled, that wide smile, and I again could see the girl in the newspaper from 1968. "Of course, babies come when they're ready, not when we are. My parents drove me to the hospital. My father never turned around from the front seat as he slowly drove the car through the snow. It got heavier and heavier, and by the time we got to the hospital, the streets were covered and we could hardly see out the windows." She smiled. "It was a good thing she wasn't in a rush to get here."

She took a sip of her tea and cleared her throat. "My mother brought me inside, with more tenderness than I had imagined possible. She stayed with me as the nurse came in and gave me an injection. I remember she held my hand as I drifted off." She set her teacup down on the table. "The next thing I remembered was waking up in a maternity ward, with five other women in the same room. It was over, done. I called a nurse over—one I had never seen—and asked if I could see the baby. She knew that I was planning to give her up for adoption, and I could see the disapproval in her eyes. But I insisted, and she promised to bring her to me."

She stopped and smiled. "*Her*. That was how I knew I'd had a girl. Of course, I had a suspicion, a feeling, I suppose, all along. I waited so long for them to bring her to me, and I was so tired from the medicine, that I must have fallen asleep."

I nodded, trying to imagine what it would be like to have a baby during that time period, when a woman would fall asleep and then wake up a mother. The moment when Abby came out and cried was such a solid part of my memory—so personal and important—that another wave of sadness washed over me for Elsie. That she didn't even get to experience that moment with her daughter, however fleeting.

"When I woke, they placed her in my arms. She was wrapped in a white hospital blanket, with a tiny fist against her cheek. She had light blond hair and the chubbiest cheeks I had ever seen." She looked out the window, and I could see her eyes were shining with tears. "And then, she was gone." She turned back to me and lowered her gaze to the table. "Another nurse came in, took her from my arms, and handed me some papers and a pen. Not exactly an even exchange."

"I'm so sorry," I said, my voice barely above a whisper. "I can't imagine."

If I closed my eyes and concentrated, I could still feel the weight of Abby on my chest right after she was born. We didn't know if we were having a boy or a girl, but all along I had suspected a boy. I had secretly even bought a couple of blue pajamas, in anticipation of his arrival. Matt, however, was certain we were having a girl. We'd even placed a bet on it: Whoever was right would get final approval on the name. I was so sure the baby was a boy that I agreed to the ridiculous terms—came up with them, in fact.

When I heard a nurse shout that the baby was a girl, I shook my head and told them to check again. Of course, I could see for myself, and she was unmistakably a girl. As they placed her on my chest and began to rub her so she would cry, I looked at Matt, stunned.

"You were right," I said.

He smiled and leaned down and kissed me, but his eyes never left Abby. I remember putting my hands on her back as the nurses warmed her. She was crying, that squirrelly, staccato newborn cry, but as soon as I touched her, she looked up and we locked eyes. She immediately stopped wailing. I felt a jolt of electricity run through my body that I would first brush off as the effects of the epidural, but later I would realize was because it felt like I was meeting someone whom I had known my whole life.

It was both the most grounding and surreal moment of my life, and I felt a deep sadness that Elsie didn't get to experience it.

She continued, "Well, it's very sad now, but at the time, I thought I was doing the right thing. It was more than difficult to hand her over, but it was what we had decided, and it was what I was supposed to do."

"Yes, but couldn't you have told them no, if you had wanted to?" I said before I could stop myself.

Her mouth twisted into a wry smile. "I was trying to be a good girl. To do what my parents wanted. I had disappointed them by becoming pregnant, and David was already gone. I wasn't to tell anyone about my pregnancy, or the baby. My mother told me I could get my life back on track if I went through with the adoption." She slowly looked around her kitchen, and then down at her hands. "If this was what she meant by 'on track.'"

"I know what you mean." So many people said to me that once the divorce was complete, that my life could go on. That I would truly Find My Way, that there was a better plan, that everything happened for a reason. And I tried to believe them. I *wanted* to believe them, more than anything. That there was some divine, all-encompassing plan for my life and I just couldn't see it quite yet. That I was too close to the Monet of a disaster in my life, and that it could only be appreciated if I took a few steps back and gazed at it from a distance like everyone else.

And yet, it seemed that the further away I got from the painting of my past, the less it seemed to make sense, and the more every decision seemed murky.

She shook her hand, and the diamond tennis bracelet slid down her wrist and sparkled in the light. "Harold gave me this, years ago. See, we tried to have children of our own. I wasn't given a choice to keep my baby the first time, and I so desperately wanted the chance to prove—even just to myself—that I could be a mother. A *good* mother." She adjusted the bracelet on her wrist and then sighed quietly. "But it never happened. I couldn't become pregnant, even after we tried for years. After we had given up, the next Christmas, Harold gave me this bracelet in an effort to cheer me up. Of course, it didn't." She smiled slightly. "But I haven't taken it off since."

"Oh, Elsie." I didn't know what else to say. I knew that I likely wouldn't have any more children, but I had Abby by my side. She was enough, and I was grateful.

I put my hand over Elsie's and squeezed. She placed a hand on top of mine, and we sat on her porch, listening to the sounds of the lake in the distance, and the boats humming across the water.

CHAPTER 20

After we left Elsie, Abby and I went home, and I started to make a gourmet meal of spaghetti and frozen meatballs. She helped me break the angel hair pasta in half and drop it into the boiling water. I started to reach for a glass jar of sauce in the pantry, but stopped. I eyed a can of crushed tomatoes and glanced over at the counter at a bulb of garlic.

"Ab, today we're going to do something special. We're going to make the sauce from scratch." I said as I opened the can of tomatoes.

"From scratch?" Her nose wrinkled, and she leaned away from the can. "What?"

"Yup. Trust me, it'll taste so much better." I pulled a clove of garlic away from the bulb, crushed it under my knife, and began to mince it, rocking the tip of my knife back and forth over the cutting board. The rhythm under my fingers took me back a few years, when I used to cook all of our dinners from scratch, back when I would keep an eye on the clock, counting down the minutes until Matt got home. Abby would be playing at my feet, pots and pans and wooden spoons surrounding the kitchen island like an obstacle course.

I sautéed the garlic in some shimmering olive oil for a moment, careful not to let it turn brown and bitter, before I emptied the can of crushed tomatoes into the pan. I brought it up to a boil and then turned the heat down to let it simmer. I threw in some salt, oregano, and a pinch of sugar and gave it a quick stir.

"It smells weird," Abby said as she sniffed the air. "Like sweaty feet."

"That's the garlic," I said. I put a hand on her shoulder. "If you don't like it, I'll make you the jarred stuff, but you have to at least try it."

She gave me a dubious look and sniffed at the pan again.

"So, Ab. Are you excited for your graduation next week?" Abby's kindergarten graduation had come up so quickly on the calendar, I barely had time to process the idea that I would soon have a first grader.

"Yup. Daddy said that we are going to have a big party with an ice cream cake afterward. Doesn't that sound yummy, Mom? It's my favorite!" She clapped her hands together.

"That sounds wonderful. I'm sure it'll be yummy, just like you say," I said lightly as I stirred the angel hair pasta. Matt had Abby that evening, although we would both be at the graduation ceremony at her school. After, he would take her back to his house, and I would go home alone so I wouldn't infringe on his time with her. Attending the ceremony was my small consolation, I supposed.

After dinner, complete with my apparently yucky sauce and the jarred stuff that Abby insisted upon, I put her to bed. I sat and opened my computer, trying to forget about whatever party Matt had planned for after Abby's graduation. I clicked on MLS listings and recently sold properties, as I did every day. I quickly scanned the list, each listing familiar.

But my finger hovered over my keyboard when I saw a date of 1902 on a recently sold listing in nearby Elkhorn. My heartbeat quickening, I clicked through the pictures of the Queen Anne–style house with a wide front porch with ornate swoops and overhanging eaves. A round tower jutted out of the center of the house, and patterned wood shingles on the roof resembled fish scales.

The inside had been lovingly restored. Every room was freshly painted, and the kitchen was just modern enough to ensure a sale with stainless-steel appliances and butcher-block countertops, but not so modern that it seemed out of place. A wood-burning fireplace with original brick and tile was in the sitting room. It had exquisite molding in the family room, and an original claw-foot tub in the master bathroom. It was a perfect blend of old and new.

And the sale price was $505,000.

I checked the real estate history and saw that the house had been under contract just a week after going on sale, and it had closed in less than thirty days. The buyer must have been highly motivated, and it was possible there were multiple offers with a closing so quick.

I sat back quickly in my chair, doing the math in my head. My house had one more bedroom; it would certainly sell for more. If it sold anywhere near as fast, and I could avoid a couple of mortgage payments, I would make more than I had ever dreamed on the house. And with the repairs from the water damage coming along quickly, no one would ever imagine that there had been a flood in the house.

The seeds of optimism watered by the comparable sale sent a shiver down my spine as I pictured handing the keys over to an eager family, walking away from the closing table with a check that meant I could pay off all my debt and still have money left over to invest in another historic house. I pictured five years down the road, when I would be known as the woman who took on old houses, saving them and renewing their beauty. Maybe I could even, someday, be able to hire out for all the work I usually did myself on a house, and not arrive home each night covered in dirt, dust, floor stain, and wallpaper glue.

Maybe this really was just the beginning.

* * *

The next morning, Abby and I arrived at the house, and I proudly shoved a *For Sale Coming Soon* sign in the front yard. It sank deeply into the soft ground, still saturated from the late May rains. I had done that only once before, since sometimes it could serve to kill the excitement by the time the house actually came on the market. But this time, I was confident it would only serve to build buzz for the house. Historic houses, renovated correctly, were a rare bird, and if there were people who lost out on the house in Elkhorn, they might want to quickly scoop up my house.

My optimism was boosted by a dream that I'd had the night before. The house was full of light and smelled like roses in the front rooms, with kids' toys in the back family room and a kitchen that smelled like warm chocolate-chip cookies. In my dream, the occupants were faceless shapes, but they moved around the house in their everyday lives, unaware that I was checking on them, making sure they were happy. They had bought the house in a bidding war, writing a letter to me complete with family pictures, to prove how much they loved the house and what I had done.

The final product taunted me—the oak gleaming with lemon oil, the front porch painted a pristine white, a porch swing slowly drifting in the breeze as it held a mother and her children, a fat, lazy dog sleeping on the steps in the summer heat, the hydrangeas lifted toward the sun and battling each other for light while the buzz of insects sounded in the trees overhead. A lazy, perfect summer morning, when everything seemed muted and watercolored, like the first few moments after waking up from a dream.

As I gave the *Coming Soon* sign one more shove into the ground, Elsie waved from her front porch. She wore a bright purple satin robe that was tied around her tiny waist and matching slippers on her feet, but her makeup was perfect. I wondered if she slept with a full face of rouge, or if she put it on while she was still lying in bed.

"Good for you." She pointed to the sign. "I saw some people driving slowly by the house last night, pointing to it, and nodding quickly." Her eyes sparkled. "I think people are talking about it around town."

"From your lips . . ." I trailed off with a smile.

"From my lips, nothing. That house is going to be the life of the neighborhood again, all because of you," she said. "I just hope whoever buys it is half as wonderful as you and Abby."

I turned back, hands on hips, and stared up at the house. The outside was still a mess, and the inside was moving slowly, but the fact that people were already thinking about it coming up for sale was a great sign. It meant that they understood its potential, just as I did.

In that moment, I knew. I knew that someone was going to buy the house, and someone was going to pay what it was truly worth. And someone was going to live there, and love it just as much as I already did. I let the optimism wash over me, and prayed it would remain until the very last moments at the closing table.

CHAPTER 21

The kindergartners were lined up, shoulder to shoulder, white paper graduation caps proudly on their heads as the parents tapped away at their phones, recording the entire presentation. Abby was in the front row, in a yellow and white gingham dress that had been mine when I was little. Her two blond braids stuck out from the graduation cap, white bows at the tops. She swayed back and forth as she sang a song about leaving school, the skirt gently swishing against her knees.

I kept my phone trained on her, thankful that I had gotten there early and snagged a seat in the front row, so I didn't have the offending head of another parent in the video. Matt and his parents weren't so lucky. Fifteen minutes after I had arrived, I heard Susan whisper, "I told you we were going to be late." I had smiled and turned around, giving her a quick wave. She rolled her eyes and held up her hands in an exasperated manner, pointing to Matt's dad, Denny, as the culprit.

Denny lifted a thick hand in greeting, his booming voice carrying across the auditorium. "Good to see you, Alex!"

I laughed, but my smile faded when I saw the two figures behind them: Matt and Julia. I gave them a quick nod, and they returned the gesture before they sat down and disappeared in between the rows of parents. I willed myself not to turn around again as we waited for the ceremony to begin.

After the songs were finished, it was time for the kids to receive their diplomas. I waited patiently for the *P* section, and tears sprang to my eyes as the teacher called, "Abby Proctor." She proudly walked across the stage, her arms at her sides, and accepted her diploma. She turned and flashed me a brilliant smile. I could hear Denny behind me, whistling and clapping, and the video on my phone shook as I laughed. I could always count on him to outdo all of us in the celebration department.

When it was over, I rushed forward and scooped Abby up. "Let me see that diploma." I read the words, not nearly believing that she was old enough to be finished with kindergarten, that she would be a first grader in the fall.

"You were the prettiest one on that stage," Denny said as his group came up from the back.

Abby giggled as Susan kissed the top of her head. "Shhh," Susan said to Denny. "Don't make the other kids feel bad." She turned back to Abby. "But you definitely were." She and Abby shared a smile, and I turned toward Matt and Julia. They stood on the periphery, looking uncomfortable. I took a step back, letting them walk forward. Matt gave her a hug and a kiss, and Julia presented her with a bouquet of pink roses.

"These are for you," Julia said. "I know how much you like pink."

Abby beamed and accepted the flowers. "They're so pretty," she said as she leaned forward and inhaled. "Daddy, did you get the cake I wanted?"

"Of course," Matt said. "Ice cream cake, just like you asked."

I shifted uncomfortably, remembering the party that Abby had told me about. I stepped aside as another family began gathering for a family photo. Mom, Dad, siblings, grandparents, and everyone all gathered around the graduate as the person taking the photo worried if they were all going to fit in the frame.

"Alex, why don't you come to the party?" Susan whispered as she touched my elbow.

I shook my head. "Oh, no. Thank you, but no." A twinge of jealousy ran down my spine as I watched Julia stroke Abby's hair and twist the end of the braids I had carefully worked on that morning.

"It's just us, at our house." Susan gestured toward Denny. "Please, come. It would be so nice for Abby if we were all there."

"For Abby?" I said quickly. She smiled, knowing full well that she was attacking my Achilles' heel. For the baby. For Abby. For my granddaughter.

"Yeah, c'mon," Denny said loudly. "Come hang out with us. You're the only one who will sit and drink a beer with me."

And with that declaration, I was locked in.

Being at Denny and Susan's house was like being in a time warp. I hadn't been there since the divorce, but the house looked and smelled the exact same. The white and green afghan was still on the couch, topped by their cat, Moses. Susan still proudly displayed a million tiny knickknacks in her china cabinet. Denny still had a plaque next to the television of his prize fish from the Delavan Lake Fishing Derby in 1995.

I don't know why I expected any of it to be different just because everything in my life had changed. It was equal parts comforting and disturbing to see that life had continued to go on for them. Comforting to know that there were some places that still existed exactly as I had remembered them, since so much else had changed. Disturbing for that exact reason. It was as though their lives weren't at all ruffled by everything that had dynamited mine.

Denny tossed me a beer almost immediately after I walked in the door, and I was grateful to have something to do with my hands other than shove them into my pockets again. Then, he went outside to the garage to have a cigarette. Suddenly, I wished I smoked. Back in college, when I used to smoke socially, it always gave me something to do at parties. If there was a lull in the conversation, or if I wasn't quite ready to enter the function, I could stand outside and have a cigarette, like a mental time-out.

"So, Alex, I heard you're working on a new house?" Julia said as she gripped a white wine spritzer.

"Oh. Yes. It's a historic property, close to town," I said as I shifted and took a long sip of my beer.

"That's awesome. Tell me about it," she said brightly.

I paused, studying her face for sincerity. Her eyes were wide, and her brilliantly white smile didn't fade. Confused, I told her about the house, and all the problems, and what I still had to do. I noticed Matt lurking in the kitchen next to us, slowly pulling out plates and plastic silverware for dinner.

"Wow. I'm sure it looks really neat inside. Does Abby love it?" she asked as she flipped a corkscrew of blond hair behind her shoulder and took another sip of her drink.

"I think so. She certainly loves to boss the crew around." I laughed, still shooting glances at Matt, who was carefully polishing the already-spotless grill tools.

"Oh, I'm sure she does." Julia craned her neck into the dark-paneled, sunken living room, and smiled at where Abby was playing with the crateful of old Barbies that Susan had bought at a garage sale. "She's just the neatest little girl."

"I'm not going to argue with you on that," I said. Which, of course, left the silent statement of, *But I will on other things,* hanging between us.

"Well, I'm going to go see if Susan needs any help with pulling things together," she said and then disappeared into the family room.

I took a step forward, to offer assistance as well, but stopped. She wasn't my mother-in-law anymore. *Should I let Julia offer?*

I am purely a guest at the party, even though it is for Abby. What is my role?

For a few terrifying moments, I stood planted while Matt stared at me, having given up all pretense of preparing utensils.

"Thanks for coming," he said, placing his palms on the scratched white countertop.

I shoved my hands in my pockets and nodded. "Oh. Of course. I'm happy to be here. For Abby. And I don't think your mom would have let me say no, anyway."

He smiled. "You never could say no to her."

The intimacy of his statement, referring back to our years together, surprised me. We were supposed to—or it *felt* like we were supposed to—pretend that we had never been in love, had never shared a life together. We were supposed to be like two acquaintances, nodding quickly at each other during the custody exchanges. An invisible cobweb between us, long thought to have been swept away, suddenly glimmered in the poorly lit kitchen.

I shifted. "Well, you know I always tried," I said. "Like the time when she asked us to all go tent-camping in November at Whitewater State Park."

"Ah, yes." He shook his head. "What a trip that was. If memory serves, I had said no, but she went after you."

"And I, of course, said yes," I said.

It was a year after we were married, and Susan insisted that we all take a family-bonding trip together. I had agreed, assuming it meant a weekend in a hotel or maybe a rustic lodge somewhere in the Dells. Instead, she proudly showed us a brochure of a state park just off the highway that advertised clean Porta-Potties, like that was a luxury feature. We spent the weekend trying to convince her to go to a restaurant for every meal and the nights freezing to death, huddled in our sleeping bags to ward off hypothermia. And on the second night, huddled alone in our tent and under our sleeping bags, Matt and I made our own heat. Our faces were freezing, but everything else was warm.

I felt my face flush at the memory, and by the embarrassed look on Matt's face, I knew he was thinking of the same thing. He looked at me, and for a moment, I didn't see both sides. I didn't see the hero and the monster. I just saw him, and who he was, and in that moment, I forgot about all the tears, screams, and silence. I saw the laughter, the hands, and the embraces.

My breath caught in my chest as I saw it reflected back to me on his face. My ears started to ring, and my head felt light as I felt something inside me, for the first time in years, hurt in a new way.

I wondered how that memory triggered so much more. If I allowed it, it could lead down a very steep path of examining everything I'd thought to be true over the past four years. If I entertained those thoughts, I would also have to be willing to let them override all that he had done, and forgive.

His eyes stopped on my ring, the ring he gave me when Abby was born. "You still wear it." It sounded like a question. What he was really asking was why.

I nodded and looked down at it, twisting it slightly before I turned back to him.

The moment was thankfully shattered before either of us said anything we might regret, when Denny busted through the garage door, reeking of cigarettes.

"Okay, time to grill! Alex, come be my wingman. Wing-woman. Whatever," he said and pointed outside.

Saved by the grill, I thought as I followed him outside, not meeting Matt's gaze.

I held an enormous platter of burgers, hot dogs, and brats as Denny carefully laid each on the grill. The heat from the fire disguised my flushed face, and I balanced the tray on one hand and took a long sip of beer, steadying my nerves.

After we cut the cake, and Abby got her fill of ice cream, I kissed her good-bye and left. Denny was already asleep on the couch, and Susan insisted that I take home an embarrassing amount of food, as though she suspected that I didn't have any in my fridge. Matt nodded a quick good-bye—he still hadn't made eye contact since inadvertently sharing that intimate memory—and Julia leaned forward and kissed my cheek lightly.

As I lay in bed that night, a million thoughts swirled through my head. *Why does she have to be so nice? I'm supposed to hate her. I want to hate her. Now I have to like her.*

And why did I get so rattled when I remembered the camping trip?

I tossed and turned for hours, waiting for sleep to come, but it never did. Finally, I got up and picked up my phone, reading real estate blogs and social media. I slowly typed Julia's name into Google, half-hoping she was one of the few people who had virtually no online footprint.

A few dozen results popped up, and I clicked on the first one. I studied her profile picture, a photograph of her on the bow of a boat, wearing a bikini. She had one arm slung across the side of the boat and a glass of champagne in the other. She wore huge sunglasses, and her hair was tossed into a messy updo on top of her head. I squinted at the picture, trying to find a flaw. Of course, I came up empty.

I turned off the computer and went back to bed, the ghost of Julia's white teeth and Denny and Susan's kitchen following me into my dreams.

CHAPTER 22

I nervously waited in the office of Richmond Burton High School, running my sweaty palms down the length of my jeans. I wore my best, least ripped and stained jeans for the occasion, and found an old button-down shirt in the back of my closet that I hadn't yet used as a rag. I had brushed my hair and pulled out my flat-iron again, thinking my straight hair might offer some level of protection.

The secretary behind the desk gave me a sympathetic glance as I fanned my face again. I cursed my sleeves, wishing I had remembered that high schools were always a little stingy with their air-conditioning.

"Don't be nervous, honey. They don't bite," she said, then frowned. "Usually."

The door to the office pushed open and Gavin appeared. "Thanks for coming," he said. He looked even cuter than I remembered. His sleeves were rolled up to his elbows, and he wore khaki carpenter pants. His hair flopped slightly into his eyes, and he brushed it back with a flick of his head. I knew that if I had had a teacher who looked like him when I was in high school, it would have been very, very hard to concentrate on schoolwork. The closest thing I had to an attractive teacher was Mr. Sherpa in tenth grade biology, who was in his mid-fifties with male-pattern baldness.

I was incredibly thankful to see Gavin again, especially after Abby's graduation and all of my confusing thoughts about Matt.

I followed him down the high school's hallway, feeling very much like a teenager myself. When he had invited me speak to his class, I thought it was one of those nice gestures without any action behind it. We would both nod about it, but it would never actually come to fruition.

Yet he'd called me the day before and asked if I was still interested. I weakly protested, thinking of standing in front of the class and slowly dying a death of sweat and stuttering—in front of a guy I liked—but he insisted. I tried to tell him that public speaking wasn't my thing, that in eighth grade I almost blacked out during a presentation on the life of Grace Kelly and accidentally muttered a four-letter word when I dropped all my note cards. From then on, college included, I would quickly scan the syllabus on the first day of class, searching for the dreaded words *Presentation* and *Speech*. Once, I even switched out of a class in college because it required weekly presentations of current events, something that seemed like the highest level of torture imaginable.

I had majored in Mass Communications at the University of Wisconsin, a subject that seemed safe and comfortable. It was as close to Undeclared as I could possibly get, since I had no idea what I wanted to be when I grew up. And then, after school, I got a job working in marketing for the Grand Geneva Resort, which was a natural progression. Move back home, find work in town. "Don't you want to find something that you're passionate about?" my dad would always ask me when he saw

me during Sunday dinners. I would shrug and pretend to be of-
fended that he didn't see me as passionate about my job. It wasn't
until I started renovating my first house after the divorce that I
realized what *passionate* actually meant.

It meant not wanting professionally to do anything else ever
again, and finally feeling like what I was good at, and what I enjoyed, had intersected.

Gavin stopped in front of the classroom door and flashed
me a smile. "They can smell fear, like a T. rex." When he saw
my face, he laughed. "I'm kidding. You'll be great." He pushed
open the door, and we stepped inside.

The students stared at me as I stood in the front of the classroom. I felt my face grow warm with embarrassment, and a
trickle of sweat ran down my back.

"Class, please welcome Ms. Alex Proctor. As I've told you,
she restores and renovates historic houses, and has a passion for
history itself. She's the best in the business, so to speak, so let's
all extend her the courtesy of listening to what she has to say.
That includes you, Peter." Gavin shot a pointed look at a boy in
back whose eyes were half-closed in boredom, and who seemed
like he would rather be set on fire than listen to one more
minute of Gavin's class.

Gavin extended an arm forward, stepping back as he did. I
stood in front of the class, still thrown by his introduction. I
began by talking about what I did, and how many houses I had
renovated, and what I knew about the history of the Maple
house.

"It was built in 1901, and it's a style considered an American
four square. A four-square house is basically one big box. It's
usually two stories, with a wide front porch. A lot of them were
delivered as a kit, with all the pieces intact and the plans, just
like you would assemble a piece of furniture," I said.

As I went on about the details and the design elements, all of the students, not just Peter, began to look like they wanted to set themselves on fire. I flashed back to the near blackout during my eighth-grade speech.

"And then, in the dining room, we discovered quarter-sawn oak built-in china cabinets, and—" I stopped abruptly and cleared my throat as I saw a student slowly nod off. "You know what? How about if we switch gears?" Slowly, life began to appear in their eyes. "So, flipping houses means that I encounter quite a few things that make me scratch my head. You wouldn't believe the idiotic things people do to houses."

That had their attention. They perked up, watching me, waiting for me to deliver on my promises.

"My first house was a complete disaster. I bought it at auction, and couldn't get inside before I paid for it—huge mistake. When we did get in, we found a ridiculously dangerous setup in the bathroom. The previous owners had installed the circuit breakers basically right next to the shower. And then, the second day, about a million flies appeared. We couldn't figure out where they were coming from, but one thing you learn quickly in house flipping is this: There's always a dead animal. Always. Without question."

They laughed, and I relaxed against Gavin's desk. I told them how we finally found the source of the flies: a duck that had crawled inside the fireplace and died, which led to a very expensive bill from the animal control people, and a chimney sweep who refused to return to the job after he discovered the decaying animal, so I had to crawl up there and remove it myself.

"Another house I bought had a problem with bats on the outside." I shuddered as I remembered the first time I walked around onto the sagging deck and saw what I thought was black mud everywhere, only to discover it was bat guano when I looked up and saw small, mouse-like figures hanging off the eaves. "Which would have been fine—call an exterminator, right? But bats are protected here in Wisconsin, so the exterminator told me there wasn't anything I could do."

A girl in the front with long blond hair that fell over her shoulder like a waterfall wrinkled her nose. "So you just had to leave them?"

"Well, the exterminator did tell me I could 'discourage' them from hanging out at the house, by applying Vaseline to the eaves to make it so slippery that they couldn't grip onto the wood. So we did, and the next day my contractor and I came back to the house to find a bunch of angry, goopy bats frantically trying to latch on to the house." I laughed as I thought of how Eddie ran right back into his pickup, shouting that he didn't sign up for bat duty.

I also told them about the strange things I had found in the walls of houses: old photographs, postcards, a few dollar bills, cigars, a snifter of whiskey.

"Clearly Grandma was having a rough time that day," I said with a smile. They laughed, and I glanced at Gavin, who smiled. I was surprised to realize I wasn't nervous anymore. In fact, I was actually enjoying myself.

I glanced at the clock and saw that my time was almost done. "Well, I know class is almost over, but I was wondering if you guys had any questions for me."

When no one said anything, Gavin cleared his throat. "If no one wants to volunteer, I'll call on someone to ask something. Your choice."

Their smiles vanished, and they looked everywhere but at me—their desks, the walls, the floors. I remembered that well: *Please don't call on me. I didn't do the homework. I didn't read anything you assigned. Just forget I'm even here. Just let me get through this period without any embarrassment.*

"I have a question, Ms. Proctor." A pretty redhead with a

peaches-and-cream complexion raised her hand in the back row. Her shiny hair fell over her shoulder, and she had bright blue eyes with a sprinkling of freckles across her nose. She confidently flipped her hair over her shoulder, and all I could think was that I'd looked nothing like that in high school.

"Yes?" I smiled.

"I was wondering what your thoughts are on the effects of preservation versus rebuilding on a community," she said, with a knowing smile. "After all, doesn't it benefit a town more if there is new business and new construction, rather than trying to save old structures?"

"I'm sorry, what?" I dropped my hands to my sides.

"I've just heard that it's usually better to just build new and revitalize an area. To make things more modern to attract better buyers," she said.

I studied her. *Who is this kid?* Before I could answer, Gavin spoke.

"Time's up, guys," he said. "I'll walk you to the office, Ms. Proctor," Gavin said as he held the door of the classroom open for me. I heard a snicker go through the classroom, and he turned back to them. "Essay on the silk trade routes through Asia in the sixteenth century next week—your choice." They immediately quieted.

"Impressive," I said as we walked down the hallway. "So, who's the redhead? The really pretty one who seems to know too much."

"Oh, Annie Sullivan? She loves to challenge everyone and everything. She even tried to correct one of my test questions last week." He laughed. "She's a total overachiever."

"Sullivan," I repeated slowly. "Any chance she's related to a Jack Sullivan, the Lake Geneva real estate developer?"

He nodded. "Could be. I think she might have mentioned something like that. Why?"

I shook my head. "She was just a little too on top of it." I sighed. "Nice to see that Jack is recruiting his family to spread his message of destruction and demolition."

"She's harmless," Gavin said with a laugh.

"Yeah, but Jack's not." I sighed. "I don't know how you do what you do. I don't think I could handle educating teenagers. They're too smart."

He laughed. "That's why I love teaching them. That, and their universe centers around themselves. Through history, I try to show them that it doesn't."

"How noble of you." We passed a girl in the hallway with long, wavy blond hair who was standing at her locker, texting.

"No phones in school, Chelsea," Gavin said as he swiped the phone from her hand and kept walking. She shrieked in protest, and he held it in the air, walking backward. "Three p.m. Office. You know the drill. Next time this happens, I'm locking you out of your phone."

Chelsea grumbled but nodded. I glanced over my shoulder at her and shook my head. "Man, where are the geeky kids around here? The braces, glasses, pocket protectors?"

"I don't think pocket protectors exist anymore," he said.

"You know what I mean. The awkward, dorky kids. The kids who look like I did when I was sixteen," I said with a laugh.

"I find it hard to believe you were once dorky and awkward," he said.

I rolled my eyes. "You have no idea. I used to—"

Gavin almost collided with me as I stopped suddenly, staring at a bulletin board on the wall.

"Ah, cicadas," he said as he followed my gaze. "One of the students got caught texting in class and had to make this in detention."

The bulletin board was decorated with pictures of the black, orange-eyed, winged creatures, and I wrinkled my nose slightly at their appearance. The prettiest bugs in the animal kingdom, they certainly weren't. In fact, they looked like something from another planet.

"Abby's going to flip," I said as I pointed to a picture from the last time they were in Lake Geneva, in 1998. Their black bodies covered the trunk of a tree in haphazard fashion, stacked on top of one another until no bark was visible. It looked like a moving, breathing black river that coated everything.

"And they're just about the dumbest things ever created," Gavin said as he put his hands in his pockets. "They literally have no sense of direction and will just fly into anything, including people, while buzzing loudly."

"Oh, I remember. Last time, one landed on my neck and I couldn't get it off. I ran into the house screaming, and my mother had to pluck it off of me. Can't wait for that." I was about to turn away and head back to the office to sign out, when a small paragraph printed in red ink, pasted on a yellow background with scalloped edges, caught my attention. "The meaning behind a 'Cicada Summer.' " I turned to Gavin. "I didn't realize there was a meaning to the invasion."

"Everything means something," he said with a smile.

I leaned forward and read the paragraph out loud. " 'The symbolic meaning of a summer when the cicadas come is one of rebirth and renewal. The cicadas only emerge every seventeen years, to live briefly, mate, and then return to the earth. Their presence encourages us to reflect on how life and the world has changed since they were last here, as they symbolize a starting over and new beginnings.' "

I read the paragraph over again, silently, before I slowly leaned back and exhaled. It was everything that I had hoped for the summer to be, summed up on construction paper. The house, Elsie, Gavin, me. Yet a corner of my mind still whispered, *Matt.* Was there a possibility of a new beginning there? Even one as simple as forgiveness? The hairs on the back of my neck prickled, and a slight chill ran through my body.

"Is it cold in here? They usually keep the AC on low, like a sweatshop." Gavin said. "But today it seems to be actually working."

I shook my head. "No, it's—" I looked at him, but couldn't find the words to express my thoughts. It was all too deep, too important, to gloss over in the halls of a high school. So instead I just smiled and relaxed my shoulders. "Yes, it must be the air-conditioning."

CHAPTER 23

"Whoa, whoa, whoa. Careful, Mark," I said as I nearly ran into a crew member who was carrying one of the broken leaded-glass doors from the dining room buffet out to the front porch.

He stopped in the foyer and gave me a fearful look. "So sorry." He set the door down carefully, resting it against the plaster wall. He motioned through the entryway. "Please, go ahead."

"Let me give you a hand," I said as I reached down to grab a corner.

He hesitated, a bewildered look flashing across his face as I smiled brightly, but picked up the opposite edge of the door.

"Let's put it right into my car. I'll take it to the restoration place myself," I said, and we carefully loaded it into my back-seat.

"Thanks for the help," he said quickly before he darted back inside. I heard him whisper to someone inside that "she" was smiling and he thought they all might get fired later.

I laughed, and climbed into my car. The smile hadn't left my face since I'd driven home from Gavin's high school. It had stayed with me as I woke up, ate Cheerios out of a mug, and even when I spilled coffee all over my lap on the drive over to the Maple house that morning. And it was still with me as I drove to Delavan, dried coffee stain covering my thighs.

Eddie had found a glass restorer in nearby Delavan, but the catch was that we had to deliver the doors over to his studio for the repairs. It would be expensive and inconvenient, but worth it to fix them. As I had first suspected, some of the lead was missing from the doors. Only a restoration company would be able to repair them, since it involved taking the whole door apart, replacing the glass, and then soldering new lead into the frame—all of which were out of the scope of any of our abilities.

As I pulled west onto Highway 50, my phone buzzed again with a voice mail from overnight. I sighed as I listened to my mother's voice.

"Hi, honey. Just wanted to let you know that we will be in town at the end of the month for a few days to see you and Abby. We would love to stay with you, but we can make other plans if that isn't possible. Let me know. Love you."

It was typical that they would choose to come visit during the busiest time of the year. They were both retired, my father from teaching and my mother from working as a school social worker. When they ended their work lives, they seemed to forget all sense of nine-to-five life, or workweek schedules. Before they moved to Florida, my mother would often call me on a Wednesday at eleven in the morning and ask to go shopping.

When they retired, they suddenly realized the meaning of the word *bored* and began to fill up their lives with various clubs, activities, and social engagements. But without jobs to anchor them to the area, they quickly grew tired of the winters and moved south to Fort Lauderdale a year prior. They had been talking about doing it for a few years, but I had some suspicion that they delayed it after everything that happened between Matt and me, almost as though they wanted to make sure I was stable before they left.

Their delay didn't dull the sense of loss when they packed up their car and drove south. Their departure meant the true end of unconditional love in a ten-mile radius.

My phone buzzed again, and I looked at it, expecting it to be my mom calling from the beach or maybe a boat, but I didn't recognize the number. It was a local 262 area code, so I picked it up. It was a woman from the Children's Society of Southeast Wisconsin. Her voice creaked with age when she spoke.

"Ms. Proctor, I did some research on the adoption you requested records for," the woman said.

"And?" I clutched the phone to my ear and sat back, the air in my car stifling.

"Well"—she cleared her throat—"I'm sorry to tell you that the child we thought might be a match wasn't a match."

"Oh." I sat back against my chair and exhaled slowly. "Are you sure? Maybe it . . ."

"No, I'm sorry. I double-checked the records, and it's not a match. That particular child was already in touch with her birth parents, so it couldn't be the same baby. I'm sorry," she said.

I cleared my throat. "So, where do we go from here? I don't really know the next step. Do you have any advice?"

"That's not really something I can tell you. Honestly, the chances of finding a match are probably very slim," she said slowly. "With the sealed adoption records in the state, it's really a matter of both parties wanting contact and having a lot of luck."

"Please? Anything." Elsie's face as I would tell her that the child wasn't a match flashed before my eyes, and I put my head on the steering wheel.

"Well, has she registered with local and state agencies that specialize in matching up birth parents?"

It was the same advice we'd heard before. It seemed to be all that anyone could offer. I sighed and told her we had, and hung up the phone. I left my head on the steering wheel, the hot sun beating down through the windshield. It now seemed suffocating, rather than warming. I turned the AC on full blast, letting the sweat evaporate from my forehead.

I closed my eyes as I realized that I would have to tell Elsie she was much further from finding her daughter than either of us thought.

CHAPTER 24

"How is it possible that there are at least ten layers of paint on this stair rail?" I muttered as I cocked my head to the side and stared at the chipped layers of rainbow paint that wouldn't budge off the wood rail. I suspected that there was gorgeous oak underneath all the dirty paint, but so far, my green, non-toxic strippers hadn't made a dent in dissolving any of it.

"Alex, you know anything's possible," Eddie said from his position on the floor. He dumped more stripper onto a rag and wiped it onto the baseboard, waiting to see if the cream-colored paint bubbled up. "People do all kinds of weird shit to houses. And with this one, you have over a hundred years of bad ideas and screwed-up design plans."

"But who just keeps painting and repainting a staircase?" I said. I ran a finger over the glossy railing, leaving a trail down the middle of dust and debris. "I imagine you'd have paint chips everywhere anytime anyone touched it."

"Probably idiots who didn't have little kids to eat the paint chips." He cocked his head to the side. "Correction: very, very smart people who didn't have little kids."

He shook his head and wiped at the painted baseboard again with the stripper. "This isn't doing anything. We need to move to the hard stuff."

I nodded. "Let's do it." Normally, I tried to avoid using hard-core chemicals and stripping agents, especially on wood that old, but there was no way we were going to get down to the grain without the serious power of chemicals. The downside was that the chemicals were toxic and flammable, and we'd have to use extra precautions when applying it.

Eddie went to his truck and retrieved the industrial-strength stripper. "On the baseboard first," I said.

He nodded and tossed me a ventilator mask, while I opened the front door to let air circulate through the foyer. He put on gloves and bent down, applying the stripper to the baseboard with a paintbrush. As we waited to see if it would work, I saw him stifle a yawn.

"Late night?" I said.

He sighed. "You could say that. Mia's got a cough and couldn't sleep . . . so we didn't sleep. She just cried all night, and Janie and I took turns holding her. I think she finally passed out around four this morning."

"Probably in your arms, right?" I said.

"Yup." He stretched his arms overhead. "Still have a cramp in my back."

"Welcome to parenthood, where you're always battling some varying degree of tired."

He wiped his forehead. "You know, I thought working at a job site for sixteen hours in ninety-degree heat was exhausting, but I had no idea what tired actually was."

"Preaching to the choir, my friend." I leaned forward and peered at the baseboard. "It's working!" I grabbed a wide putty knife and moved it gently across where the paint was beginning to bubble. A small piece of cream paint flaked off. Underneath another light layer of paint, I could see wood grain.

"Great. Now only about a thousand square feet of moulding to strip," he said as he slowly gazed around the foyer. "And then the rest of the house."

For all of the painted wood trim—of which there was some in virtually every room—we would have to scrape all of the paint, and then go over any leftover residue with steel wool. Then, we would have to fill in any cracks or chips in the wood-work before sanding it with a handheld sander before we stained and sealed it. A lengthy, tedious process for sure, but like most good things, worth the effort.

I headed toward the stairs, paintbrush and putty knife in hand, and began to methodically apply the chemical. As I waited for the paint to start bubbling, I let my thoughts drift to earlier that day.

I had stopped over at Elsie's house that morning before I started work and told her the news about the adoption agency not having a match. She smiled and thanked me for my work, again stating that she was sure we would find her daughter, but her eyes brimmed with sadness. As she closed the door, I called out that I would keep looking, and checking to see if there were any more leads, but she didn't respond. Or if she did, it had been too quiet to hear.

The sound of someone walking up the front porch pulled me away from the memory. A pretty, blond woman in a black suit and wearing aviator sunglasses appeared at the door.

"Eddie, watch this spot and scrape it when it's ready," I said over my shoulder as I walked outside. I pulled my respirator down around my neck. "Yes? Can I help you?" As I opened the screen door, I sized her up and down. Realtor, I thought. A few of them had wandered into my renovations in the past, looking to drum up business.

"Alex Proctor?" she said with a frown. When I nodded, she thrust her hand forward. Instead of Realtor business cards, it was a manila envelope with an official seal on the front.

"What's this?" My heart began to pound when I saw *County*

of Walworth on the seal. "All of our permits are legit. I can go grab them. . . ." I trailed off when she shook her head.

"I'm from the office of the county assessor." She stuck her hand out, but I waved my dusty fingers, covered in paint chips, at her, and she quickly withdrew it. "Well," she said as she pointed at the envelope. "Were you aware that there's a tax lien on the property?" she said with a sympathetic look that meant she suspected that I was clueless about the situation.

I shook my head, tore open the envelope, and scanned the document. The most recent owner, a Mae Sweeney, had fallen behind on the property taxes before the house went into foreclosure, an amount that had compounded with interest. My hands started shaking as I read the money due: ten thousand dollars.

"So, you're saying what? That I owe this amount?" I said, my eyes darting from the zeros back to her.

She nodded. "As the current property owner, you are responsible for the debt. And you can't transfer the title to anyone else before the lien is paid off. Since the property was in foreclosure when you purchased it, you are the responsible party."

"I—" I looked down again. "I know what a tax lien is, but . . ." I trailed off. "No. This has to be a joke," I whispered.

"Sorry, I don't make those kinds of jokes," she said before she turned and walked down the steps.

The paper floated from my hand onto the porch. I stood very still, breathing heavily, as I watched the assessor get into her car and back out of the driveway. "Shit," I said. "Shit. Shit. Shit!"

"You alive out there?" Eddie called from inside.

I didn't answer, just bent down and picked up the statement, hoping I had mistakenly added a zero. The ten-thousand-dollar figure stared back at me. I would have to pay that amount just to unload the house. I had paid off tax liens on properties before, but never more than a couple thousand. It was a risk understood when buying a property at auction, but at this stage in the game, I had all but forgotten about the possibility of a lien. Usually the assessor had come knocking almost immediately after the property was sold, his or her hand out, to collect their monies.

"Far from it," I called to Eddie. I tried to calculate what I had left in my accounts. With the hit taken to my contingency fund due to the flood and other repairs, and all the other monies spoken for, this amount would come directly out of my own pocket. And it would clear out my savings account.

Eddie came outside, wiping his hands with a rag. He pushed up his face mask. "Matt?" he said when he saw my expression.

I shook my head. Blood rushed through my ears like a freight train.

"Abby?"

I handed him the paper.

"Wow." He gave a low whistle. "We've never had one this high, right? The bungalow had what? A couple grand?"

"Not even," I said.

He handed the paper back to me and lifted his scraper in the air. "No time to waste, then." He disappeared back inside, and I heard the scratching sound of the scraper working on the stairs.

It was a good five minutes before I could move again, and I went back inside. I remained planted there, as though my feet were nailed to the warped wood floor. I didn't know how it was possible that one house could have so many problems. I had certainly expected hard work, disasters even, but nothing like the half of which we had already experienced.

I rubbed my forehead as I fought back tears.

A mantra began to run through my head that told me I was an idiot for taking on a project of this size and scope, that I should have just stuck to what I was good at: remodeling beige condos, like Jack Sullivan—and his granddaughter—had said. Painting and replacing the windows in a few outdated bungalows. That I was in over my head, and my ambition was going

to lead to financial ruin. That Matt would end up with full custody because I was going to end up living under the marina
bridge.

"Boss, I'm outta here. You okay?" Eddie said when the sun
began to disappear over the horizon and dusk began to settle in
the delicate nooks and crannies of the molding.

I didn't answer, and he grunted good-bye. I stayed at the
house, laser-focused on the stairs. I tediously scraped and scraped
until my arms began to shake and burn, and I tried to ignore the
feeling in the pit of my stomach that told me the worst wasn't
over yet.

CHAPTER 25

Two days later, I felt the sun move over my closed eyelids as I lay in bed. Not that I had been asleep; on the contrary, I had been up for hours. Since midnight, likely, as though my body had some weird sixth sense of time and refused to allow me a moment of peace once the day had officially started.

It had been the same way years ago, on the day when Matt and I got married. I remembered I woke up some time around three in the morning, stared at the clock on my nightstand, and then screwed my eyes shut but never really fell asleep after that. Too many details swarmed through my head—whether the flowers would arrive on time, whether Traci's bridesmaid dress would hold up despite barely being able to be zipped up. She had ordered a size two sizes smaller than normal, since she said it would be motivation to lose weight. Except, of course, she didn't lose anything, and her dress had to be practically duct-taped to her body.

I had worried about whether Matt was nervous. The week before, I'd caught him reading over the vows from the wedding booklet given to us by our priest, reciting them in different tones. He confessed that he was worried he was going to say the wrong thing and screw everything up. Or drop my ring. That was his other fear, that he would drop the ring instead of putting it on my finger and it would go bouncing across the church and under a pew.

Looking back, it was strange that we worried about so many small things, so many details, when we really didn't think at all about the reason we were there: to get married. Throughout the entire planning process, I didn't spend more than five minutes thinking about what it all meant and what would be the end result. Or what would be left after the cake was cut and the dance floor empty. We never worried about the marriage, only about the wedding.

I remember when the wedding day started, it was as though an invisible force was turning the wheel, and I was just a bystander. Each event: hair, makeup, pictures, the ceremony, more pictures, the reception, seemed to happen on its own, with or without my presence. I made it through the vows without messing them up, but I remember the corners of my mouth trembled as I said the words, nerves making my chin wobble and my lips stick against my teeth. And Matt didn't say the wrong words or drop the ring, although his hands were shaking so hard that I thought his worst nightmare was about to come true.

I slowly sat up in bed, and waited for the crush of emotions—disappointment, anger, loss. They slowly washed over me, and I remained helpless in their pull. I put my head in my hands and sighed.

It was the fifth wedding anniversary since the divorce, and it hadn't gotten any easier. I thought with the passage of time, the date would become more and more of a footnote on my past and lose importance. It seemed to be the contrary; the more time that passed between then and now, the closer all the memories became, like time was moving in a circle and doubling back toward me instead of moving in a straight line forward.

The first anniversary after our divorce, I didn't leave my bed. My parents came and picked up Abby, and I slept the entire day. The second anniversary, Matt had her, so I met Traci and drank way too much wine and passed out on her couch. The third and fourth years, I spent at my houses, replaying nearly every moment of my marriage in my head. But this year, I was determined to do something other than wallow and obsess. Except, of course, that was always easier said than done.

I pushed my feet into my slippers. *Were there signs? Should I have known? Was I really that stupid?*

Yes, and no. Maybe. Probably. Not likely. I had never reached an answer, and I was so tired of asking the questions, but they never ceased.

I stared in the mirror, toothbrush still raised, and studied my face. I was older, yes, but I didn't think I looked that different. A few extra lines on my forehead and around my eyes were the biggest evidence of my age.

Am I that different? What happened?

Impossible questions to answer, at least on my own, likely because the answers didn't exist, at least not in a way that could be expressed cleanly. The answers were in some alternate universe where two plus two didn't equal four, it added up to the square root of purple.

I set my toothbrush down and slowly walked into the basement, toward the box marked *Misc.,* shoved against the back wall that sometimes leaked. I reached into it and pulled out our wedding DVD. I hadn't watched it in at least four years, and I didn't think Abby had ever seen it. She certainly wouldn't have watched it at Matt's house.

It was the last memento from that day. After Matt told me about the affair, I threw all of our wedding photos into the garbage. Burned a couple of them in a very *Waiting to Exhale* moment. Tossed my wedding ring onto the lawn. But I didn't remember the DVD existed until almost a year later, after the papers were already signed. I was alone when I remembered, so it seemed worthless and anticlimactic to destroy it then. Besides, it felt strangely gratifying to have one piece of evidence left that showed that what I thought happened, actually did.

Or did it?

"What do you know?" I said to the video as I narrowed my eyes. I was about to toss it back into the box—and to pray that the leaky basement would finally leak enough to destroy the damn thing—but stopped. I could watch it. I could watch it and see whether he loved me on our wedding day as much as I thought he did. Whether he loved me on the day when he was supposed to love me the most. It would all be downhill from there, of course, so if he started out lukewarm, if I saw it on his face with the benefit of time and divorce papers, maybe I would feel vindicated that the outcome was inevitable. There was nothing I could have done.

I could watch it and make myself as miserable as possible on such a crappy day. After all, wasn't I allowed at least one day of emotional-train-wreck behavior?

"Mom?" Abby's voice made me jump. She was on the basement steps, still in her nightgown. "I was looking for you." She padded over to me and hugged me. "What is that?" she said as she pulled away and pointed to the video in my hand.

"Nothing." I quickly dropped the video back into the box and stepped forward, but she picked it up.

"Is that you and Dad? At your wedding?" She pointed to the smiling bride and groom on the cover and I reluctantly nodded. "Can I see it?"

I tried to protest, but she began to beg. "Please? I want to see your pretty dress and veil. Please?" she said again until finally I obliged.

She and I sat on the couch, her eyes transfixed on the screen as we watched the ceremony. I tried to look away, check my e-mail, close my eyes, but I couldn't escape it. My eyes remained on the images of a young, pretty woman easily smiling at her new husband, who gazed at her with admiration and love.

As we watched the first dance to "The Way You Look Tonight," I wrapped my arms around my stomach, to try to plug the hole that grew larger and larger. I bit my lip as I saw Matt lean down and whisper something in my ear. On-screen, I threw my head back and laughed. Our eyes twinkled as we stared at each other, smiling.

"What did he say, Mommy?" Abby asked me.

"I don't know," I said. Although I very much did know. I had forgotten about it until just then. As we danced, he had glanced around the room at our guests.

"Don't look, but your cousin Melissa brought her damn dog in her purse," he had said. Melissa, a second cousin who'd barely made the invite list, had RSVP'd her and a "plus one" and had asked that her guest's meal be served on the floor. Which seemed . . . odd. So my mother called her and she confirmed that she couldn't possibly leave her dog, Stella, at home for the whole evening, so she would be bringing her. We, of course, told her that wasn't allowed, but on the wedding day, she didn't listen. That damn dog ran around the dance floor all night, yapping and biting at people's ankles, until my father unceremoniously locked it in the handicapped bathroom. Melissa had pounded on the door, screaming, "Stella! Stella!" in the most Marlon Brando–esque way.

Everyone was worried that I would be upset, but I laughed it off, saying it would be good fodder for reminiscing. And it was, for years after. Matt and I would sometimes look at each other and just yell, "Stellllla!" before we dissolved into laughter.

As the dance finished and the alien couple on-screen kissed, I grabbed the remote and turned off the television.

CICADA SUMMER / 171

"Why did you turn it off?" Abby said in protest.

"Time for breakfast!" I said as cheerfully as I could muster.

Later that night, I sat on my couch with a beer and thought, *How did this all happen?*

The answers all came rushing in bits and pieces, like a scattered puzzle. The stress of having a colicky baby. His focus on work. Both of us being exhausted all the time. Intimacy feeling like another point on the never-ending checklist. The constant, weary bickering.

All of those things were small. They could have been adjusted, improved. It wasn't until his affair that the gauntlet was truly thrown down. I couldn't help but wonder what would have happened if we had both turned to each other, maybe during one of those intense fights over something insignificant like emptying the dishwasher, took a deep breath, and allowed ourselves to come together.

I pictured it, Matt and I, living together. Abby never having to pack her overnight bag; me never having to say good-bye to her. Never having to hug her when she returned and recognize the smell of Matt's deodorant. Matt and I, laughing when she told us corny jokes. Slipping away for a date night, maybe taking a boat out to the middle of the lake, turning the radio on, and sharing drinks from a cooler.

Sharing a bed, a house, a life together again, as though the divorce had never happened and I was able to forgive.

I pressed my fists into my eyes as I realized that part of me still hoped that would happen. That some small part of my brain still believed that our story wasn't over. I was still clinging onto an impossible future.

Before I could stop myself, I walked outside and threw the DVD into the trash can by the side of the house. I emptied the kitchen trash on top of it, leftover spaghetti sauce and all. I also dumped my beer on top of the mess, enjoying the way it glugged and fizzed down over the case, before I closed the lid with a bang.

In my kitchen, I poured a glass of water and sipped it slowly, my hands still shaking. It seemed so unfair that Matt was still intruding on my life. I didn't know when I would have any freedom from him, if ever. And if that didn't happen, I couldn't possibly move on with someone else. Even if that someone was wonderful, charming, and attractive like Gavin.

I picked up my phone. It was time for reinforcements. I dialed Traci, and the day's events came spilling out before I could censor them or consider how crazy I sounded.

"Hello?" I said when there was a pause.

"You wasted a whole beer?" she said. Her voice was muffled and hoarse, like she had been sleeping.

"Yes. Listen, I'm sorry to bug you. I'm sure you were asleep. We can talk about this another time," I said quickly.

"No. No. I mean, yes, I was asleep, but you're not bugging me." I heard her yawn. "Chris has had a hard time sleeping the past few nights, and I've been up with him from about two to six a.m. for the last three nights."

"Oh, Traci." I sank down on the couch. "I'm so sorry. Why is he awake?"

She sighed. "Why does he do half the things he does? He wakes me up, asking questions about the year I was born and what color did we paint the living room in 2005. It's like a computer database that keeps shorting out, and he won't rest until I answer every single question. Until I make the database work again. I never imagined that I would be up all night with him at eighteen."

"So, not the best week for you, either, then," I finally said. I knew Traci's problems were completely different from mine, but it was hard not to think that she knew exactly what I was feeling: that the lives we were living should not have been.

"Not exactly. But look, I've learned something that might help you, too. Don't you think I have days when I see photos of Chris when he was a baby, and remember that feeling of hope? That I used to wonder what Ivy League school he would attend? And then I realize that we're more likely to pick out which cartoon he will watch before work, and if he can learn to tie his shoes without tears. That all of those dreams come crashing down the second that I remember reality, or when he walks into a room and starts flapping?" She paused and sighed again. "But I can't live my life in that space. I have to move on, and function. For everyone."

"I know. You're right," I said as I slowly nodded.

"It's time to move on, Alex. Live your life, and stop looking back to what you thought would happen. It is what it is, and you have to just deal with it. I do it with a hefty dose of denial mixed with a glass of wine and compartmentalization. You're welcome to use my formula," she said with a laugh.

I took a deep breath and slowly nodded. "Am I crazy?"

"Yes," she said immediately. "But it would be crazier if you didn't still think about the two of you being together. He's still around, and you guys were together forever. For starters, though, you need to take off that ring."

I looked down in surprise at the gold band that Matt had given me. I had worn it almost every day since Abby was born. When Matt and I got divorced, I had sold my engagement and wedding rings and used the money to pay for my used Ford Explorer. But I hadn't taken off my gold band, figuring it was a present for having Abby, something I would never regret.

"It's from him," she added. "It ties you to him."

I hung up with Traci and sat back against the couch, staring out at my backyard until the first rays of morning light began to peek through the trees. Finally, when the trees outside were fully lit, with tears in my eyes, I slid the band off and put it on the side table. I flexed my finger, my thumb immediately finding the soft indentation of where the ring used to be. I rubbed the joint, trying to make the indentation disappear, but it wouldn't go away. I let the tears fall down my cheeks, but didn't wipe them away. Instead, I went upstairs and grabbed an old costume jewelry ring and stuck it over the groove. It didn't fit quite right, but it was enough. Enough to remind me to forget.

CHAPTER 26

"Now would be the time to start that prayer circle," Eddie said as he sprayed down a section of the popcorn ceiling in the dining room with a garden mister. We silently waited five minutes before he climbed back up on the ladder and stuck a putty knife perpendicular to the texture. He gave me a look before he put his weight into the ceiling. Only the smallest flake of the texture came raining down on the plastic sheeting on the floor.

"Well, we got lucky with the asbestos testing, so, of course, this popcorn ceiling stuff won't be easily scraped away. Can't win 'em all," Eddie said with a sigh. The popcorn ceilings were practically the only possible surface in the house that was free of asbestos, but they were going to be a nightmare to remove.

"So, now what?" I said as he climbed down the ladder.

He craned his neck upward, and I could see the blue bags under his eyes from lack of sleep, thanks to Mia's restless nights. "Well, since it looks like they used some kind of plaster to texture the ceilings, it's going to be impossible to scrape off." He looked pointedly at me, waiting for an answer.

"No. We can't just leave them like this. It looks awful, and prospective buyers will think it's the apartment building from the 1980s style of acoustical ceiling. It won't matter if we tell them it looks like shit but it's okay because it's not cheap material."

He sighed wearily. "We can skim-coat the entire surface with joint compound, I guess. We'll end up with a smooth surface, and then we can paint it. It's going to be—"

"A lot of work," I finished. "I got it. Can we just agree to stop saying that phrase? I—" I stopped and peered out the window. A silver Toyota Camry was slowly driving past the house, and at the wheel an older man with sunglasses was leaning forward, scanning the property. I remembered what Elsie had told me about prospective buyers driving by, but the memory of the county assessor paying us a visit was also fresh on my mind.

I had driven to the county office the day before and swallowed hard as I forked over a check for ten thousand dollars. My hand shook as I wrote all the zeros out, trying not to think of how long it had taken me to save that amount, and how many things I could buy with it. Clothes for Abby, a new microwave. A dishwasher. A new pair of jeans for me. A night in a hotel with Abby and me. All of the above, and I would still have had thousands left over.

The clerk accepted the check without so much as a smile. It was just normal, everyday business for him, not someone handing over what represented the last of their savings. Their last safety net. He gave me a receipt, and I walked away. A small square of paper was the only proof that I had once had that money in my account.

At least when I had spent that kind of cash on a house before—hello, new windows in the bungalow—I had something tangible. I could open and close the windows, clean them. With this, it was merely paperwork, an administrative problem that I had to pay to make go away.

So when I saw another car slowly drive past the house, I immediately began to wonder, *What else?*

"Hang on," I said to Eddie as the car slowed to a stop.

I jogged down the still-cracked front steps, careful to side-step the broken concrete, and approached the car with a smile and a nervous wave. I thought maybe if I looked pleasant, the reason for his visit might be pleasant, as well. The man in the car glanced at the road, like he was considering driving away, but slowed the car to a stop instead. He didn't return my smile, and my pulse quickened.

"Hey there!" I leaned down and placed my dirty hands on my thighs. "Can I help you?"

When he didn't answer, I added, "Are you interested in the house?" I jerked a thumb back in its direction. "It's not for sale yet, but hopefully in a few weeks it will be." I smiled again, but he frowned.

"I gathered as much, based on your sign." He pointed to the *Coming Soon* sign waving in the lake breeze. "Do you have an asking price in mind?" He didn't take his sunglasses off, but placed his arms casually on the steering wheel, his shoulders rigid.

Warning bells began to go off in my head. My smile faded, and I pressed my hands into my legs. "I have something in mind." I glanced back at the house again, and Eddie appeared on the porch, wiping his hands with a drop cloth, as he watched. I could see his expression probably mirrored mine: *Not again.*

"Well, I'm sure you've heard that there is a developer inter-ested in expanding this area, yes?" he said. "And this house is in a prime location for a hotel or commercial development."

My stomach dropped, and I stood, quickly taking a step back from the car. I raised my eyebrows at him. "Who are you?"

"Look, I'm from Waterview Developers. We're expanding our commercial interests on this block, and we would poten-tially be interested in this property." Only then did he remove his sunglasses and stare at the house for a brief moment. He frowned again at Eddie, before quickly putting them back on.

"To tear down," I said.

There was a pause before he answered, "Of course."

The heat started to rise in my face, and my scalp prickled with anger. "Well, that will never happen. I'm not restoring this house just so you can tear it down. I'm sorry, you'll have to find some other poor house to rip apart."

His face didn't flinch. "Thanks for the information. I'm sorry to hear you feel that way." His tone was measured. Placating in the most disturbing way. He had heard all this before, and it hadn't mattered. They had always gotten what they wanted. "If we are interested, we would be prepared to offer you the market value on the property plus an incentive bonus." He glanced at the house, grimacing at it before smiling.

"Everything okay?" Eddie called from the porch. "Who's here?"

"I think you should leave," I said to the man. "I don't care what you've done before, but you'll have to bulldoze through me to get to this house."

He briefly smiled. "If I had a dollar every time . . ." He shook his head before he drove down the road.

I sank down on the lawn, my legs suddenly Jell-O.

Eddie appeared next to me. "Uh-oh. Let me guess: another tax lien?" When I didn't answer, he continued. "Former resident trying to take the property back? Insurance adjustor? Contractor looking for work? Someone who hates old houses?"

"You're getting warmer," I said without looking at him.

"Waterview?"

I didn't answer as I put my head in between my knees and took a deep breath.

"Shit," he muttered. "Those assholes. Only interested in destroying, never fixing." He let out a long breath. "Well, they can talk all they want, but we won't let them get near our girl."

"Eddie," I mumbled into my arms, "I might not have a choice. If no one buys the house, I might have to sell to them. After the flood, the wiring, the plumbing, the everything, I'm already into this house for way more than I planned. There's no contingency fund left. If anything else goes wrong, it doesn't make any sense for me to even fix it. I'll have to sell to Water-view and watch them tear it down."

And Matt might be the one to sign off on the paperwork, I added silently.

"That won't happen," he said firmly.

"Even if I do find a buyer, though, what's to say that they won't sell to Waterview a few years down the road? They're patient. They'll wait." I glanced at the leafy oak in the front yard. "Like the cicadas."

I thought about calling Matt, asking what he knew about Waterview's interest, but I knew he couldn't, or wouldn't, tell me anything.

Eddie and I sat on the lawn for a few moments, before he said, "Can we get the historical society involved somehow? They have to want to keep the house around, for . . . historical reasons."

I picked my head up as I thought of Shannon and her perky zingers. "Historical status. If the house had historical status, then Waterview couldn't tear it down," I said slowly.

Eddie shook his head. "Do you have any idea how to get historical status for this house? I've heard the process is an ad-ministrative nightmare. They don't like to give it out unless the house is truly a landmark, since it kind of screws everything up for development."

"That's exactly what I want. I'll figure something out, some way to get it." With renewed determination, I stood and brushed my hands off on my jeans. I extended one forward and pulled him up. "Let's get back to those ceilings." While Eddie and his crew were working on skim-coating the ceilings, I walked around the side of the house, frowning at the bubbling stucco up near the roof. I had hoped that it could be fixed with a patch. In theory, it could be scraped off and a new layer of wet stucco could be applied, and then sanded, textured, and painted, but we wouldn't really know until we got up there and surveyed the damage. I doubted that there was much insulation left behind the façade, and we might have to replace that, as well. I just hoped that in the meantime, no pests decided to nest in there and pull out whatever was left of the insulation.

In my house growing up, the exterior walls were cedar, and woodpeckers had a serious love affair with the material. At least twice a year they would drill a hole in the side of the house, pull out insulation, and nest inside. They became my father's biggest enemy, his mortal rival.

I was almost to the backyard, close to where we'd found the old arbor, when I heard a loud *thud* from next door. "Elsie?" I said. I carefully tried to peer into her window, and at first didn't see anything, but I could make out what looked like a foot on the ground, near the front stairway.

"Elsie?" I called again as I knocked on the front door. I thought I heard a weak moan in response, so I opened the door. As I stepped inside, I saw Elsie collapsed in a heap at the bottom of the stairs, cradling her arm. I rushed to her side. "What happened?"

She weakly looked in the direction of the wooden staircase with white painted risers.

"Oh, no," I whispered. I lightly touched her shoulder. and she winced in pain, clutching her forearm. "Let me get some help. I don't want to move you."

An ambulance arrived fifteen minutes later. The medics carefully lifted her onto a stretcher, stabilizing her forearm. They said she likely had broken both bones in it, by the way it was bent downward at an unnatural angle. I rode with her in the ambulance, and grabbed a crappy cup of coffee from the vending machine as I sat in the waiting room of the ER.

I stared at the fish tank in the wall and an eerie sense of déjà vu came over me as I recognized a big blue fish swimming near the bottom. Five years ago, Matt and I had sat in this very waiting room and watched that same fish while I waited to be admitted for suspected early labor.

I was only six months' pregnant, and it was far too early to be having contractions. I had ignored them for most of the day, thinking it was false labor, and that they would stop. But they continued, and by dinnertime, my doctor told me to go to the hospital so they could figure out what was going on. I hung up the phone and immediately burst into tears. Matt walked in the door at that moment, and put an arm around me and led me out the door to the car.

I think we only waited in the ER for about ten minutes, but it felt like an eternity. Every second that ticked by was another moment that my child could have been in danger. My agitation was only calmed by watching the fish in the tank swim around, oblivious to what was happening around them.

"Everything will be okay. I promise," Matt had said to me as we waited.

Finally, we got into a room and they hooked me up to a monitor. They found the heartbeat, turning the sound up so we could hear the strong *thump thump*, and watched the contractions on the monitor. A steady stream of paper with wavy lines spit out from the machine, indicating heartbeat and contractions. Matt and I held our breath and stared at the output.

"The baby's fine. The contractions are just strong false labor. You're not going to have a baby anytime soon," the doctor finally told us after I had been hooked up to the machine for close to an hour.

Matt put his head down on my lap and exhaled slowly. It was only then that I realized how worried he had been. He had shown little emotion up to that point, instead being the calm parent to my crazy parent.

He looked up from my lap and smiled. "Already causing heart attacks, isn't he or she?" He sat up and kissed me on the forehead, and I remember thinking that we had endured the worst. That the night in the ER was our biggest scare, and that things would be perfect after that. The next time we were at the hospital was when Abby was born.

The blue fish nudged a red fish with its nose, before it hid behind a plant, and I came out of my memory. I shifted in the hard plastic chair and took a sip of my coffee, wincing as it burned the roof of my mouth. Years ago, I had expected that we would be back again, that we would have more kids and more births and more excitement. In another life, maybe I would have been at the hospital for that reason. That I would be up on the maternity ward, having another baby. Giving Abby the sibling she so desperately wanted. Adding to the family that Matt and I both had dreamed of.

I could picture it all so clearly, that other life. Holding a new baby in my arms in one of those blue and white hospital blankets, introducing Abby to him or her. Taking pictures of her holding the baby. Watching Matt change a diaper in the Isolette as I fiddled with the hospital bracelets around my wrist. The beeping of the machines down the hallway and the sound of approaching footsteps in the middle of the night from the nurses. The smell of a new baby as it lay against my chest. Matt and I, parents again.

The life that I had planned for.

Instead, I was sitting in the ER, watching the fish swim again, all alone. I forced another sip of coffee into my scalded mouth as I tried to remember what Traci told me: that I needed to move on. That that life was something that didn't exist, and would never exist.

I forced the hot liquid down my throat as I pushed the memory and the daydreams away and instead watched the fish swim around, focused on one second to the next.

CHAPTER 27

Even though Elsie had only broken her wrist, the doctors suggested she stay overnight at the hospital so they could monitor her blood pressure. It had dipped low, and they were concerned she might have a concussion due to her fall down the stairs. I asked her if she wanted me to stay overnight with her, but she refused, practically kicking me out of the room.

As I was leaving the hospital, I got a text from Gavin. *Would love to meet up again. Dinner on Friday night?*

I stopped in the lobby and smiled. *Sounds great,* I sent back. *Call you in a few,* came back as the response.

I squared my shoulders and walked out of the revolving doors, reminding myself that I didn't have to feel lonely anymore, that I had a new beginning right in front of me. That Traci was right, I was only torturing myself by looking backward and to the side instead of forward.

My phone buzzed, and I laughed as I pulled it out of my pocket. "Eager for a date, are . . ." I stopped when I saw that the caller was Matt, not Gavin.

"Sorry to bother you," he said quickly.

"You're not bothering me. What's going on? Is Abby

okay?" I started walking quickly toward my car, keys in hand. Matt was supposed to pick her up from the house, with Eddie, when I went to the hospital with Elsie.

"Yes, she's fine. I just wanted to call and . . . talk to you about something." His voice dimmed for a moment before he cleared his throat. "Her sixth birthday is next week—"

"I know that," I said. I got into my car and turned the air-conditioning on full blast, bracing myself for whatever might be his request. I imagined he might ask to take her somewhere extravagant, somewhere overnight, meaning she would miss spending the day with me.

"I mentioned maybe taking her tubing on the lake for her birthday, and—"

"No. It's my turn. She'll be at my house." In the divorce agreement, we agreed that she would alternate years of where she spent her birthday. Last year, Matt had her on her birthday, and I spent the day in a heap on my couch, trying to unsuccessfully distract myself with reality television.

"I know. I'm not asking for that day. This weekend, before her birthday. On Friday. I told her I would take her tubing and she said yes . . . and asked if we would both take her," he said.

"Both? Like you and me, together?" The words sounded so strange. *You and me. Together.* A unit.

There was a pause before he said, "Yes."

"Well, will . . . anyone else be on the boat?" I didn't have the strength to say "Julia." I didn't think I could fake pleasantries for hours with both of them, at the same time. While trapped in the middle of a lake. Life jackets or not, if that happened, there would be a fifty-fifty chance of someone going overboard. Or at least of me swimming to the shore regardless of how far it was.

"Just the three of us. You, me, her," he said. When I didn't answer immediately, he added, "She asked me to call."

"She did? She asked you to call?" I knew I was being intentionally obtuse, but I enjoyed listening to his discomfort.

"Yes, she did." There was a pause. "So, what should I tell her?"

Friday night, I thought. *When Gavin wants to go on a date.* I sighed and rubbed my forehead. For Abby, I would go and pretend that everything was fine between Matt and me. But for myself, I would meet Gavin after, and let my guard down.

"Now, stop. It's really nothing. There's no need to fuss over me." Elsie waved her good arm in the air from her hospital bed, shaking her head at the chocolate-chip cookies that Abby and I had baked for her. She pointed to the countertop that lined the circumference of the room. "Leave it there for the nurses. They'll make sure to give me the good drugs, then." She winked at me.

I set the white bakery box down on the counter, next to a box of latex gloves. I reached into the shopping bag from the Piggy Wiggly grocery store on the floor. "At least let me give you some lunch. The food here is abysmal, that much I remember." I held out a turkey sandwich and she nodded, pointing to her food tray next to the bed. I unwrapped the sandwich and put it in her good hand.

"You really shouldn't be fussing over me," she said again.

I glanced down at her splinted arm, the purple and black bruises peeking through the black fabric. Her face was bright with makeup: blue eyeshadow, pink blush, and red lipstick. She had tried to conceal the angry, red bump on her left temple, but it still sprouted from her face like a molehill.

The orthopedist had told her that she wouldn't need surgery to reset the bones, but that they were both displaced. He said she was lucky that neither had broken the skin, and become a compound fracture. I had shuddered when she told me that. I had only seen a compound fracture once, when I worked on the docks in Fontana. A drunk guy had gotten off his boat and stumbled around on the pier, before tripping over his cooler and landing straight on his arm. I could still remember the ear-piercing sound of his shriek as he held up his flopping arm that was gushing blood.

"It's really no trouble. I needed a lunch break from the house, anyway," I said as I pulled out a matching turkey sandwich and sank down on the pea-green vinyl chair across from the bed. I told her about the Waterview developer I had seen on the day she fell and how I wanted to get historical status for the house.

"And how difficult is that?" she said as she nibbled at her sandwich.

"Difficult. Beyond difficult. We have to prove that either someone famous lived there—historically significant, as they say—or that the house is a landmark for some other reason." I took a large bite of my sandwich and rolled my eyes.

"And is it? A landmark, I mean," she said.

I smiled. "Depends on who is asking. In reality, no. But Eddie and I are going to try to figure out something, some angle to pitch to the town council to get them to consider our position. But it's still a huge long shot."

"Ah, so not quite as easy as you had hoped," she said with a knowing nod. She glanced down at her turkey sandwich and smiled. "Most things aren't."

I swallowed hard. "I'm sorry that we haven't made much progress with finding your daughter. I'll make some more phone calls, contact some more agencies. Something will shake loose." I gave an encouraging nod, but my words felt fragile, easily shattered.

In a hospital gown, without the benefit of her usual brightly colored clothes, she looked older than I had ever seen her. I had a terrible thought that she might not have many good years left.

"Maybe some things are meant to stay in the past," she said quietly. Her red lips fell downward and seemed to bleed into her paper-thin skin.

"Sure. Of course. Some things." I thought of Traci's words again about Matt and me. "But not this. We'll find her," I said again.

"You know, I spent the first few years after I had the baby searching for a sign of her in every child that I saw. I would be at the market and see a towheaded two-year-old, and I would search her face for any sign of me, or of David. Or at church with my parents on Sunday, I would see a tiny girl with bows in her hair and pray that she would turn around and flash me deep blue eyes just like David's. Sometimes I would try to bargain in my prayers, say that even if the child wasn't mine to raise, just to give me a sign. Some moment in which I would know that she was safe. Loved." She placed her good hand lightly on top of her splint. "I would promise that I wouldn't try to contact her, or think about her again, if I could just catch a glimpse of her." She smiled, her eyes watery. "Maybe I'm not meant to find her. Maybe I wouldn't like what I found."

"Or maybe this is your second chance, like you said. Right now, there's just a few bumps in the road," I said.

A nurse walked into the room, and Elsie's face brightened. "Paige, my favorite! How are you today, dear?"

Paige smiled as she grabbed Elsie's pink water pitcher. "Same as yesterday, love. Ready for the weekend." She turned to me. "You look familiar. What's your name?" She held the pitcher in the air, mid-thought. "Did you go to Badger High School?"

I nodded, a familiar feeling of dread coming over my face in the form of a flush. "Alex Proctor, but I graduated in 1999."

"Hmmm. I was 1997. I don't think we ever met, though." She narrowed her eyes at me as she searched the corners of her brain. "Proctor . . . Proctor . . . Proctor."

I decided to pull off the conversation Band-Aid right away. "Matt Proctor. My ex-husband. You graduated with him."

"Aha!" She triumphantly lifted a finger in the air as though she was the one who had solved the familiarity puzzle. "Matt, right. How is he?"

"Honey, she said *ex*-husband." Elsie's voice crackled through the air, shooing away the building discomfort in the room.

Paige smiled. "Right. Sorry." She put a hand on her hip. "Well, if he let you go, he can't be doing that great." She gave me a wink, before she walked out of the room with Elsie's pink water pitcher.

"She should see Julia," I muttered. "I think he's doing pretty well. Me, I'm not so sure."

"Oh, stop it," Elsie said. "You have that teacher."

"Well, for one, I don't 'have' him. I'm not even sure how I feel about him." I didn't tell her about pushing my date back to after-dinner drinks to go out on the boat with Matt and Abby, or that I couldn't seem to push Matt out of my head long enough for Gavin to take over.

"It will all work out," Elsie said as she stared out the window at the sunshine that spread across the fields. The bright green hills were crisscrossed with horse fences and dotted with the occasional barn and silo. In the distance, the trees parted and the landscape sloped down toward the lake.

She turned back to me. "Good things will happen."

I nodded. "For both of us."

CHAPTER 28

I pulled into the Lake Como boat launch, my heart pounding. I immediately spotted Matt and Abby and exhaled in relief when I didn't see Julia with them. Even though he'd told me she wouldn't be there, I wouldn't have been surprised to see her perky blond head next to his.

Matt gave me a quick wave, and I noticed he seemed as uncomfortable as me. I couldn't decide if that made me delighted or irritated. Abby jumped up and down with excitement as she showed me the giant red tube with a back, like a floating couch, that Matt had hooked up to the back of the boat. Except it wasn't a boat that I had seen before. It was new. A Cobalt. And it likely cost more than his car. Or, at least, *my* car.

"Nice boat," I grunted as I hopped on board, ignoring his outstretched hand to help me on.

"It's . . ." He trailed off as he sat down at the captain's chair.

"Yup," I said. I pulled Abby up front with me and sat at the bow with her. Her little body shook with excitement as the wind whipped through our hair and I cuddled her to me. I felt Matt's presence from behind, but thankfully didn't have to turn around.

We reached the center of Lake Como quickly, it being a much smaller lake than Lake Geneva. While Lake Geneva had quickly become a favorite spot for wealthy families at the turn of the century, Lake Como had never gained the affection of the rich in the same way. For starters, in addition to being smaller, it also had more weeds and water lilies in certain areas. The shoreline was dotted with modest houses and a few restaurants, like Mars Resort, a staple in the community for decades.

"Beautiful afternoon," Matt said as he slowed the boat. "Nice and empty."

Whereas Lake Geneva was probably still filled with cocktail cruisers and dinner boats, Lake Como was quiet. The water shone like glass from shore to shore. Perfect for tubing. Across the lake, I could see people gathered on the deck of Mars Resort, having cocktails under the blue umbrellas advertising different beers. The signature red light shone from the top of the restaurant, to signal to boaters that they could dock and come inside for a drink.

I smiled as I thought of meeting Gavin there later, after I got off the boat. He'd mentioned that he wanted to go to a real Wisconsin supper club, and there was no place that fit the bill better than Mars.

"All right, Ab. Want to go?" Matt said when we were stopped.

She leapt out of my arms and ran toward the back of the boat.

"Help her," I shouted, but he was already waiting for her. He held her hand as she climbed onto the tube and then unhooked it from the back and let it trail in the water, the line straightening.

"Ready?" he shouted and she gave a quick thumbs-up.

Matt started the motor and the line grew taut, snapping her into place slightly as we towed her behind. He drove slowly, just enough for the tube to remain flat on the water, but not enough to knock her off. There being no other wake on the water, she slid across the surface with barely a bump.

After a few turns around the lake, Matt slowed the boat to a stop. I tried to ignore the fact that we were facing the clubhouse for Geneva National on the south shore of the lake. Just to the right of the clubhouse was Matt's new house, with the elevated white screened porch that probably caught the cool lake breeze on even the hottest summer afternoons. It looked like it had been there for decades, and maybe the untrained eye would assume that it had, but I could tell that it had been built maybe two, three years ago.

Sitting on his boat, in view of his new, beautiful home, made me feel more like a guest than normal. I felt like I didn't belong on the same lake, or even in the same zip code as him. I was the "plus one," included on their afternoon.

I turned my focus to Abby, waving to her in the water. Abby floated happily on the tube, her spindly legs crossed at the ankles and her arms outstretched over the back.

"Do you want to go again?" I called to her.

She shook her head and kicked her legs a little, so the tube drifted around in the water. "In a minute. Not now."

"Drink?" Matt gestured toward a small white cooler on the floor.

I slowly nodded and he handed me a beer.

"How is your house project?" he said carefully as he glanced at Abby on the water and then leaned back in the chair.

I sighed slightly. "It's not just a project—it's my job."

He winced. "I didn't mean it like that." He looked down at his drink, his shoulders sagging slightly.

There was a pause, and I cleared my throat. "It's going well. We've had some hiccups, and there was a tax lien issue. And an issue with a developer. So I'm looking into getting it historical status." It was more than I had planned to say, but the words propelled out like popcorn popping.

"What would that do?" Matt said. The sun was beginning to set, and the light moved across his face, the oranges and reds highlighting his five o'clock shadow.

"Protect it. From anyone ever tearing it down, messing with it, or . . . hurting it." My voice unexpectedly shook, and I took a quick sip of my drink. My head started to feel light, and I put the beer down. I didn't need to show up tipsy to my date with Gavin.

"Is that hard to do?" he said as he turned toward the radio. "Music?"

Before I could agree, he flipped on the radio.

"Yes. Harder than you might think." I paused, considering whether I should continue. I figured it couldn't hurt. "Well, and I have another problem with the house, one that you are familiar with."

His brow furrowed. "What do you mean?"

"Your good buddies over at Waterview. Seems they're interested in my property, too," I said. I carefully watched his face for a reaction, for some sign that he knew about it.

His face lifted in surprise, and a tiny part of me exhaled in relief. "Well, would you ever consider their offer?"

I shook my head. "Not in a million years."

He nodded and looked out at Abby on the tube before he turned back to me. "They're tough, but you can go against them. People have done it before." He paused and gave me a small smile. "Not many, but I'm sure if anyone could fight them off, it would be you."

"Thanks." My stomach dropped a little at his compliment, and I looked down at my drink, unsure of how to respond.

He didn't know what to say next, either, so we floated in silence, listening to the radio, before the DJ came on, talking about the delayed appearance of the cicadas.

"Do you remember those from when we were kids?" he said with a half smile.

"Yup. It was my first summer home from college, and it made me want to turn around and drive right back to school." I smiled. "I think Abby's going to freak out when they arrive. If they ever do," I said as I tucked my legs under me.

"Man, that was the first summer I started working on the Fontana pier. They mostly stayed away from the water, but occasionally some tourists would arrive and be waiting for their boat with a cicada clinging to the back of them. I'd point it out and watch them run around screaming, trying to bat it off." He laughed, his eyes crinkling at the corners. "One lady jumped in the water. Of course, she then started screaming about the seaweed she was standing in." He paused. "Never a dull moment on the piers during the summer."

I nodded, thinking of the time when I saw parents wrangling their four screaming, tantrumming kids on the dock as they waited for their boat rental. And then we watched from the snack shop as the parents drove away in the boat and left two of their kids on the pier. It was hard to say if it was intentional or accidental, but after watching the kids try to push each other into the water, I suspected it was on purpose. One of the dockhands had to drive around the lake with the kids, since it was back before the golden age of cell phones, and try to locate the parents.

"Wouldn't it be nice to go back to that time, even just for a day?" he said.

I swallowed hard. I wasn't sure if he meant the lack of responsibility, or the casual summer jobs, or . . . us. The way we used to be.

I glanced at his face and from his expression I knew the answer: us. I wanted to nod, to tell him I wished we could go back, that I did think about it. But then my thumb went to the ring on my finger, the one I had put in place of Matt's gold band.

He noticed the gesture and looked down in silence.

For a moment, we were both quiet, lost in the past. The smell of boat fuel mixed with lake water permeated the air, and the gentle rocking of the boat seemed to say *shush, shush*. The sun felt the same as the sun when we were younger. And if it wasn't for the memories of what had happened in the past five years, everything else would be the same, too.

"Look, Daddy! Julia's waving to us!" Abby's voice brought me to the present.

I followed her outstretched finger to the shore, and my stomach dropped as I saw Julia's perfect blond form on Matt's porch, a hand outstretched. She wore a hot pink bikini and sunglasses, drink in hand.

"Just like she said she would!" Abby added. "Did she finish making my birthday cake?"

I swallowed hard as I realized that while Matt had told Julia she couldn't come on the boat, she had still made plans to make her presence known. His face flushed, and he rubbed his forehead with his hand as irritation crossed his face.

"Does she always bake birthday cakes like that?" I said. "That bathing suit looks a little . . . unsafe. What if she got burned somewhere sensitive?"

He shook his head in response and turned back to Abby. "Want to go around the lake again?"

She nodded so enthusiastically I thought her head might loll off, and any further conversation was halted by the roar of the motor and the sounds of Abby's shrieks.

I saw Gavin's broad figure sitting at the bar at Mars Resort. His back to me, I studied his well-defined shoulders and a chill ran down my back as I looked at his strong, tanned hands. I sank into a bar stool next to him and smiled.

"Thanks for waiting," I said. I didn't lean back after I sat, and our legs were touching.

"Of course. Manny here recommended an IPA." He lifted a finger to a bored-looking bartender, who nodded. He slid the beer toward me. "Want some?"

I nodded, taking a sip of the hoppy, bitter ale. "Not really my thing. Different from what I usually order."

"Different can be good. New can be good," he said as he placed his forearms on the bar and gave me a crooked smile.

"I'm beginning to agree with you," I said.

He leaned forward and dropped his chin. "Beginning to?" His eyes sparkled.

He looked so handsome, but the tension and confusion from the boat ride with Matt still lingered on my shoulders. I needed to think of something—anything—other than the fact that before I saw Julia, Matt and I were getting along and showing some shred of the people we used to be. That I almost allowed my guard down long enough to be pulled toward him and act on the thoughts that haunted me.

Before I could stop myself, I moved forward and kissed Gavin. He didn't respond at first, in surprise, but then kissed me back, putting a hand on my cheek.

I felt my face flush and my pulse quicken, and I leaned into the kiss once again.

My flush deepened, thanks to a slow clap from Manny. "What was that?" he said. "Thirty seconds? Has to be a new record." He made an exaggerated gesture of turning around and pointing to the taxidermied fish clock on the wall.

I sat back in my stool, taking a long swig from Gavin's drink, and then ordered another, waiting for the embarrassment to subside.

I had never been big on blatant PDAs. Or even subtle PDAs, I suppose. I never really wanted to hold hands or kiss while out with Matt. It was a constant source of irritation to him. He seemed to want to hold hands over romantic dinners, whereas those things always felt unnatural and cheesy to me, like the overly sentimental Hallmark cards at the drugstore. Even at home, I suppose, I was never a big cuddler or spooner. There was sex, intimacy, and then there wasn't. Sleeping time was for sleeping. His side, my side. Often separated by a wall of pillows in an almost-reluctant bed sharing.

I swallowed hard at the memory of Julia waving from the dock, and wondered if she always held his hand at dinner and cuddled him all night long. Probably, I thought. I shook my head, pushing her away. Matt had already dynamited enough in my life, and I couldn't let him ruin this, too.

"So, how's the house coming? Almost finished?" he asked, putting his forearms on the bar. As he did, the short sleeve of his polo shirt inched up, and I saw a black design on his bicep.

"A tattoo?" I said as I pointed to his arm.

He glanced down and flashed me an embarrassed smile. "Oh. It's an armband tattoo." He lifted the sleeve up slightly so I could get a look at the black swirls that went around his bicep, before he quickly pulled the material back down over to cover it. "It was a dumb college thing. A couple of friends of mine and I got them all at the same time."

"Like friendship bracelets?" I said with a laugh.

"Something like that. It seemed cool at the time, but now . . . less so." He shook his head.

I put my foot on the base of his stool, turning toward him. I pointed to my hip. "Shamrock. When I was eighteen. My college roommate and I were bored one afternoon."

"Matching shamrocks?" He raised his eyebrows.

"Nope. She got some kind of flower, but on her toe. I was glad that I went first, because watching her scream in pain while this guy was tattooing her foot was kind of terrifying," I said and then took a sip of my drink. "Although, maybe it would have been better if she'd gone first. It might have prevented me from getting any ink myself."

"It could be worse. It could be one of those awful lower-back tattoos," he offered.

"Like a tribal tattoo?" I said.

He laughed. "Exactly. And yours isn't visible unless you're at the beach or—" He stopped and twisted his mouth into a small smile.

I smiled, feeling the spark between us, crackling like newspaper under a flame. This time, he was the one who leaned forward and kissed me. He tasted like hops and breath mints, a strange but appealing combination. As we kissed, I heard Manny whistle again from behind the bar. Clearly, none of the other patrons had been as successful on their dates in recent memory.

When we broke apart, Gavin placed a hand on my shoulder and whispered into my ear, "I think we're turning Manny on. Should we go somewhere else?" He paused. "Like, another bar?"

At the same time, I said, "Like, my place?"

He lifted his eyebrows, and I almost laughed it off as a joke, but gave him a small smile instead. "Well, yeah. Or that," he said.

Manny appeared with the tab and a wink.

"I'll follow you in my car," Gavin said as we walked outside. He grabbed my hand, but I didn't pull away. I did wish I had another gulp of liquid courage before we left, though.

At my house, he leaned forward and kissed me again, his lips pressing to mine. I grabbed the back of his shirt and pulled him toward me. His hands were in my hair, pulling the strands off my warm neck.

"I should go," he said when we broke apart.

"Yes, you should," I said.

Moments later, our clothes came off in a tumble, leaving bread crumbs of a trail toward the bedroom. I wished that I had thought to straighten up my bedroom before our date, but I never thought we would end up back at my house. I had planned to clean before my parents came into town, but hadn't gotten around to it yet.

I brushed the laundry and piles of contractor notes aside onto the floor, and gave the adoption research a shove to the other side of the bed as we sat down.

"It's great," Gavin said as he kissed my neck.

"What is?" My eyes were half-closed.

"Your house," he said.

"This one? Or the other one?" We lay back on the bed, and my legs intertwined with his.

"Both," he said as I rolled over on top of him.

I hadn't been with anyone in over a year, since a minor flirtation with Jonathan, the guy I met at Home Depot. And that was only a couple of times. The sex was vanilla, basic. Fine. Even though it was only twice, it felt scripted. So I don't think either of us minded when I never called him back after the second time. Besides, he kept asking me for advice on tiling his shower. Once while we were making out, he stopped unbuttoning my shirt to bring me into his bathroom and show me the subway tile.

But that night, when Gavin and I were together, subway tile was the furthest thing from my mind. I focused on turning off my brain and existing in the moment. I concentrated on feeling every brush of his fingertips, and kiss of his mouth. I willed myself not to worry about how my body looked or if we were moving too fast. I was fueled by the knowledge that I had just watched my past have his own future, and so it was high time I took a step into mine. I tried to push all thoughts of Matt and the way he used to touch me, kiss me, and hold me out of my mind. I tried, but when I closed my eyes, I still thought of him, so I kept them open to remind myself whom I was with and what was happening.

And when it was over, Gavin and I lay next to each other on my unmade bed. My limbs were sore and my lips were tender from being kissed, but I still felt unsettled.

CHAPTER 29

I woke up the next morning and drove over to the Maple house. My lips still felt bruised from the night before, and my hair was thrown into a messy ponytail. Gavin had kissed me before he left, gathering his clothes in a trail to the front door. Without the added benefit of darkness, the drinks, and desire, the early morning took on an awkward quality as I waved good-bye and shut the door behind me.

As I drove to the house, flashes of the night before interrupted my drive: the softness of where his neck met his shoulder and the way he kissed the inside of my wrist, and how I had to concentrate to stay in the moment. I couldn't stop the flush from moving across my face as I thought of the moment he told me to slow down, relax. I didn't realize my cheeks were still pink as I pulled up to the house at the same time as Eddie.

"Wow. Where did you spend last night?" he said as he fastened a loop of heavy wire between two screw eyes on the edge of the broken pocket door.

"Nowhere. My house." I could feel my cheeks reddening further, so I turned and paid close attention to the wire on the door, my gaze not meeting his.

"Who was with you?" he asked with a laugh.

"I was alone in my house this morning." It was the truth. By virtue of admission, since Gavin had left last night.

"All right. None of my business, boss. I got that. Nice to see you had a good night, though. It's about damn time," he said.

I rolled my eyes at him before I turned back to the pocket door. I watched as he pulled the wire and dragged the door out of the pocket. We each took a side and lifted the door out of its track after we pried off the top and bottom jambs.

Eddie peered inside the pocket. "Can't see a thing." He slowly extended a narrow piece of wood into the dark, narrow opening. "I really don't want to lose another finger," he said. After poking around for a moment, he nodded. "Just as I thought. The studs at the back of the pocket are warped. We'll have to straighten them out and then rehang her back into place." He glanced at me. "Are you listening?"

"What? Yes. Pocket door. Go for it," I said absentmindedly. My entire body felt like it had been wrung out, like a wet sponge that had been sitting on a kitchen countertop for days until finally someone had discovered it.

"Boss?" Eddie said, his eyebrows raised.

"I'm going to start patching that plaster in the living room," I said without looking at him.

I sat down on the scuffed floors of the living room, pre-mixed joint compound next to me. I slowly began to apply the compound with a wide knife, spreading it to several inches on either side of the crack. Then, I taped down the center of the crack, and applied another layer of compound. The methodical, rhythmic motions made me settle further into the floor.

As I worked, I glanced next door, at Elsie's empty house. The windows on the second floor seemed to frown, their chipped wood sills sagging in the sunlight as they waited for their owner to come home. I wondered if this was the longest time she had been away from home.

Some people don't believe that houses have souls, but I know they're wrong. Every person who lives in a house leaves an imprint on it, like a ghost that won't ever leave. The tears, laughter, and smiles are all soaked into the surfaces of a house. The wood, the tile, the paint, all absorb the energy of those who live there. The house is a forever witness to the peaks and valleys of those who live there. It knows the deepest sadness and the greatest pleasures of a family, and will always keep their secrets.

As I moved over to patch another crack, Eddie appeared from around the corner.

"Hey, listen. I just got a text from Janie that Mia's cough is getting worse. She thinks she might have croup. It's probably not a big deal, but . . ." He trailed off, his shoulders sagging.

I waved my hand in the air. "Go. I remember what that's like. I hope she feels better," I added when he turned to leave.

I settled in front of a wide, horizontal crack that was next to the paneling close to the fireplace. I was about to spread more joint compound on the crack when the edge of the paneling caught my eye. I leaned in closer, putty knife in hand, and realized the last section of the paneling stuck out more than the others. I ran a finger along the wood, and then lightly pressed on it.

I moved back as the paneling swung open, releasing a cloud of dust and stale air. It was a section only two feet by two feet, with a small alcove inside. It was just big enough to hide a small box, or a bottle of liquor. Or, in this case, a yellowing envelope.

I winced as I stuck my hand into the small space, certain a tarantula or giant centipede was making a nice home inside, and pulled out the envelope. The front was blank, and inside was a folded piece of paper.

At the top of the document was the name of a lawyer, a Mr. Thomas J. Regan, Esq., and it appeared to be a sort of contract, signed by Mr. and Mrs. Moore and Elsie's parents, Mr. and Mrs.

Slattery. As I read the text, my eyes widened at the words *adoption* and *baby*. I nearly dropped the paper when I saw the sentence: *The birth families agree to relinquish all familiar claims to the child, and to never contact the child in the future.*

"They knew about the baby. They knew and . . . they gave her up." My arm drooped down to my side as I took a long, deep breath. I shook my head and read the paper again, certain I had missed something. Yet it was the same: They had given up all rights to ever having a relationship with their granddaughter, even though their son was dead.

I couldn't imagine their logic in signing the agreement. It was so hard for me to say good-bye to Abby when she left for Matt's house, yet that was only for a few days at a time. I supposed they did what they thought was right at the time, but I knew from my own life that decisions made in the past sometimes don't seem quite as clear-cut when examined in the present.

I realized that Elsie didn't know about the agreement. She believed the Moores never knew about her pregnancy. Her parents must have told them, though, and gotten them to sign the agreement so the adoption could go through without any hesitation. It didn't make sense that Elsie wouldn't have been asked to sign the contract, as well, but maybe her parents figured that she would go along with whatever they decided. And, for the most part, she had.

I put my forearms on my knees. Elsie would be devastated if she knew about the paper, if she knew that they had all conspired to send the child away. I wondered if the child somehow knew, if she knew how quickly she was given up for adoption, and what she might assume about Elsie.

I shook my head. I wouldn't tell her. It wouldn't make any difference. But now I had a name: a Mr. Thomas J. Regan, Esq. He was someone who might know something that had happened with the adoption. He likely wasn't still alive, but I thought that maybe I could track down a family member or a colleague. I would investigate the lead on my own, and if it turned out to lead me somewhere, I would try to find a way to explain it to Elsie.

I tucked the paper into my back pocket and turned my attention back to the cracks in the plaster.

CHAPTER 30

"And how did you strip all the painted door hardware?" my dad asked as he surveyed the doorknobs that were laid out on a tarp on the front porch.

"Soaked them in a Crock-Pot and then scrubbed them all with a nylon brush, of course. Wouldn't have dreamed of using stripper or a wire brush," I said with a smile. "I was taught by the best."

"And the windows?" he said, his gaze moving toward the restored sashes.

"We saved and fixed them all. Rebalanced all the weights, replaced the glass, and patched the rotting wood. We even saved the leaded-glass doors in the dining room buffet. Just got a call this morning that they're ready for pickup from the restoration company."

He turned to me and nodded. "Great job, honey. I mean, really."

"Thanks. There's still a lot to be done, but we're getting there. Despite all the setbacks, I still want it to be done by the end of the summer, before the winter sets in and people enter hibernation mode."

"Well, it looks just fantastic." My dad looked at my mom and smiled. "I told you."

My mom threw her hands in the hair, her hot pink fingernails flashing and her bright red bob moving around her shoulders in one piece. "I told you I knew she would do a great job on the house." She shuddered and looked at me. "Those pictures that you first sent us, though."

I saw her sneak a glance in one of the windows.

"They're all gone, Mom. All the dead animals are gone. Promise," I said.

"Yeah, it was really gross." Abby wrinkled her nose.

"And how would you know? Were you the one scooping them all up?" My dad lifted Abby off the ground in one swoop and hugged her to his hip. Even at almost seventy, he still retained the shape of an NFL quarterback, and the fitness level. Last year, he ran a half marathon and beat out a bunch of men half his age. He had always seemed like a superhero to me, a fact that continued into his golden years.

We walked inside the house, and my mom surveyed the baseboards and trim, her white linen tunic floating behind her. "Isn't the wood a little dark, though? Are you going to paint it white?"

My dad and I both gasped at the same time, and I nearly fell over on the spot. My mother's decorating style could be described as more Palm Beach circa 1987, with lots of mirrored walls, gold accents, and tropical print furniture. They even had a giant, built-in shelving unit covered in white and brass as their headboard. Their entire condo looked like the Golden Girls had hooked up with the cops on *Miami Vice* and went into real estate together.

"Evelyn, we're going to pretend that you didn't say that," my dad said as he shifted Abby on his side.

"What? There's nothing wrong with painted wood, Gary," she said as she rolled her eyes.

"Sure, Mom. But, I mean, look at this." I ran a hand along the doorway trim in between the dining and living rooms. "It's imperfect, but it's beautiful." I traced the grain in the wood, swirling my finger along the color variations. "I don't know why anyone would want to cover this up."

"Like I said, I knew she would do it right," my dad said with a smile as my mom shook her head.

She glanced at her watch. "An hour. We landed an hour ago, and that's how long it's taken you two to fall into your routine." She threw her hands up in exasperation, but I saw the sparkle in her eyes. She walked over to Abby and plucked her from my dad. "C'mon, sweetie. Come tell Grandma all about your school before we leave for dinner."

"Really, I couldn't be more proud," my dad said before we followed them into the kitchen. He paused and looked into the powder room, at the original porcelain sink.

"Yes. I'm patching the flaking porcelain, too, Dad." I rolled my eyes. "Eddie was supposed to do it today, but he's home with his sick daughter." He had texted me before dawn, asking for a day off since Mia was still having a rough time, and Janie had come down with the same thing. I hated to lose him for a whole day, but I told him to stay home.

"You know, I patched that damn sink about a hundred times in our old house," my dad said with a frown. He stared at the black cracks and missing pieces of porcelain near the drain.

"Be my guest," I said.

He grinned and set to work in the bathroom with some fine-grit sandpaper, porcelain filler, a few toothpicks, and a bottle of surface glaze. My mom took Abby back to my house, and I worked on patching more plaster cracks in the dining room. I found the Milwaukee Brewers game on the radio, and my dad and I worked together, the baseball announcers' voices carrying us through the afternoon.

When it was nearly dark out, my mom dragged us away

from the house to grab some dinner. There wasn't a discussion as to where, since it was understood that we would go to my parents' favorite restaurant, Anthony's, as we always did when they visited. A leftover from decades ago, the restaurant was literally in the middle of a giant cornfield off the main highway, and proudly boasted red leather booths and old world Wisconsin charm.

As we walked in, the maître d' ran forward, arms outstretched to greet my parents. While they hugged and exchanged pleasantries, Abby sighed.

"Mom, what am I going to eat here?" she said in a drawn-out, whiny tone.

"Noodles, like you always do," I said firmly.

She rolled her eyes and sighed again, and I saw a flash of her teen years. "We'll have a nice dinner," I said brightly, but she didn't respond.

We took a step forward to follow the maître d' into the dining room, toward one of the corner, red leather booths when I heard a familiar voice slur across the restaurant.

"Well, well, well. What a nice family reunion." We turned and saw Jack Sullivan sitting at the bar, on the opposite side of the host stand. He lifted a martini glass, sloshing the liquid onto the bar.

"Oh, boy. Why does that jerk have to be here?" my dad said under his breath before he smiled at Jack and walked into the bar. My mom, Abby, and I followed him, but remained in the reception area, letting my father do the dirty work.

"Jack. Looking good. How long has it been?" my dad said.

"Since we last saw each other or graduated high school?" His words ran together in one long sentence, the syllables barely distinct from one another.

My dad ignored the question and clapped him on the back, in the jovial, former high school quarterback and prom king way that he always had with people. "How are things?"

Jack took a long sip of his drink before he set it down. "Does that explain it?" he said with a laugh that sounded like a hiccup. "Eh." He shrugged. "Still divorced. My kid still hates me. You know how it is." His glassy eyes focused on the rest of us, behind my father. "Well, maybe you don't."

"No, I suppose I don't." My dad turned around, motioned his eyes toward Abby, and nodded his head toward the dining room. "Listen, we should really get something to eat before the little one falls asleep on the table. It was great to see you."

"Your daughter doesn't know what she's doing," Jack said in response.

I took a step forward. "Please, continue."

My dad held up a hand to Jack, and my mom grabbed Abby's hand and cheerfully asked her if she had to go to the bathroom, not waiting for her answer before she led her away.

"That house. You're going to lose all your money in that house," he said. "Come to work for me, and you won't have to worry about any of that."

I shook my head. "You're crazy if you think I would want to work for you."

"Not so crazy that I would ruin my life for some hunk of junk that's been rotting away for over a hundred years," he said with a smile. He lifted his martini glass again in a toast.

"Jack, it looks like you've been a little overserved. It was good to see you, and take care," my dad said firmly before he turned to walk out of the bar. When I didn't immediately follow, he put a hand on my shoulder. I shrugged it off, and grabbed the glass out of Jack's hand, and downed the liquid inside. It burned my throat and my eyes immediately started to water, but I fought the urge to cough.

"Lay off the booze and maybe your life wouldn't be such a disaster," I said before I turned and walked out of the bar.

"A pleasure, as always," he called from his bar stool before I heard him order another drink.

"He's really gone downhill," my father said under his breath as we walked into the dining room.

As we sat down in the booth, we ignored questioning looks from my mom and Abby.

"Let's get you some bread," I said to Abby as I reached for the basket of bread sticks and cheese spread.

"Some things never change in this town," my dad said as he opened a menu. He scanned the menu that hadn't been altered in thirty years and added, "Some good. Some bad."

After dinner, Abby fell asleep on the way home, and my dad passed out on the couch while watching *SportsCenter*. My mom and I settled at my tiny kitchen table with glasses of wine. It seemed impossible, but the longer she lived in Florida, the younger she seemed to get. As I studied her smooth forehead and unlined cheeks, I wondered if she really had found the fountain of youth.

"So. How's it really going?" she said as she folded her hands in front of her. On her left hand was the modest engagement ring my father had given her over forty years earlier, and on her right was a simple gold band with a missing stone. It was a tiny ruby, from her grandmother, lost before she was even born. I had once asked her if she was going to replace the stone, but she told me that it didn't seem right to put another stone there that wasn't original. For all of her *Miami Vice* decorating and suggestions to paint antique wood, she still knew that original was better when it came to certain things.

"Great. The house is probably going to kill me, but I'm great," I said as I shifted under her gaze. I took a long sip of my wine and avoided meeting her eyes.

She made a murmuring sound and didn't look away. Finally, I caved. "Stressed at times. But really, I've started dating someone new, and things are looking up."

Her eyebrows lifted in surprise. "You're dating someone? That's wonderful."

I nodded as I trailed a finger along the stem of my glass. "So far, so good. Traci set us up."

She nodded approvingly. "Well, good. I want to see you happy. You deserve that."

"Thanks. I hope so," I said.

She considered her wedding band for a moment. "Relationships are never easy, that much you know."

I laughed. "I think I've earned my literal stripes in that category." I leaned back and tucked my legs underneath my body.

"At times, I think we all have," she said.

"Yes, but you guys are still married. Not the same thing," I said.

She smiled. "We're still married, because we stayed married. Trust me, there were more than a few bumps in the road."

I sat back in surprise. "What do you mean? You guys have always been happy."

She shook her head. "Happy? No. Married? Yes." She leaned forward and lowered her voice. "It has been peaks and valleys, good times and bad. The for better and for worse." Before I could say anything, she put a hand on mine. "I'm not saying what you think. I'm not telling you that you and Matt should have stayed together. All I'm saying is that things sometimes get tough. Really, really tough. No one gets the fairy tale, even those who love each other to death, like your father and me."

"Well, that's the most depressing thing I've ever heard," I said quietly. I thought back to the night I spent with Gavin, and how I had to forcibly push Matt's ghost away, out of the bedroom. Even in the heat of the moment, he still hovered over me.

"It shouldn't be. We fought—fight—all the time, but we work at it, and we know we are both in it for the long haul." She leaned forward. "Besides, fairy tales are boring."

"Oh, I don't know. Living in a castle might be fun. Plus, tons of money, a tiara, and a handsome husband? Not the worst thing in the world," I said with a laugh.

"Yes, but I know you. You get bored with easy after a while.

You've always wanted a challenge—just look at that house. Cinderella, I'm afraid you'd steamroll right over Prince Charming."

I took a long sip of wine before I said, "Bulldoze, Mom. I'd bulldoze him."

Two days later, my parents loaded their luggage into their rented sedan, ready to make the two-hour trek to O'Hare airport and return home. My dad had spent the better part of their trip helping me on the house, patching plaster cracks and scraping the woodwork, while my mom took Abby shopping and to lunch, two activities that I was never interested in. Finally, my mom had a girly companion.

Before they left, my dad kissed me on the cheek and said, "Give 'em hell," before he scooped up Abby and squeezed.

"You know I will," I said. As I hugged my mom good-bye, she whispered, "Stay away from any bulldozers."

"Not a chance," I responded with a smile.

Later that night, sleep washed over me quickly, and when I woke to the sound of my phone buzzing on my desk across the room, the bedside table light was still on. Fumbling around with the covers, I fell out of bed onto my knee, hard onto the wood floor. I grabbed my bed and hoisted myself up, quickly limping toward the phone. I glanced at the time as I answered it: 4:45 a.m.

White-hot terror coursed through my body as I saw an unrecognized number. I had had enough of middle-of-the-night phone calls lately.

"What is it?" I said quickly as I began to walk down the stairs, my hands shaking.

"You the owner of a house on, uh, Maple Street?" a gruff voice spit out. "You're listed as the owner of record."

"Yes. What's the problem?" *What can possibly be wrong now?* I thought.

"Well, this is Officer Miller with the Lake Geneva Police Department. There's been a fire at the residence at 4723 Maple

Street, and this number is listed as the primary owner's contact."

"A fire?" I started walking quickly down the stairs again, my stomach in knots. "What do you mean?" I gripped the phone with one hand as I grabbed my car keys in the other.

"You better come down here," was all he said.

CHAPTER 31

Nothing could have prepared me for what I saw when I arrived at the house. Thick black smoke poured out of the second-floor windows, billowing into the night air like the fire was exhaling from the inside. The red and orange from the police cars and fire trucks projected multicolored strobe lights against the newly repaired stucco, and I could see a section of the replaced roof buckling inward from the heat. The roof, which was supposed to protect the house from water, was now succumbing to the fire.

I ran toward the house, but was stopped by a firefighter who held his arms out. "That's as close as you're gonna get," he said. His face was illuminated against the flashing lights, giving him a strange, demonic quality.

"But it's—it's my house—what's happening?" I cried out as I gestured toward the house. I didn't wait for him to answer before I tried to rush toward the door again, but he held up an arm and pushed me back firmly. I leaned against his arm as I felt the breath go out of my lungs, sucked away like a vacuum. "Tell me what's going on!" I said as my shaking hands went to my mouth.

"Sorry. Fire started in the attic, we think. At least that's our best guess right now." He glanced at the house and frowned. "With these old houses, they usually have old wiring. I've seen it a million times. Anything and everything can cause a spark with that old stuff."

"I know, but almost all of it has been replaced." My voice screeched through the air, swept away by the wind and the ash.

The firefighter shrugged. "It's just a guess. I'm not really sure what could be the cause. Sometimes these things just happen. We won't know the details until we get it under control."

I sank down on the sidewalk in front of my house, the same sidewalk where I had stood and watched the house lift in the air, and watched as they fought the fire that wanted to destroy everything I had done. A few neighbors came out and gathered on the sidewalk. I heard their condolences and their offers to get me something to eat or drink, but everything seemed underwater, like it was moving through gelatin. I shook my head in refusal of their help, not able to take my eyes off the house as it burned.

Five hours later, the fire hoses were off, and the firefighters were loading back into their trucks in the driveway. A few neighbors still gathered around me on the sidewalk around me, watching the spectacle of the house. My gaze remained on the house, as it had been the whole time, as though I could will it to resist the fire. Yet, black smudges of smoke trailed upward from the upstairs windows, and portions of the roof were burned away. I couldn't imagine what it looked like inside. There was so much wood, and so much lath and plaster, that the fire would have had perfect conditions to destroy everything in its path. The firefighters had broken most of the re-stored windows to allow the heat and flames to escape.

The air was still heavy with smoke, and tiny pieces of ash rained down around me, like a terrible baptism.

"You the owner?" A police officer with a gray goatee appeared in front of me.

I nodded mutely as I wiped at my face. I still hoped that I could shut my eyes and reopen them to find it was all a terrible dream, a nightmare that seemed too real.

"As someone probably already told you, the fire looks like it started in the attic. We still don't know the cause yet, but it could be faulty electrical wiring. Is all the electrical updated from the knot-and-tube?"

I nodded. "Yes, it was all done weeks ago."

He frowned. "You said there had been water damage?"

"The roof. It leaked in the storms a couple of weeks ago."

"Ah. I would imagine there was moisture still left somewhere and maybe that got into the electrical . . ." He trailed off and pointed to the charred roof. "We'll have a full report for you, since I'm sure you'll want to file an insurance claim." He paused and looked at me critically. "You look a little pale. Do you need something? You need to see a doctor?"

I shook my head, and he put a hand on my shoulder. "There wasn't anything you could have done. It was the middle of the night, and no one was here."

I glanced over at Elsie's darkened house, and remembered her promise to watch the house. Of course, that only worked if she was home, and not at the hospital. I knew if she had been home, she would have spotted the fire earlier, and called the police.

"Who called it in?" I asked.

The police officer pointed down the block. "Neighbor about seven houses away was sleeping with his window open and thought he smelled smoke. You're lucky. It could have been worse."

The police officer walked away, and I remained staring at the house. *Lucky. It could have been worse.* I thought those were the worst words in the English language, for they implied that I should be grateful for the horrible situation in front of me. And after all, can't everything always get worse?

I tried as hard as I could, but I couldn't picture the house decorated for Christmas, with the evergreen garlands and red bows strung across the porch. I couldn't picture the tree in the front window, or the arbor in the back painted a pristine white. I could no longer hear the sounds of the children playing throughout the halls and the neighbors laughing over cocktails.

I had lost the image of the house as a home. It seemed as though the fire had destroyed not just the upstairs, but my dream for it, as well.

And on top of that, to make things worse, I knew that getting historical status to preserve the structure was all but impossible now, due to the extensive damage.

I put my head down on my forearms and screwed my eyes shut, fighting back the tears that would never stop if I let them fall.

After the firefighters and police had left, I stared at the open front door, and took a step toward it. My foot wobbled in the grass, and I stopped. I couldn't handle going inside and seeing the damage from the fire. From what I was told, almost all of the upstairs had been touched by the fire. The downstairs, mercifully, was saved, but covered in inches of water that would warp the floors and soak the plaster. Again.

In a daze, I looked up at the sky and saw the sun had risen high overhead. I looked at my phone and realized that I was supposed to pick up Abby that morning, and I robotically climbed into my car and drove to Matt's house.

"What the hell happened to you?" Matt's eyes were wide with concern as he opened his door. When I wordlessly shrugged and lifted my palms, the terrible explanation escaping me, he gently pulled me inside by my shoulder.

He shut the door behind me, and I looked down at my ash-stained white tank top and the dirt smudges across my gray sweat shorts. My hands shaking, I tried to brush off the marks, but just made them worse.

"Alex," Matt said quietly. "What happened? Are you all right?"

"There was a fire. At my house on Maple," I said, my voice barely above a whisper. Saying the words out loud didn't make them more real. If anything, it seemed even more like a dream. My head felt light, like I had drunk the better part of a bottle of wine, yet my feet were heavily planted in his shiny marble foyer.

"Oh. Oh, no. I'm—shit. I'm so sorry. Is there a lot of damage?" he asked as he rubbed his face. I then noticed that he was wearing his blue Turkey Trot 10K T-shirt. I remembered when he ran that race. It was when he had just started as an associate at the Wynn & Ryan law firm and took up running as a way to relieve stress. It was that or start screaming obscenities in the office. I cheered him on as he reached the finish line, and then we headed to Chuck's for after-race beers. A couple hours later, tipsy and happy, we sat on the beach in Fontana and sipped smuggled red wine out of a plastic flask and talked about when we might be ready to have a child.

He always wore the T-shirt to bed, and I realized that he still had stubble covering his face and his feet were bare.

I glanced at the giant silver and gold clock above the mantle. It was only 6:30 a.m.

"It's early. I'm so sorry. I thought it was later. I'll drive home. I can come back later for Abby," I said as I turned toward the door, my whole body shaking.

"Are you crazy? Come sit in the kitchen. Have some coffee and settle down. You shouldn't be driving anywhere."

I followed him into his kitchen, with white cabinets, a gray island, and white and gray quartz countertops. As I sat down at the island underneath a row of Edison lights, I noticed that the

218 / *Maureen Leurck*

countertops had silver flecks in them that reflected the light like diamonds. It all looked shiny and new, a contrast to my dirty and smudged appearance.

Matt turned and poured me a cup of coffee from a giant, expensive-looking silver coffeemaker that looked like a space-ship. He opened the fridge and put two splashes of heavy cream into the mug and slid it toward me. Then, he poured himself a cup. Black, no sweetener.

I took a sip, the ease of the routine washing over me. I set my forearms on the cool island and dropped my head.

"Is it salvageable?" he asked quietly.

I shrugged, not lifting my head. "Probably. I think. For a price. Always for a price." I sighed and then sat back, tucking my feet up on the chair, drawing my knees to my chest. "Of course, historical status will be all but impossible, assuming I can even find the money for the repairs."

"Insurance?" he said.

"Sure. There will be insurance money to cover some of it, but I can guarantee it won't be enough. And, like I said, histor-ical status is . . ." I shook my head, the images of Waterview's bulldozers threatening from the corner of my mind. I rubbed my face, covering my eyes with my hands.

I jolted slightly when I felt him put an arm around my shoulders.

"I'm so sorry," he said.

My shoulders stiffened, pulling back at first. Then he said, "Everything will be okay."

The same words that had comforted me for years caught me off guard, and I softened like room-temperature butter. I turned slightly toward him, and he wrapped both arms around my shoulders.

"I'm so sorry," he said again.

For what? I wanted to ask. *Which part?*

My head rested on his chest, fitting perfectly in the space

where it always did. I wanted to tell him that it *wasn't* okay. That he always said that, but things didn't turn out that way.

Most of all, in that moment, I wanted his words to be true. I wanted him to tell me that again. I wanted to hear him promise.

"Don't give up. Everything can be fixed, if you try," he said, his voice quiet.

My body shuddered under the weight of his words. Before I could respond, the moment was broken, as we heard a *thud* from upstairs, and then the rhythmic motion of small, bare feet padding down the stairs. We broke apart, not making eye contact. Not willing to acknowledge that something strange had just happened.

"Mommy!" Abby came flying into the kitchen, clutching her pink blanket. Her hair was a tangle down her back and she wore a light blue nightgown.

"Oh, honey." I scooped her up and held her to my chest, tears falling from my face. I pressed her tiny body to mine.

"Mommy, that hurts! What are you doing?" She giggled into my shoulder.

I didn't answer as I let her go, brushing her sun-streaked hair from her face.

She looked at me critically. "Why are you all dirty?"

"Oh, it's nothing. I was just working at the house," I said quickly. I couldn't handle explaining what had happened again, especially not to Abby.

"I'm glad you're here," she said as she rested her head on my shoulder. "I had a dream about you."

"What was it about?" I said.

"It was that I got to live in the house you're fixing up, like a real princess," she said.

My heart caught in my throat as I thought of the fire burning the upstairs and how, likely, no one would be living there.

"But then a dinosaur came and ate a bunch of McDonald's and then the house," she added.

I laughed and wrapped my arms around her and closed my eyes. They snapped open, though, when I heard another set of footsteps coming down the stairs.

My stomach dropped as I looked at Matt, and his eyes grew wide before he nervously set his coffee down on the counter and started toward the stairs. He only took one step before Julia appeared in the kitchen. She wore black leggings that came down over her ankles, giving her already long, skinny legs the appearance of a ballet dancer. She also had on a bright pink tank top that fit her like a second skin. I remembered Matt had said she was twenty-eight, but that morning, I could have sworn she was even younger.

Julia stopped suddenly when she saw me, her hands at her sides as she slowly looked from Matt to me.

"Good morning," Matt said quickly as he took a few steps toward her, holding out the cup of coffee that he had poured for himself. She gave him a questioning look, but slowly accepted the cup. "Alex had an issue—a fire—at her renovation project."

"A fire? Did it get ruined?" Abby cried out from my lap, her bottom lip turned outward.

I looked at Matt, a different kind of fire in my eyes, and then forced a smile at Abby. "No, honey. It was just a little problem, but Eddie and I will get it all fixed up."

"Good," she said as she relaxed back down and rested her head on my shoulder.

Sorry, Matt mouthed to me, his shoulders slumped forward. He rubbed his face again, and I realized how old he looked, especially next to Julia. I wondered if he realized how they looked together, how people probably instantly had ideas about why they were together when they saw them. And I couldn't be sure that all those judgments weren't correct.

Julia recovered from her initial shock and set the coffee cup down on the island next to me. "Can we help you with anything?"

I nodded my head slightly. "I'm going to take Abby home. If you could gather her things, that would be great."

She quickly nodded and turned and went back upstairs, but not before she shot Matt a questioning look.

There was an awkward pause when she left, Matt opening his mouth but no words coming out, and me slowly rubbing Abby's back, happy to have her, as much of a security blanket as the pink one she held in her hands. I didn't say anything, either, because I wasn't sure how to process what had happened between us a few moments ago.

Sorry, for what? kept running through my head like a mantra.

Moments later, Julia handed me Abby's suitcase, and I saw that she had put on makeup and brushed her hair so that it fell in waves around her shoulders. Her lip gloss and blush gave me a strange sense of satisfaction. I obviously looked awful, but the fact that she felt the need in some way to fix herself up, to show me how pretty she was, rang as somewhat pathetic. For the first time, I felt sorry for her.

"Would you like us to keep Abby for another day? Until you get things together?" she asked.

I shook my head, the silent daggers of "*us*" landing heavy against my chest. As Abby and I walked to the front door, Julia added, "I'm so sorry about your house. At least you don't have to fix it up now, right?"

I placed a hand on Abby's shoulder and turned to Julia. "Just the opposite. There's a lot of damage, but I'm not giving up on it."

"Well, I admire your . . . persistence," she said with a smile, yet *stupidity* rang in my head. "I would just take the insurance money and run. Find something easier to work on, and cut your losses."

"She's better than that," Matt said quietly. Julia looked up at him, and he squeezed her shoulder. They shared a long, silent conversation filled with private innuendo before I put Abby in the car.

As I drove away from Matt's house with my daughter in the backseat, still in her nightgown, I wondered why exactly I had felt like a bolt of lightning had struck my chest when he said those words. *"Everything can be fixed."*

CHAPTER 32

It took me two days to get the courage to go into the house after the fire. The floors on the first floor were still soaked through, and it took every ounce of willpower not to start shop vac–ing everything. The police officer who had followed up on the fire told me not to repair anything until after the insurance inspector could get into the house to assess the damage. So, I had to wait and allow the beautifully restored floors to once again warp with moisture. What was new, was old again. I had made my way up to the second floor, a lump growing in my throat. The walls were singed with black marks, like the flames had quickly shot against the wall before they were extinguished. The floors had scorched marks running across them, and the wood was buckled in the hallway where the flames had licked at it.

In each of the four bedrooms, plaster had melted off the walls and fallen to the ground, exposing the wiring and the plumbing. Yet the room that took the most damage was the smallest bedroom. Not only was the plaster missing from the walls, but the plumbing had been exposed and damaged, and the wiring was burned to a crisp.

I had run my hand lightly along the only strip of plaster that remained in the room, and it collapsed with an exhale, all the damage complete.

I sat down on the floor, my head in my hands, the darkness of the house around me. I thought of Matt's words—*"Everything can be fixed"*—and wondered how that possibly could be true. It didn't seem like anything this badly broken could ever be fixed.

And I let myself go back to that terrible day.

It had started like any other morning. Abby woke up in her crib around 6 a.m., first talking to herself for a few minutes and then quickly progressing to screams, interspersed with the occasional "Mama! Come!" as I hurriedly brushed my teeth and stumbled around for my glasses. Her cries still produced a fight-or-flight response in my bones. An *oh, shit* reaction of panic, even though I knew she was fine and just hungry for her breakfast. But every morning I would rush through the basics to fling her door open and rescue her from the crib like there was a tornado down the block.

She immediately stopped crying when I went in and picked her up, her fat, eighteen-month-old hands slapping at my shoulders in excitement as she said, "Pancakes!"

I made my way downstairs, and noticed that Matt had already left for work. The bundle of rumpled blankets and his pillow on the couch were empty.

He had started sleeping downstairs when Abby was about nine months old. She wasn't sleeping through the night, and I was still nursing her one or two times before dawn. So when I would return back to bed, Matt's snores made me irrationally angry in the way that only a sleep-deprived person can be. I would shake his shoulder until he turned over, and the snoring would stop for a few moments, just long enough so that I almost felt back asleep, before it started again. This would continue for several more turns, until I would wake him up and angrily hiss that I was exhausted, and he would go downstairs and snore on the couch until morning.

Usually he would be awake when I came downstairs with Abby, in the shower or shaving in the bathroom downstairs, but that morning he was already gone.

"I guess Daddy had an early meeting," I said to Abby as I strapped her into her high chair. She immediately began trying to climb out, shrieking, "Out! Get down!"

I began to methodically slice up a banana, tossing the pieces onto her tray as fast as she could squeeze them in her fingers and aim them toward her mouth.

I glanced down at my to-do list for the day. Every night before I went to bed, I made a list of tasks for the next day. At times, it was embarrassingly pathetic, and filled with things like laundry, mail bills, and buy diapers. Yet, it gave me a sense of accomplishment, of control. I used to do the same thing when I worked in public relations for the Grand Geneva Resort, taking great satisfaction in crossing things off with a scratch of my black pen.

The adjustment to staying at home with Abby had been a hard one for me. It wasn't anything like I had pictured. I imagined walks to the park, a regular naptime, and blueberry pancakes made from scratch, with berries we had picked from the farm down the road. Instead, I experienced a profound sense of loneliness, that had progressed to mild panic every time Matt left the house for the day. Every day was so long, and her needs so constant, and the job was without a sick day policy or even the positive reinforcement of an annual review and salary increase. But Matt still thought I was living a dream life.

I didn't yet have any mom friends, despite a few friendly conversations here and there. So my only real social interaction each day was with my husband.

I glanced down at the to-do list and sighed. Abby screamed, and I handed her another piece of banana. It was only 7 a.m., and I was already exhausted.

I forced a smile. "Let's do something fun today, okay?"

Abby grinned, banana squished into her teeth.

"How about we get some sandwiches from the deli and take them to Daddy at his office?"

She grinned again in agreement.

If I had been watching the scene unfold in a movie, it would have been so clearly obvious what would happen next. It was so cliché, so suburban. So expected.

Matt wasn't in his office, but his assistant told me that he was in a meeting across town and due back in about twenty minutes. Abby and I waited in his gray-toned office, and I tried to occupy her with pens and my car keys, instead of her heading straight for the computer wires like she really wanted.

From the desk, Matt's cell phone buzzed, and I realized he had forgotten it, which was why he didn't see my text that we were headed over. It buzzed again, and I reached over to check the message so it would stop impatiently trying to deliver it.

On the text preview, was my message from an hour before, but that was at the bottom of the screen. On top were two other texts, from an unknown number with a Chicago area code. The first read: *Great to see you again. It had been too long.* And then the next message said, sent just a few seconds before: *I hope you had as much fun as I did. Next Thursday still work? Can't wait to see you again!* Followed by a winky face.

I grew very still, but the phone in my hand began to shake. I wasn't stupid. I knew exactly what those texts meant.

There was a crash as Abby pulled herself up on the other side of Matt's desk and yanked his monitor over, the screen cracking on the ground. I dropped the phone on the desk and grabbed her, right as Matt walked through the door.

"What the . . ." he said as he took in the sight of his computer. "What happened?"

I clutched Abby to my side, my insides burning. I felt my face flush. "Exactly. Or, what's been happening?" My voice shook, and tears sprang to my eyes.

"With what?" he said.

I pointed to the phone on his desk. "Better respond. Sounds like you had a great afternoon."

His walk from his doorway to the phone was the longest few moments of my life. A small, miniscule part of me hoped he would give me some plausible explanation. Lie, or at least try to lie. He read the text and didn't look up for a long time.

I shifted Abby on my hip and detached her hand from my hair. "Not going to say anything?"

He slowly put the phone down and exhaled, a sound that cut through my heart. He was relieved. I assumed it was because he didn't have to sneak around anymore.

He tried to apologize, say that it looked worse than it was. That it had just been a flirtation and nothing had happened.

"Yet," I finished. "And you don't have to sleep with someone to have an affair. Who is she?"

"Just a client," he said slowly.

"Which one?" I volleyed back.

He sighed, and rubbed his forehead. "She's an assistant to one of my clients from Waterview Developers."

"Sounds like she must have her hands full with all of the *assisting* she's been doing," I said.

He reached for me and said that things between us had been different, but he didn't want them to be.

But I just walked out the door, away from him, and back to the house. I called Traci, and when she arrived, I had thrown all of his clothes onto the front stoop, just like in the movies. She played with Abby while I made phone calls, ignoring his repeated calls and texts. And when he showed up an hour later, she ran interference and made him leave.

I refused to speak to him for almost a week afterward, packing Abby up and taking her to my parents'. He had said his family meant more to him than anything, and keeping Abby from him was the one thing I could do to hurt him back.

I don't know where he was when they served him the divorce papers two months later, but I do know that he didn't fight me on any of it. I found that the hurt deepened again when he didn't contest anything. I was angry, but where was my big show? Of him chasing me down the highway and making me pull over so he could beg me for forgiveness? Where was my big Hollywood moment of him showing the world just how stupid he had been and how much he wanted me back?

I didn't realize it until later, but if he had done something like that, I might have taken him back. I might have agreed to stay together and work on things. Instead, he gave me everything that I asked for, and nothing that I hadn't. It was easy, and all he did was sign on the line. Within days, I had the divorce agreement back in my lawyer's office and it was done.

A couple of months later, we went to court and filed the papers, and I walked out divorced. During that waiting time, I think a part of me still didn't really believe it, like it didn't fully register. Yet, on that morning, it was all finished so quickly. What had taken years to build, only an hour to dissolve. I remember that I got into my car and read the document over and over again, in hopes that it would sink in. It never really did, and I went and picked up Abby from my parents' house without saying a word to them.

I am divorced. We are done. It's over, I wrote later that night after she went to bed. I made the period at the end of each sentence large, finite. There was no comma at the end of the story. It was done.

CHAPTER 33

Two days later, I met the insurance inspector at the house. After the walk-through, he said later that afternoon he was going to work up a report and send it to me for how much they were going to cover. Even as he said it, he had a hard time looking me in the eye. We both knew that whatever amount they were going to front, it wouldn't be near enough to fix the house the way it should have been.

After he left, I went to the hospital to visit Elsie and told her about the fire.

"I'm so sorry that I wasn't home, Alex. I just can't imagine what you're describing." Elsie lifted a shaking hand to her forehead, rubbing it so that the wrinkles moved back and forth, sticking in one place before they returned.

"It's probably better that you don't," I said. "Enough about me, and my house. How are you feeling?" I asked her, forcing a smile onto my face.

Her eyes grew soft. "The doctors say I'm healing, but . . ." She lightly touched the bruise on her forehead, which had changed to an ugly purple slash. Her left eye was still swollen shut, and it gave her face a lopsided appearance. She, too, forced a smile.

I hadn't told her about the document I'd found in the wall, with the name of the original adoption lawyer. I had exhausted Google searches for his name that morning, trying to find any connection or living family member to contact, but I came up blank. And if there was anything else hidden in the walls, any clues as to where the baby was, it would have been destroyed in the fire.

I had also scanned all of the adoption message boards and public registries posted by people wanting to find their birth parents, but there was nothing that matched.

"Just as soon as I get this mess with the house figured out, I'll keep looking for your daughter," I said quickly. My voice was thin, easily broken, and barely reached her.

"Don't worry yourself about that. You have enough to think about right now." She looked down, and folded her hands in her lap. "Besides, it might be that I'm never to find her. I made choices long ago, and I shouldn't keep looking back. Maybe we should give up." Her eyes grew watery, and she twisted the hospital blanket under her hands.

"No, I'm sure there's more we can do. More searches, maybe we could hire a lawyer to look into it for you," I said quickly.

"If it's that difficult, it might just be that I should let this lie. She might be happy, and this would disrupt her life. No, I think we should stop here," she said.

I opened my mouth to protest, but she shook her head again. I slowly closed it and leaned forward, putting my forearms on my thighs. My head dropped down, and I exhaled.

She looked out the window, and pointed toward the trees that sloped downward toward the lake in the distance. "You know, David once took me on a boat, a few weeks before he died." She smiled, but her gaze was still out the window. "It was a wooden boat that belonged to the parents of one of his friends from school. Oh, it was just beautiful, with gleaming sides and a brightly polished steering wheel. Of course, those boats were all over the lake during that time, before the kind you see now."

I nodded. Wooden boats used to be all the rage on the lake in the 1950s and 1960s, before fiberglass boats became popular. Now, they were relegated to the very rich who could afford to buy them from collectors and restoration companies. Whenever a wooden boat pulled up to a dock or passed others on the lake, people would always crane their necks at it and smile with nostalgia.

"We drove over to Buttons Bay on the town, and stopped. It was the middle of the afternoon, and there weren't any clouds in the sky. It was hot and hazy, and we lay back against the back of the boat, dangling our feet in the water. The lake water was still cold from the winter, but I remember how good it felt against our hot skin." She looked at me, and folded her hands over her lap. "I remember he put his arm around my shoulders and it felt like I was going to melt right there in the boat."

I nodded; the teenage memories of butterflies and nerves felt like they weren't that far in the past.

"It was the first time I knew we were meant to be together. And later that night, well, we were." Her eyes twinkled at the memory, and she leaned forward and whispered, "We were still on the boat, after sundown, of course."

I laughed. "Well, that was certainly a memorable evening cruise, I'm sure."

She didn't answer, but looked out the window toward the lake again. "Some days it feels like it was yesterday. Some days, I *wish* it was yesterday."

I tucked my legs up on the chair and wrapped my arms around them. "I get it. I really do."

"I loved Harold," she added firmly. "We had many wonderful years together. But . . ." She trailed off.

"It wasn't like what you had with David," I finished, and she nodded slightly.

After a pause, she shook her head. "Letting go is hard," Elsie said with a sniffle. "Sometimes we don't get a second chance, and we have to accept that. We don't always get to live the lives we imagined."

I didn't lift my head but nodded in agreement. I knew that statement to be true more than just about anything. With the house, with my love life. It all seemed to be just beyond my reach, and I felt like I had been grasping at air for so long. I was afraid that things that I so desperately wanted would always remain on the horizon, a mirage that would convince me to keep going instead of stopping and looking around, accepting where I was instead of where I wanted to be.

CHAPTER 34

"Mom, when can I see the house again?"

Abby and I sat on the white public pier in the town of Williams Bay, tossing stale bread to the sunfish below. She had paused, bread crumb pinched between her forefinger and thumb, and asked about the house before she flicked another bread crumb into the water.

"When it's safe, honey." I tossed a piece of bread into the water and watched as the biggest sunfish darted forward and nudged the others out of the way to grab the crumb.

"Hey! That wasn't very nice," Abby shouted to the fish.

"No, it wasn't. Those big fish tend to take everything from the smaller ones," I said. *Like Waterview Developers,* I silently added.

"Well, I'm going to throw some bread to the side, away from the big guy, so everyone else can eat," she said confidently. She threw a handful of crumbs in the farthest possible direction from the big fish, but he still darted forward and ate most of it. She frowned. "How do I stop him?"

I sighed and looked out onto the water. The sun was just be-

234 / *Maureen Leurck*

ginning to lower toward the shoreline, the trees growing closer and closer. A few boats remained out on the water, basking in the last few minutes of daylight. I could see a boat pulling a wakeboarder—something that could only be done, really, after the busy daytime rush of boats—and a group of people anchored not far off the shore in the bay, enjoying a few sunset cocktails.

It was so beautiful, and so full of different memories. Of Matt and me as kids, of Elsie's description of her and David. Of the future that I had hoped for the buyers of the Maple house.

The sun fell behind the rows of trees ringing the lake. I turned to Abby and kissed the top of her head. "I don't know how to stop him. Sometimes we can't."

As we left the pier, my phone buzzed with a text message from Gavin. I had given him the CliffsNotes version of the fire at the house, and he asked if we could meet for dinner this weekend. He added at the end, *If you're not up for it, I totally understand.*

I wasn't at all up for it, and I knew he would understand. I just wished that I understood myself why I felt like when the house caught fire, when all the work that we had done had been destroyed, that it was time to let Gavin go. And after sharing the small moment with Matt in the kitchen after the fire, I knew it wasn't right to string him along. He deserved to have someone who wasn't such a mess, whose life didn't keep imploding with disaster. Someone who didn't feel confused about her ex-husband.

I knew that it wasn't fair to keep him around in case I ever became ready for him. Dating him would have been like painting over wallpaper, or gluing layers of linoleum on top of one another—a temporary solution. Yet at some point, it would all have to be scraped away, and it would be much harder than if it had been done the right way the first time.

I thought about Elsie's words, that we didn't get a second chance, and I knew she was right.

* * *

That evening, I tried to tuck Abby into bed, but she protested and insisted on sleeping with me. I lay down next to her in my bed, staring at the ceiling fan, until I heard the rhythmic breathing of sleep. I picked up my phone and took a long, steady breath before I started typing.

I first typed a text to Gavin. I realized I should have called him, asked to meet in person, but I had to do it while I still had the courage from the recent depressing events.

Thanks so much for the invite for this weekend. I'm afraid I can't make it. Right now is kind of a tough time for me, with the house and Abby and everything. I'm sorry to do this by text, but I would love if we could be just friends for now.

I hit Send and closed my eyes, waiting for a buzz when he texted back. When nothing came through, I thought he might be asleep, but underneath the text bubble it said that he had read it.

Sadness washed over me, but I didn't let myself think about it. I had one more message to send, and that one would be even more difficult.

I typed out the e-mail, swallowing back my tears, pushing the image of the Maple house filled with laughter and children out of my head, and hit Send. That future was already gone, burned by the fire. Maybe it existed in some kind of alternate universe, where Elsie reunited with her daughter, and the house welcomed a new family into its restored structure. Maybe Matt and I had never gotten divorced in that universe, and Abby didn't have to live in two places at the same time.

Maybe all of our wishes and hopes for the future came true in this fantasy. It gave me some peace to think that maybe it did exist, in some ethereal plane. That in some small corner of the universe, all was well.

Yet this was my corner of the universe, my reality, and it looked much different. And I had to live in that world, and make decisions based on what had happened, rather than what I wished had happened.

And so I went to bed that night, but it took me hours to fall asleep, as I waited a response from Waterview Developers about my proposal to sell the house to them.

CHAPTER 35

I woke up the next morning to the smallest, quietest of *tap tap taps* on my bedroom window. I could feel the sun on my face, and I tried to will my eyes to open, but I had only fallen asleep an hour or two before. I knew the second I sat up in bed, I would reach for my phone and check to see if I had a response from Waterview. Then, it would all begin, and the roller coaster would sail down the hill. So I decided to remain in bed, still, until the last possible moment.

That plan was quickly thwarted by the rapping on my window, like the cord from window blinds hitting against the slats. I turned toward it, squinting. I could see black ovals, about an inch long, rhythmically hitting against the glass like they were dive-bombing the house.

"What the . . ." I was careful not to wake Abby next to me as I crawled over her and peeked out around the drawn Roman shade. I grabbed the pull and yanked it upward, flooding the room with light.

Across my front yard, as far as I could see, were cicadas. Their newly hatched black bodies and delicate, lace-like wings flitted back and forth across the yard, flying erratically. They knocked into each other in midair, buzzing in surprise. The trunks of the trees were covered in their tan shells, and I could spot several in the grass. I opened the window slightly, and the buzz became louder, a constant hum of energy. It was the end of June, and they were late, which only made it seem as though they had waited to make a grand entrance.

"Ab, Ab. Wake up," I said as I shook her slightly. She rolled over and buried her face in her pillow. "No, really. You have to see this."

She slowly sat up, her eyes barely open. She knelt on the bed and peered out the window. "Ew! What are those things?" Her eyes snapped fully open and her nose wrinkled.

"The cicadas. Remember?"

"Oh. Why are there so many of them?" She tucked her messy hair behind her ears.

"Because they only come every seventeen years. This is their big chance," I said. "And they're even late for that. About six weeks, in fact. Don't you remember I told you about all of this?"

A cicada landed on the windowsill, and we leaned in closer for a better look. Its lace-like wings rested on its black body, and its orange eyes had a perpetually stunned look.

"I think they're kind of weird-looking," she said as she leaned closer to the windowpane. "When are they going to go away again?"

"In a couple of weeks," I said as I rubbed her back. "So, don't worry. But I can promise you'll remember this for a long, long time. Think about it—the next time you'll see them, you'll be twenty-two years old."

"That's really old," she said with a whisper. She wrapped her arms around my waist. "Don't worry, Mom. I'll still live with you when I'm twenty-two so you won't be by yourself."

I swallowed hard as I hugged her to me. "I'll be okay. Don't worry. You can live wherever you want when you're older."

"Can I go outside?" she said.

We stepped onto the front stoop, and watched as the cicadas circled overhead, occasionally buzzing close to us in curiosity, but never landing near, a fact that I was happy about, since although Abby seemed to have mild curiosity about them, if one landed on her I was sure her feelings would turn to sheer terror. And then I would have to battle with her every time we left the house. I could picture her staying inside like an agoraphobic until they were gone, her arms crossed over her chest, glaring at the insects as they buzzed around the yard.

"I think they're kind of cool, but a little bit scary," she said.

"Well, a lot of stuff that's cool can be scary." I laughed. "But don't be afraid. They won't hurt you. I promise."

I heard my phone vibrate from my pocket, and I slowly lifted it, my heart beating fast as I remembered my e-mail to Waterview. I relaxed when I saw it was Traci calling.

"Can you believe this?" she said when I answered. Abby and I moved inside, although her nose remained pressed to the glass on the side of the front door.

"Just as they predicted, albeit six weeks late. So far, Abby seems okay with it, which was my main concern," I said as walked into the kitchen and poured myself a cup of coffee. I threw a frozen waffle into the microwave for Abby.

"Well, Chris is completely freaked out. He woke up at five a.m., and came into our room in a panic because he heard them buzzing outside. For the life of me, I couldn't hear it, but we went outside, and sure enough, those jerks were starting to hatch. It's so bizarre—he won't respond when I'm practically shouting his name from two feet away, but this? This he heard." She sighed. "I have to get him out of the house. He's so lost in the summers when school is out. And I tell you what, those things better be dead by the time school starts or else my students are going to go buck wild. Speaking of school, how's Gavin?"

I set my coffee cup down and frowned. "Oh. Well . . ."

"Shit. You broke up with him, didn't you?" she said.

"We were never a couple, so I don't know if 'broke up' is the right term," I said evenly. "I just said that I would love to be friends."

"You're deflecting the question. Why? Didn't you like him?"

"Of course I liked him. He's a great guy. That's not the issue. It's just—"

"Please, please don't do the whole 'it's not him, it's me' thing. It too early and my lawn is covered with black bugs from outer space."

I didn't respond as I tried to think of a reason she would accept.

"It's Matt," she said. "You're still in love with Matt."

The silence over the line was deafening as words escaped me. I would never have said the sentence, but now that she had, I couldn't deny it. She was right. Even after everything that he had done, and all that we had gone through, I still had feelings for Matt. And I couldn't move on with Gavin because of them.

It was as though I was swimming in a pool—drowning, more likely—and holding on to the edge, but desperate to reach the other side. But there was no way I was ever going to reach it without first letting go of the edge. And I just couldn't do it.

"I had hoped that Gavin would help you get rid of those feelings, but they must be pretty strong if even really great sex didn't stop them," she said. "But you are always going to worry that you made a mistake in filing for divorce after everything happened. You worry that you didn't stick it out longer, and try to make things better." She paused. "So, what are we going to do about this?"

"Do? Nothing," I said. "It's just something I have to get over. Manage. Make go away."

"Yeah. And how's that been working out for you for the past, oh, five years?"

I rubbed my forehead wearily. "Please. It's too early for this."

"All right, but at least you're admitting it now. And think about what you're going to do about it as you're replastering walls and staining floors or arguing with the insurance people about whatever it is you're doing to repair the fire damage," she said.

I swallowed hard, thinking of my e-mail to Waterview. I couldn't tell her that I was giving up on the house, too. So I just said, "Will do," before I hung up.

CHAPTER 36

"Oh, dear. No, you cannot do that. No." My mom's voice crackled over the phone, and I heard her cover it and whisper something to my dad in the background. "You cannot sell the house to those people. Please, that would be just terrible if they tore the house down after everything."

I rested my head on my steering wheel while parked in my driveway. It had been a week since the fire, and I had just dropped Abby off at Matt's house, with Susan. She hugged me and told me how sorry she was to hear about the house and that she knew I would make it great again. I couldn't bear to tell her that it would likely never be fixed, so I just nodded and smiled.

"It's not something that I want to do, it's something that I might have to do. All that work, money, is gone. The insurance money isn't going to cover it."

As if on cue, I had received the estimated settlement from the insurance agent, delivered straight to my voice mail. The amount they were willing to pay was laughable, and tens of thousands of dollars below what it would cost to recoup all of the work.

"I have to think about my finances, and about Abby. Cutting my losses and moving on is the only way to get out of this situation."

I had already received an e-mail back from the CEO of Waterview. She wanted to set up a meeting the next day to go over a preliminary plan for sale. It was that simple. We would hash out the arrangements, and then sometime soon after, I would come back, sign a few documents, and receive a check for the fire-damaged house that would be far more than whatever I might get from the insurance company. I could deposit the money and move on, like it had all never happened. But, of course, it had.

"Except you're not so good at moving on, Alex," she whispered.

"What do you mean?" I sat up straight and frowned.

"You know what I mean. You can't let go of him. Things for you were difficult, yes, but then you gave up."

I cleared my throat as my back began to prickle with anger. "I'm sorry, but that's not fair at all. He cheated on me. He had a girlfriend while I was at home with our baby. He was the one who 'moved on' without our family, not me."

I heard her exhale slowly. "That may be true, but sometimes life leaves room for a second chance. Have you considered that?"

"So, I'm supposed to be the one who just forgives? He gets to mess up, and it's on my shoulders to fix everything, to give him a second chance?" I spat the words out quickly, in a rat-a-tat fashion, surprised at the heat in my tone.

There was a pause. "Honey, sometimes. Yes. Sometimes we have to accept the bad to get back to the good. Some things, some people, deserve a second chance. Not everyone, or everything, but some."

"Right. Not everyone," I said quickly.

"What matters is how you feel about it. You haven't been able to move on, that should tell you something," she said. "I'm not telling you to forgive him and just forget what happened.

I'm just asking you to think about what you really want." She paused. "That goes for him and for the house. You don't really want to sell the house, do you?"

I shook my head slowly. "Of course not."

I heard a rustling, and my dad came on the phone. "You can't sell it. Find a way to repair it. Don't give up, not yet. It can be the beauty that it once was, it just takes some extra love and special care. I saw how much you love that house, and I know you can make it great again. Think about how you always pictured it, and what you wanted to do."

Tears sprang to my eyes as I thought of the white painted porch with the swing gently moving in the breeze, the scent of the rosebushes floating around the house. It was summertime, and a mom sat on the swing, moving back and forth with a little girl tucked under her arm. The air was getting hot and humid, and the afternoon bugs were just starting to buzz. Two cold glasses of lemonade were on a white wicker table by the swing. The hot sunshine reached the grass in the areas not shaded by the giant maple tree in the front yard.

The little girl was getting sleepy on the swing, and her head drooped from the motion and the hot air. The mom smiled and hummed quietly, waiting just a few more minutes, savoring one of the dog days of summer when everything was effervescent and silent at the same time. She looked up at the house and smiled, knowing that other mothers had sat out there with their children, smelling the sweet scent of the garden and listening to the leaves rustle in the trees overhead.

Back and forth, back and forth they rocked, until the mother carried her daughter inside the cool house, their shelter from the summer afternoon heat.

Shame washed over my shoulders and down my back, and I put my head in my hands. I sniffled into the phone and took a deep breath.

"Honey, don't cry." My mom was back on the phone. "Don't waste your energy on tears. Save it for the house. You know, there's an old superstition about living in a house that's had a fire. It's actually a good thing, because it cleanses all the old energies and brings forth good fortune . . . and new beginnings," she said.

"A new beginning," I repeated slowly before I nodded.

I dreamed that night of the family at the house, but this time, they weren't anonymous faces. This time, it was Elsie and David at the house. They held their little girl on the front porch, rocking her back and forth in the summer heat. The little girl turned her head toward me, her hair sticky against her forehead, and I saw it was Abby. And when I looked again at the couple on the porch, it wasn't Elsie and David anymore. It was Matt and me.

CHAPTER 37

I doodled on the edge of the notepad that contained my budget options for restoring the fire damage. Even with the check from the insurance company, I was still coming up several thousand dollars' short. It had been ten days since the fire, and I hadn't had any brilliant ideas to raise money. I made a row of dollar signs across the bottom of the page as I looked around my desk. I didn't have anything of value left to sell, and my checking and savings accounts didn't have enough to cover the overages.

I sighed as I closed my eyes. I had started with such a healthy contingency fund, and it was long gone, swallowed up by the leaking roof, electrical rewiring, plumbing issues. Not to mention the fire.

I couldn't go to the bank and ask for more money. I was already maxed out on what I could borrow against the property. Nor could I mortgage it against my own house, not that I thought that option was financially prudent.

I sighed and sat back in my chair, slowly typing in the address of a few local real estate blogs, hoping something would spark a brilliant, light-bulb plan. On the second one that I clicked, Jack Sullivan's scowling, lined face popped onto my screen. The blog was about how he had sold his latest renovation project—a row of town houses near downtown—for a six-figure amount, and that he was looking for something new to start.

I thought back to when I saw him at Harpoon Willie's, and his warnings about Waterview Developers. He hated them as much as I did, and now he had some serious cash to burn. Before I could talk myself out of it, I grabbed my car keys.

I found him once again at the bar, a tall beer in front of him. He signaled to the bartender as I fought off a drunk woman for the bar stool next to him.

"Sparky's drinks are on me," he said. When I started to shake my head, he raised a calloused hand. "It's the least I can do instead of saying I told you so." He leaned forward and smiled, that creepy, gap-toothed smile. "By the way, I told you so. Those old houses are full of nothing but problems."

Anger began to bubble up inside of me as I thought of my poor, charred upstairs, but I took a slow, deep breath and relaxed my face into a smile.

"That you did," I said as nicely as I could muster. I took a sip of the beer in front of me when the bartender placed it down.

"So, tell me one thing: Has Waterview contacted you yet?" he said as he folded his thick forearms on the bar.

I nodded. "Of course."

"Signed with them yet?" He laughed.

" 'Yet'? You say that like it's a foregone conclusion." My shoulders settled downward, comfortable in our banter, and drawing out the conversation.

"Well, it is. Unless you got a whole bunch of cash lying around to fix that blackened house of yours," he said.

"Not really. But here's the thing: I want to finish the house. I want to finish what I started. It's a good house, and a good investment," I said.

He laughed. "Sure, after all new plaster, new drywall, electrical work, plumbing, and whatever else that fire destroyed." He leaned forward and lowered his voice to a whisper. "You know, if you were the one who lit the match, I wouldn't blame you at all." He slapped the bar. "In fact, I'd happily pay for your drinks all year."

"Yeah, I know. But listen." I turned and faced him, putting a foot on the bottom rung of his stool. "Do we really want Waterview to win? Aren't we all kind of in this together? If they start taking over all of our properties, don't you think that we'll all soon be out of business?"

He narrowed his eyes and shook a finger at me. "I see where you're going with this. Nowhere good. The answer is no. Before you even ask, before you even say whatever it is that you think you want to say, no."

"As much as I would hate to work with a snake like you—"

He cut me off with a slice of his hand. "Exactly. Think of all those beautiful, historic properties that I tore down, without one moment of feeling." He leaned forward. "And I would have torn down that house of yours, too. Still would, in fact."

"I'm fully aware of that fact. But I don't have a whole lot of other options right now," I said. "If you can believe it, you're the lesser of two evils."

He downed the rest of his beer and reached into his pocket, throwing money down on the bar. "Never heard that one before. Kinda like it. But sorry, answer's still no. We're much better as enemies, not partners. I mean, what would people think if we went into business together?" He laughed. "I might lose my reputation for being such an asshole if I help you on this."

"Trust me, everyone will still think you're an asshole. I don't think that can be remedied," I said. "But don't you want a second chance? You said it yourself—your personal life is a mess. Don't you want to do one good, decent thing before you drink yourself to death?"

He stopped in surprise, slightly wobbling back and forth as

his eyes focused on me. For a moment, I thought he was going to sit back down. But he stepped back.

"Good luck to ya," he said. Then, he turned and walked out of the bar.

I stayed and finished my drink, part of me hoping he would come back and reconsider. When he didn't, I slumped my shoulders and silently wondered how much more pathetic I could get, how much further I could slip.

The next morning, my doorbell rang as I was getting out of the shower. I wrapped a towel around me and peeked my head out the door. I saw Jack Sullivan's Ford pulling down the driveway. His white hair was askew, and I could see deep lines running down his cheeks. He lifted a cup of coffee in greeting. Even from my front stoop, I could tell that he was hung over.

"Say hi to your parents for me," he shouted before he turned down the street.

On the concrete stoop was a manila envelope. I shooed off a cicada, and opened it. I pulled out a piece of paper and almost dropped my towel when I read it.

It was a contract. He would put up the money to renovate the house, the difference between what the insurance company would pay and the actual cost. All cash, available immediately. In return, we would split the profits on the house. I would do all the work, of course, but it would be finished. The house could be repaired just as I planned.

I leaned against my doorway as I scanned the contract again, searching for the catch. And the last few lines, in print smaller than it should have been, I found it: If I didn't find a buyer in sixty days, we would sell to Waterview with no contingencies and then let them tear down the house.

CHAPTER 38

"You've had a lot of bad ideas in the past, but I'm pretty sure this one takes the cake." Eddie shook his head and rubbed his forehead with sweat. He ducked down and swatted at a cicada that flew past.

We were working in the upstairs master bedroom, clearing the debris from the fire before the restoration company could come in and begin to fireproof everything. It had been only four days since my deal with Jack, but we needed to move quickly. First, the restoration company would set up ozone generators, to get the smell of the smoke out of all the surfaces. Then, they would have to clean the entirety of the house, removing all the soot so that the walls could be fixed, primed, and painted again. Any walls with extensive damage would have to be replastered, and we would have to rebuild the wood baseboards and trim where the fire had eaten away, and the roof needed to be fixed—again—but it all could be done. For a price and time, of course.

The holes in the roof and the walls from the fire meant that the cicadas had entered the house in droves. I could almost see the confusion in their weird little eyes as they flew around the house, wondering what happened to all the trees. The smartest beings in the animal kingdom, they weren't.

"And what was my other choice? The money tree in my backyard isn't exactly flowering these days." I shoveled a pile of charred plaster and roof shingles onto the tarp in the hallway.

"Sure. But still. Jack Sullivan? You couldn't have found some other investor who isn't such a . . . snake? No, *snake* is too kind of a word." He carefully lifted a charred, splintered piece of what I assumed had been the window framing. We had so carefully preserved all of the quarter-sawn oak in the first go-around, and now we had to dump it all and rebuild with what we could salvage. "Whatever is worse than a snake."

"I could have, if I had the time. The mortgage on this house is—weird concept, I know—due every month. And I'm out of money as of yesterday. It was either find an investor immediately or sell to Waterview. Pick your poison, Eddie," I said. "And actually, since you aren't paying that mortgage, you don't get to pick anything."

I had called Jack immediately after he dropped off the contract and asked him to reconsider the contingency clause about selling to the developers if we didn't find a buyer in sixty days, but he held firm. I had sent an e-mail to Waterview, backing out of the deal even though I knew I might end up at the table with them if we failed to sell the house. The sand in the hourglass had already begun to fall, and there was nothing I could do to stop it except finish the house and pray that a buyer popped up immediately. I had called Eddie and told him the good/bad news, and asked him to triple his crew to get the work done.

He held up his soot- and dirt-stained hands. "Fair enough. Too bad he's such an asshole."

"Now, come on, I'm not that bad." Footsteps echoed through the hallway as Jack made his way up the stairs. "I'm not always an asshole. Just almost always." He appeared outside the bedroom and leaned against the doorjamb, crossing his arms over his chest.

"I stand by my original statement," Eddie said. He tossed his shovel in Jack's direction. "Give us a hand, would you?"

Jack let the shovel clatter to the ground in front of him. "Nope. My money's doing the work here, not me. Hopefully, some nice family will buy it, who will put an addition on it, or maybe"—he looked at me—"paint all that woodwork so it looks halfway decent." Before I could strangle him with an extension cord, he added, "There's some lady outside, poking around, asking for you."

I set my shovel against what was left of the wall. "Saved by a stranger," I said before I walked down the stairs.

A woman in her thirties with bright red hair stood on the front porch, phone in hand. "Alex Proctor?" she said as I walked onto the porch.

"Yes. Why?" My heart started to pound as I wondered if she was from Waterview, or maybe another county office, here to deliver some other fine or citation. Visitors at the house never seemed to come bearing good tidings or nice surprises.

"I'm Jill Springform, from the *Lake Geneva Regional News*. I was wondering if I could get a quote from you on the house fire that happened here a few weeks ago." She tapped on her phone and poised her finger above the screen, waiting for me to speak.

"You guys already ran a story on it, didn't you?" I had seen the front page of the newspaper the day after the fire, accompanied by a photo of orange flames shooting out of the roof. In the bottom corner of the picture was my shadowy figure as I stood on the lawn and stared at the house. I had crumpled up the newspaper, bile rising in my throat.

"Of course. But I'm doing a follow-up. I heard a rumor that you and another investor have teamed up to fix the house."

"Yes, that's true." The news that Jack and I were working together had hit the real estate blogs almost immediately. It was no surprise, since Jack seemed to want to tell everyone he knew that he was helping me on the project, to show that he could be a decent guy. Charitable, even. "You want a quote about that?"

She shrugged and rolled her eyes. "Slow news day." She glanced down at her phone again. "So, how's the cleanup coming?"

"As well as can be expected." I told her about how we first had to haul away all of the fire-damaged materials, and then start from scratch in most of the bedrooms. Not to mention a whole new roof and rewiring the melted electrical components.

She nodded. "And the other investor?"

"Yes. Jack Sullivan." I glanced upstairs and prayed that he didn't come sauntering down the stairway, eager to toot his own liquor-soaked horn for the reporter.

"Right. Isn't he kind of known for tearing down historic properties? Building McMansions, that sort of thing?"

My eye twitched. "Yep. But I guess he wanted to try saving something instead of ripping it apart." I crossed my arms over my chest. "I convinced him that old houses are worth restoring. They've stood for how many years and we should preserve their history. They have a soul, a life to them. They've seen more than we ever have, and we should respect that."

She smiled. "That sounds almost poetic." She pushed her sunglasses back on top of her head. "Look, my editor wants me to run this small column on the property, just a short update on the fire and the cleanup process. But I'd love to talk to you more about what you're trying to do for the house, and include any neat historical tidbits you've uncovered." A cicada landed on her blouse, and she made a squeaking sound. I reached forward and plucked it off, sending it on its merry way through the air. "Thanks," she said. "Those things kind of freak me out."

I watched as the cicada flew toward Elsie's house, eventually landing on her empty front porch. I thought of the article that ran in 1947 about the Moores' house, and the details about the family. Then, an idea sprang to life as quickly as the cicadas had emerged.

I turned to Jill. "I'd love to help you with a longer story. I have a bunch of pieces of historical information that I think you'd really be interested in, including some great human-interest stories about the people who used to live here. Really compelling," I said brightly.

We made a date to meet in a few weeks, after some of the fire damage had been fixed so she could see the progress, and I returned upstairs to where Eddie and Jack were arguing about old windows, and if it was worth the effort to rebuild rotten frames or just replace them with vinyl windows.

"You're not taking into account that the windows were made for the house," Eddie said, his voice rising. "You can't ever duplicate that."

"Why in the hell would I want to duplicate that when I can have something better? You're out of your mind," Jack said, his face reddening.

"Enough. Eddie, we have work to do." I bent down and threw him a shovel. I turned to Jack. "Enough for you, too. Let us get back to work, if you ever want to get a dime out of this place." I made a waving motion toward the stairs.

"Fine. But for the record, I hardly expect a dime from this place. Pennies, maybe," he said.

"Then why the hell did you put up the money?" Eddie said as he threw a charred piece of plaster into the debris pile.

Jack smiled, and ran a gnarled hand through his white hair. "Because it makes me look good."

"You still look like shit," Eddie replied evenly.

"Out!" I shouted to Jack before he finally turned and went down the stairs.

"Good luck with the crap upstairs. Remember to drink lots of water and stay hydrated," he said before he walked out onto the porch.

I could feel Eddie staring at me as I kept my head down, sweeping up bits of plaster. "Not a word," I said.

* * *

Two days later, we had most of the fire debris cleaned out from the upstairs. As the last pile was hauled away in a Dumpster, Traci arrived at the house with Chris. He slowly followed her up the steps, clapping his hands in excitement at the house.

"Is this your house?" he said, his eyes wide.

"Sure is, Chris. And hey, your mom said you might want to help us with some stuff. Is that true?" I asked, my hands on my hips.

"I would like to help," he said quickly. He walked right inside, pushing the door open with one swoop.

"Sorry," Traci said with a smile. "If you can't tell, he's been looking forward to this all week." When we got inside, she lightly touched my arm. "Do you actually have something for him to do? If not, that's totally fine."

"Yup. The fire debris is finally gone, but we still need to sweep out any remaining dust to get everything ready for the ozone machines." I pointed to a collection of mops, brooms, and rags in the corner of the foyer. "Hey, Chris?" I called through the house, but there wasn't an answer.

"He's probably doing a home inspection," Traci muttered as we walked into the living room. We stopped when we saw he was standing in front of the fireplace, staring at the cracked and damaged stones on the floor outside the hearth.

"Yup. Those are broken," I said. "Our crew is going to come in next week and replace those after all the fire damage is repaired." In addition to fixing the windows, painting, refinishing the floors, and many other tasks that I didn't want to list off.

"Rocks. Like the ones I have in my room in my house," he said, his gaze never leaving the fireplace.

"Yes, we have to fix those," I said with a nod. Traci stepped forward to redirect him, but he didn't turn away from the stones.

"My rocks." He pointed to the broken and missing pieces. "My rocks there. We can put my rocks there." He turned and looked at me, his eyes sparkling.

I smiled. "I think that's a great idea. Would that be okay? Do you mind giving us some of your rocks to use? It would be a big help."

"Yes. They would like to go there," he said. He looked back at the fireplace and hummed with happiness.

"You don't have to do that," Traci whispered.

"I want to. That's what this house is—a collection of pieces of the people who came before." I glanced back at the fireplace. "I love the idea."

CHAPTER 39

Eddie and Chris were again hard at work on the house with mops and brooms when I left a week later and went to the hospital to bring Elsie home. As I helped her out of my car, she froze when she saw the cicadas covering her property. They were dotted on the rails of her porch and moving through the grass in her front yard. A couple clung to the screens on her front door. She slowly turned her head to my house and put a hand to her mouth.

"It's just as I remember it." She pointed to the few insects hanging off the porch eaves. "Oh, yes. Mrs. Moore would be out there with a broom, trying to shoo them away from the porch to quiet their racket, but they never listened." Her eyes clouded for a moment, lost in some memory, picturing Mrs. Moore standing on the porch frantically waving her arms.

"We didn't have air-conditioning back then, so they flew inside and couldn't figure out how to get back out. At first, it scared us, but after a couple of days, we would just pluck them off the floor and toss them back out the window." She laughed.

I pointed toward her house. "We should go inside. The reporter from the newspaper will be here soon," I said and she nodded, placing both hands on my forearm.

"And you said she had a small wing-shaped birthmark on her right shoulder?" the reporter, Jill, asked as she furiously wrote notes on a black-and-white composition pad. Her phone was next to her, recording the conversation also. She had just finished surveying the progress on the house, which was coming along quickly due to a near-constant presence of crew members funded by Jack's checks.

Elsie nodded. "It looked like someone had drawn it on her shoulder, it was so distinct." She twisted her hands in her lap. "Would you like more coffee?" she said nervously.

Jill glanced down at her full cup and shook her head. "Oh, no. Thank you." She smiled. "This is a great story, and really adds a human-interest element to the house restoration. We do have a place to start in all of this, so I really hope that the sidebar helps in your search."

"When will it run?" I asked. I had called Jill after her initial visit, and pitched the idea of including a sidebar on Elsie's search for her daughter. She loved the idea.

"Oh, soon. I think. End of the week, beginning of next, barring any breaking stories. And I'd also be interested in turning this piece into a series. Maybe do a follow-up on the new owners, and of course, when you find your daughter," she said.

Elsie smiled and looked at me.

"See? When," I repeated. "Not if."

"When, not if," I muttered into the darkness as I stopped to rub my shoulder. "These floors will be done when, not if." I looked across the expanse of the upstairs, the patches in the wood floor finally done, but the sanding just begun. Due to the delicate nature of the wood, having been sanded down once before already, I was using a hand sander on the entirety. Wood floors could only be sanded down so many times before they became too thin to refinish again. They had just enough juice left for one final refinishing, but I had to be careful and take my time. It had taken me all day to do just one bedroom, and I wasn't sure that my arm wouldn't fall off before I finished the rest.

I wiped the sweat from my forehead with my arm and clicked the sander on again. The pad whirring, I slowly began making concentric circles on the floor, eating away the old stain and damage and leaving beautiful, pristine oak. If I had just stained and refinished the patches to match the existing floor, it would never look right or even. So I was stuck doing the whole thing over again. After the floors were sanded and any stains removed, we would have to seal the wood, buff it, and then apply the varnish. And we would have to do all of that on a day when it wasn't ridiculously humid, a rarity during a Lake Geneva July.

The repairs were moving quickly along, and the house was starting to take on her once-glorious appearance. The end was in sight, and needed to stay that way so we could find a buyer before Jack's contingency clause kicked in.

A flash in the hallway made me jump and nearly sand a divot into the floor. I quickly switched the sander off and stood. The floors didn't need to be any more uneven than they already were.

"Hello? Who's there?" An image of the squatter I'd found in my last house made me grab the nearest weapon: a pointed plaster drivel. It likely wouldn't even break the skin, but it looked threatening despite being only a few inches long. "I said, who's there? This is private property. Get out before I call the police."

I heard footsteps and I lifted the drivel, ready to stab downward, when Matt appeared in the hallway, his palms up.

"It's just me. Don't shoot . . . or stab," he said. He took a step backward. "Or call the police. It's just me," he repeated. "Or would a criminal be more welcome?"

I dropped the drivel, and it clattered to the floor. "Funny. What are you doing here? Where's Abby?" I bit my tongue back from asking if she was with Julia. Mainly because I didn't think I could say her name without scrunching up my nose like I had ingested lemon juice.

"She's with my mom, getting ice cream in town," he said as he slowly looked around the upstairs. "Wow. This place looks great." He slowly moved a palm across the newly plastered walls. "You can't even tell there was a fire here. None of it seems to be damaged at all."

"Well, that's good. I've had about a million crew members here over the past few weeks to make sure that would be the case. You could only find evidence of the damage if you opened up the walls." I reached back and tightened my sweaty pony-tail. "That's the thing, Matt. Some scars are easier to hide than others." I laughed thinly. I meant for it come off as a joke, but my words hung in the air, lightly bouncing off the wood and lath. I thought of the last time we were alone together, in his kitchen, and my heart beat faster.

He didn't respond, but just looked at me with a weary look, like he had run cross-country with a pickup truck on his back. I bit my lip, wondering what he might say. Before he could speak, I blurted out, "Why aren't you with Abby and your mom?"

"I had some business to do at my office, some papers to deliver, so she offered to take her for an hour," he said.

Papers to deliver. I wondered what kind of papers those might be. Good ones? News of a settlement, or maybe a favorable decision? Or maybe it was bad news, like a lawsuit or a divorce. Either way, he might have just been a lawyer, but the things he dealt with were far from the cut-and-dried nature of the law.

He looked down at the manila folder in his hand, something I hadn't noticed before. He extended it toward me. "Here."

"Oh. I didn't realize the delivery was about . . . me." I almost said *us*. "What is this?"

"Open it," he said.

I tore open the envelope, half-expecting to find another legal document pertaining to our marriage, another piece of paper to remind me that we were divorced. But it wasn't about us at all. It was about *it*. The Maple house. I scanned the document, not absorbing what it said. "What? I don't understand. . . ."

He smiled, leaning against the door frame. "It's all legit. As long as the fire damage is repaired, you'll have historical status on the house. Well, provisional status, pending a city council meeting."

"I'm sorry . . . what?" I said.

He simply nodded.

I stood very still, tears threatening to fill my eyes. "How?" I whispered.

"Oh, well. A few of my clients are city council members—who shall go unnamed, by the way—and I spoke to them about your situation. I had some help from some others." His face slightly flushed, but he pressed his mouth into his serious, lawyer face that I had seen so many times.

I looked down at the document again. I reread the words: *The town of Geneva Lake hereby grants the house at 4723 Maple Street provisional historic status.*

"From who? What favors?" I said.

"Oh." He cleared his throat. "I called the historical society. The woman who is the director over there went to our high school and—"

"Shannon," I finished. "She helped me find a photo of the house when I was there a few weeks ago."

He nodded. "She mentioned that. She said that she knew all about you, and the house, and she gave me some key words to use in my appeal to the city council. She said because of the house's age and its period details, it can be qualified as a historical icon. She also said she wanted to help, that you and she had some things in common."

"Yeah, divorce." I laughed. I shook my head slightly, read-

ing the words on the paper again. My eyes welled up, tears
drip-dropping on the paper. I thought of his business. "What
about Waterview? Aren't they going to be pissed off when they
realize it was their own lawyer who undermined their prospect?"

He gave me a half smile and shrugged, his hands outstretched. "Probably."

"Why? Why would you do this?" I said as I quickly wiped
my face on my sleeve and brushed my hair back from my forehead.

He opened his mouth, but no words came out. He lifted his
palms in the air and shrugged slightly. "I thought I could help.
I *wanted* to help."

"Why?" I said again, my voice barely audible.

He looked around the room, considering the walls and the
trim and the floor again. We stood in the tiny room for those
moments, before he said, "Because I know how important it is
to you."

I couldn't think of anything else to say, other than, "Thank
you so much." I looked down at the provision, skimming it
again to make sure I wasn't dreaming.

Jack wouldn't be happy about the historical status, since it
would all but negate the deal with Waterview, but after I calmed
him down with a libation of his choice, I was sure he would understand what it meant: that someone would buy the house that
much more quickly. It was now a certified historic gem, recognized by the town.

"You're welcome." He gave me one more glance before he
turned to walk back down the stairs, the wood creaking underneath his feet. "I'll let you finish sanding." He smiled. "You
know, those floors at the house on Lawn Avenue would have
looked great if you had gotten your hands on them."

If. The word echoed in my head. If only we had lived there
long enough for me to work on them. If only we had stayed to-

gether and restored that house. If only our marriage could have been sanded and stained, all signs of trauma removed.

"If only," I whispered, wishing I could say more, that I could find the words to tell him how I felt, and what I might still want.

As he walked down the stairs, they creaked under his weight and I called down, "Thanks again. And—" My voice faltered and I cleared my throat. "Say hi to Julia for me." As I said it, I realized I truly meant it.

The footsteps stopped. "Oh. Well—"

I held my breath and braced myself for some unpleasant news—that they were taking Abby away together, that things were getting more serious, or maybe, that he was going to propose to her. The air seemed to stand still as I waited for whatever bomb he was about to drop. The stairs creaked again under his weight.

"Sure. Will do," he finally finished before the front door squeaked open and he left.

I exhaled as I walked to the master bedroom and watched in the darkness as he got into his car and drove away. I imagined whatever sensitive news he had, he figured could wait. He would tell me after I allowed the softening of the historical status to set in, so my reaction wouldn't be one of fire and brimstone. Maybe they were getting married and the house was the final gift to me before he started a new life.

I clutched the manila folder in my hand as his headlights illuminated the darkened street before disappearing.

CHAPTER 40

"Restoring History," Traci said triumphantly as she crossed her arms over her chest. The lights of the carousel in the distance bounced off her face as the sun began to go down across the shoreline. We were in Reid Park, near downtown Geneva Lake, at the annual St. Daniel's Festival. Held in mid-August, it was an annual fund-raiser for the local Catholic church, complete with corn dogs, a Ferris wheel, and games rigged to empty the pocketbooks of exhausted parents.

The lights from the games and rides reflected off the lake water and against the bottom of the boats docked on the piers, giving the illusion of fireworks exploding underneath the surface. I settled back against the bench next to Traci and smiled. "Restoring History," I repeated with a smile. "I couldn't have picked a more perfect headline."

The article on my house had run in the *Lake Geneva Regional Newspaper* four days prior, complete with a glamour shot of the almost-finished house. I had staged the outside with potted impatiens, a porch swing, and an antique yellow mailbox next to the door. Of course, the inside of the house wasn't quite as pretty, and we still had a lot of work to do before it was done, but the outside made it look like the crown jewel of the street.

The article detailed my preservation efforts, and outlined the provisional historic status on the property. The photo made the house look even larger than it was, like a warm, welcoming estate just waiting for a family. In the picture, Abby and I sat on the front porch swing, smiling at each other. It was perfect, better than any advertisement I could have run in a real estate catalog or magazine.

"And it's almost done?" she asked.

"Just about," I said. I shook my head slightly as I thought of that day's challenge: Alex versus calcimine paint. I had started to paint the living room a beautiful blue-gray color, and paused for lunch. When I returned, I found the paint beginning to peel and bubble away on the walls. I immediately knew it had to be calcimine. It was a type of paint that was used in the early part of the century that was water-based, and usually made at home. It was inexpensive, so it was attractive, but it had to be washed off before another layer could be applied. As with most things in the house, corners had been cut, so layer upon layer had been painted on, causing a buildup and peeling.

To fix the problem, we had to steam off the old paint and scrape it before we could apply anything new. Of course, we could have just painted over it with an oil-based paint that wouldn't react with the calcimine, but it would likely chip in a year or two. So, the steamer and I were best friends that day.

"How many calls have you gotten about the house so far?" Traci said as she craned her neck before she saw Chris, riding on the carousel next to Abby. His eyes were closed with a smile, his consciousness transported somewhere far away, maybe to a land where he didn't have to sit on a carousel to feel like a part of the world. In contrast, Abby's eyes were wide open as she clutched the gold pole of her white horse as it careened around and around.

"Four. I've gotten four calls about the house," I said with a smile. Every one of the callers had asked that I let them know when it went on the market—or before, if possible—so they could come see it. Two of the calls were from Realtors who had been searching for historic homes for their buyers, but hadn't found anything quite right.

A feeling of warmth moved over my shoulders as I thought of showing the house to the potential buyers, of seeing the looks on their faces as they pictured themselves in the house. Yet as I thought of the moment when I turned over the key, a sadness pricked at my happiness. The house had been a part of my life for the past few months and, like with anything special and important, moving on would be bittersweet.

At least I knew that Jack and I likely wouldn't have to sell to Waterview. The house would remain standing, and I would find a buyer well before my sixty-day deadline.

"You look happy. Finally," Traci said with a smile.

I nodded. "I am. Finally." I looked at Chris again. "He looks happy, too," I said.

She gave me a half smile. "He is. For the moment." She leaned back on the bench and put an arm on the back, shifting toward me, and looking around in the trees. "Cicadas are almost gone."

I nodded. Their numbers had started to dwindle considerably in the past few days, and their deafening buzzes had dulled to low background music. All of the newscasters and papers said that within a week, they would be gone for another seventeen years.

"Seventeen years," she said slowly. "Can you imagine where we'll be the next time they arrive?"

I considered her question as I looked out over the lake. The water was calm, and I could see only two boats out, bobbing in the water. I turned back to her. "No, I can't. But I feel like I'll be . . . okay. For the first time since the divorce, I feel like the future isn't this thing that has to be endured. Feared. Mistrusted, if that makes sense. I feel like there might be hope yet."

She nodded. "I get it." She looked at Chris again and smiled. "Thank you so much for letting him help on the house. He really loved it, and it gave a sense of purpose to his day."

"Of course. He was a hard worker. We'd love to have him back on the next project." Even though Eddie or I had to repeat instructions to him a few different times, and in very simple terms, Chris worked harder than most of the crew. He was always the last to drop the broom, and the first to arrive on-site.

"You know, we came up with a plan for him. For when we're gone. We found this really great living situation." She looked down and laughed. "Let's call it what it is—a group home. But a good one. One where he'll be safe and have friends. Shit, that's all we want, you know?"

I nodded and gave her a sympathetic look.

"Me, too," I said quietly.

"What about Elsie? Any hits on that situation?" Traci asked. The carousel came to a stop and we rose, waiting for Chris and Abby at the exit. His large frame lumbered next to her, as he clapped his hands and hummed while walking over to us. She skipped along with him, eventually grabbing his hand and leading him toward us.

"No. Nothing yet," I said with a frown as I reached for Abby. A sidebar had accompanied the article, like we had asked, but it hadn't gotten us any closer to finding Elsie's daughter. While I had received calls on the house, the phone was silent on Elsie's daughter.

"What do you guys want to do next?" Traci asked Abby and Chris.

"Funnel cake! Funnel cake!" she said and gave a little bounce up and down.

"Funnel cake! Funnel cake!" Chris repeated.

We followed the overpowering sugary smells of the funnel cakes and patiently stood in line for one of the sticky, dense creations sprinkled with powdered sugar.

Abby barely sat down at a picnic table before she stuck her

fingers into the center and began pulling it apart. Chris slowly began to dismantle his, Traci carefully watching and hovering over his shoulder.

"Slow down," I said to Abby.

She wiggled sticky white fingers at me. "Help," she said.

"Napkins," I muttered as I glanced over my shoulder toward the other food vendors. "One second. Don't move." I grabbed a stack of napkins off the corn dog stand and headed back toward our table. My eyes flashed to the beer truck, and were about to return to Abby when a familiar flash of blond hair made me stop, causing a couple behind me to nearly run into my back. "Sorry," I muttered to them as I tried to quickly look away from the truck, but it was too late.

Julia pretended that she didn't see me, either, and turned her back toward a group of attractive friends, all varying copies of her. They were dressed in bright pinks and greens and wore white jeans with metallic wedge heels. Long, sparkly earrings dangled to their tanned shoulders, and they clutched plastic cups of wine with perfectly painted nails.

I thought of Matt's olive branch, and took a deep breath. "Hang here," I said to Traci as I walked over to Julia and her friends. They pretended they didn't see me until I was practically on top of them, a comically awkward avoidance strategy.

"I don't want to bother you, or intrude, but I just wanted to come over and say hello," I said.

Julia gave me a questioning look before she slowly nodded. She looked over my shoulder and waved to Abby at the picnic table. "I'm sure she's having fun here." Her tone was measured, cautious.

"She is. Like I said, I don't want to bother you. . . ." I trailed off, but none of her friends so much as smiled. "Although it seems that I am, so I'll get out of here." I turned to leave, my face flushing in discomfort.

"Good luck with the house," she said.

I turned back. "Thanks. Matt's help really made a lot of difference."

At the mention of Matt, Julia's friends all looked at each
other before turning their collective, angry gaze on me. Julia
looked like she had been slapped, and then her eyes narrowed.
"I'm sure it did." She turned her back to me, leaving me on the
outside of the circle.

I was about to walk away, but the irritation building in my
chest made me tap her on the shoulder. "I'm sorry, did I miss
something?"

"I guess so. See you around," she said without turning back.

What was that about? I thought as I walked back to Traci. I
rolled my eyes and shook my head when she asked me what
happened.

"So, what else? More rides, or should we head out?" I said
brightly before she could ask any more questions.

She looked down at Chris, whose eyes were glazed over as
he looked at the ride. "Maybe head home."

I nodded as my phone beeped. I pulled it out and saw that I
had a new e-mail. It was from Jill Springform. A forward, from
a woman named Corrine Griffin. As I scanned the text of her e-
mail, my hand began to shake.

I glanced up at Traci, my eyes wide. "We might have
found her."

"Who?" she said without looking up as she wiped Chris's
hands.

"Elsie's daughter. A woman named Corrine e-mailed the reporter. She thinks she might be her. Same birthday, geographic
match, and—get this—she has a wing-shaped birthmark on her
shoulder." My voice broke and I shook my head.

Traci dropped the napkin in Chris's lap. "You're kidding."

I reread the e-mail again and smiled. "I'm going to call her in
the morning. I'm going to make sure it's her, and then I'll tell
Elsie."

She put her hands on her hips. "Wow. That's amazing."

I put my phone in my back pocket and leaned down and gave Abby a hug. "Should we do one more time on the carousel?" I whispered.

She shrieked and grabbed Chris's hand, and they ran toward the spinning horses, happily handing over their tickets and climbing aboard.

As Traci and I watched them spin around and shriek in delight, a cicada landed on the bench next to us.

"See you again in seventeen years, buddy," I said as I plucked it off the wood and held it in the air until it took flight and disappeared somewhere over the lake.

CHAPTER 41

I watched as Eddie threw the paintbrush down into the tray. He stepped back and put his hands on his hips, surveying the dining room. I had chosen a light blue for the room, to accent the beautifully restored woodwork, finally free of all that white paint. It was the last room to be painted, and Eddie just needed to touch up a few spots.

"Boss?" he said without turning around.

"I love it," I whispered. I could see, in my mind's eye, a cherry dining table in the center of the room. A china cabinet would fit on the wall across from the giant window, six feet tall by three feet wide. The newly restored leaded-glass doors on the built-in buffet waited for glassware to be placed inside. The pewter and wrought-iron chandelier in the center of the room perfectly fit with the original woodwork. I had bought the chandelier years ago at a garage sale, intending to use it in my old house with Matt. I couldn't think of a better Plan B place to hang it.

Eddie turned and smiled, saluting me. "Same here." He looked around and whistled. "She's a beaut, that's for sure. Not so much when we got her, though."

272 / Maureen Leurck

I slowly walked through the dining room into the kitchen, gleaming with refinished cabinets, butcher-block countertops and an island with four stools. Frank, the electrician, had hung two pendant lights over the island that I fitted with Edison bulbs. Since there really wasn't anything we could salvage from the previous kitchen, I used it as a modern space, incorporating everything that any home buyer would look for today.

I pictured two, maybe three, kids sitting at the island, scarfing down breakfast as their parents frantically made coffee and packed lunches before school.

In the living room, I swept my hand across the wall, where I imagined someone might place a couch, across from the wood-burning fireplace. Chris's rocks were sunk in the floor of the hearth, ready for their first fire. We had hung a new mantle, since the old one was too singed after the fire, but before we did so, Eddie, myself, his crew, Abby, and Chris all signed our names on the wall behind it.

I eyed the corner where the Moores used to put their Christmas tree, and thought about how the multicolored lights would bounce against the detailed plaster trim along the ceiling that had thankfully survived not just the past century, but the recent flood and fire. I had painted that room a warm gray, a touch of modern style to complement the historic elements. The wood trim around the original windows gleamed with linseed oil polish that showed off the beautiful variations in the wood.

Upstairs, the four bedrooms had wood floors, and new paint (and plaster, electrical work, plumbing, and just about everything else). The two bathrooms had pedestal sinks and subway tile, with wood trim around the doors. I was able to find wood doors for each room at a resale place, along with antique doorknobs. I would have dared anyone to guess that the pieces weren't original to the house.

Before I walked outside, I gave one last glance to the staircase, stained a deep brown and also free from layers of paint and shellac, and took a deep breath. Eddie followed me.

"So, is this it?" he said. Before I could answer, he squinted across the lawn and put a hand to his ear. "Hear that?" I shook my head. "Nothing. They're gone. The cicadas are finally all gone."

I cocked my head to the side and listened. Their buzzing and chirping had grown quieter with each passing day, with more crawling back into the earth to begin another seventeen-year slumber. "You're right. It's over. It's amazing how quickly I got used to their sound. And now, it's like they were never here. They're gone."

"As am I." Eddie turned to me. "Well, boss, on to the next one, right? Any idea what that will be?"

I shook my head. "Not sure yet. I need to get this one on the market and then figure out my plans." I rolled my eyes slightly. "And see what kind of profit I have left over after I have to split it with Jack." I wasn't about to tell Eddie that I had already spotted a few historic properties in nearby Burlington, each one in worse condition than the Maple house. I figured I could give him a few days of rest and serenity before he wanted to bang his head against the wall.

"Don't give that snake a dime." He laughed. "I'm going to grab my stuff and then get out of here."

I nodded and stayed on the porch. I slowly went over and sat on the porch swing, gently pushing my feet against the light blue–painted porch floor. As I waved good-bye to Eddie, I stayed, swinging on the porch.

I inhaled the deep scent of the rosebushes that surrounded the porch, and the roses that once again climbed up the arbor in the backyard. I closed my eyes and could feel the peace running through the house, through the wood floors and up the plaster walls.

I stood, and pulled the heavy wooden front door closed, rubbing a tiny spot out of the leaded-glass transoms. I put the key in the lock and turned until I heard a *click*. I gave it one last glance before I got into my car, tears pricking my eyes.

My work was done. The house was ready.

CHAPTER 42

I drove the *For Sale* sign into the ground, giving it a hard shove with my shoulder until I felt it sink into the dirt. I stood back, admiring the way it looked in front of the house. It was the moment that I had dreamed of since I bought it, yet it was still sad to think of letting it go. It was similar to what I felt on Abby's first day of kindergarten. Pride mixed with the emptiness of letting go. Bittersweet in the sharpest, most beautiful way.

I turned to Elsie's house, and she gave me an encouraging smile. Her arm was healing and had been placed in a brace. She was once again dressed in bright colors, beautiful inside and out, just like the house. On that morning, she wore a Kelly green pantsuit and gold jewelry, with a lapel pin in the shape of a peacock. I smiled as I thought of her as the peacock, showing off her extraordinary feathers.

I started to walk over to her house, but stopped when I saw a silver Audi pull into the driveway. The woman behind the wheel had short blond hair and a square jawline. Even while wearing sunglasses, I could tell that she was Elsie's daughter, Corrine. I knew that she and Elsie had spoken, but I didn't realize they would be meeting so soon.

Corrine got out of the car slowly, and I could see her hand shaking as she closed the car door. She didn't take her glasses off, but stopped when she saw Elsie, her hands dropping to her sides. I watched as a million different emotions flashed across her face. Shock. Sadness. Confusion. Surprise.

Elsie slowly rose, her legs wobbling. I stepped forward instinctually to help her, but stopped. This was their moment, not mine. So I remained on the lawn, an observer.

Corrine walked up to the porch, and I saw them grasp hands and then slowly embrace. They sat down on her front porch, their knees touching in intimate conversation.

I walked back to my house, and sat on the porch swing. I occasionally glanced back at them, and saw each wipe their eyes at times. Finally, Elsie and Corrine rose and walked over to me. I met them on the front yard, near the *For Sale* sign.

"And this is her," Elsie said as she pointed to me. "She's the one who did all of this. She made this all possible." She looked up at the house and then to her daughter.

Corrine met my eyes, and it nearly took my breath away when I saw that she had the same aquamarine-blue eyes that sparkled when I had heard Elsie describe David.

"Thank you," she said, her voice breaking. "I'm not sure what else to say but . . . thank you." She turned back toward Elsie, who put her hand on hers. She looked up at the house and smiled. "It's beautiful."

"It was your father's," Elsie said simply.

"Would you like to see the backyard?" I said.

As we walked around the house, Elsie smiled and said, "Corrine has two sons, A.J. and Patrick."

"You're a grandmother." Corrine smiled at Elsie. She turned to me. "They're seventeen and twenty, and act every bit their age."

"Two sons. What a wonderful blessing. A family," Elsie said.

"Well, I suppose it's your family now, too," Corrine said.

I saw Elsie swallow hard, and she brushed at her eyes as she nodded. "That's what I've always wanted."

My chest tight with emotion, I stopped in front of the maple tree in the backyard and pointed to the carvings on the back. Corrine leaned forward and traced the letters *E.S.* and *D.M.* "Elsie and David," she said. She turned to me. "It's like something out of a movie. Lost love, a child. A reunion."

I smiled. "Like a storybook."

Elsie and Corrine went into her house for lunch, and I remained at my house. They invited me in, but I knew they needed time alone, and I also had to wait for Matt to drop off Abby.

I swung on the swing, back and forth, back and forth, watching the butterflies flit around the hydrangeas, and the bumblebees lumber around the roses, before I saw the Yukon pull into the driveway. I stood and outstretched my arms, pulling Abby toward me as she came flying up the restored front porch steps, her hair streaming behind her like a ribbon.

"Mommy, can I swing on the porch swing?" she asked when I set her down.

"Of course." I was about to sit down next to her, when I noticed Matt was still standing on the driveway, leaning toward his car but facing me. "I'll be there in one minute," I said to Abby before I walked down the steps.

"Alex, the house looks . . ." He trailed off as he craned his neck upward, shielding his eyes from the sun. I noticed the same gold glint in the center of his eyes, the shimmer that I had once studied all those years before. "Unbelievable," he finished.

I glanced back at it, and the same familiar feeling of pride ran down my arms to my fingertips. "Thanks." I turned back to him. "And thanks again for your help, with the historical status."

"You're welcome. Do you think it'll help sell the house?" he said. He leaned back against his car and shoved his hands into the pockets of his tan khaki shorts. I noticed he was dressed more casually than I had seen in a while, in an old Gordy's ball cap, blue T-shirt, and flip-flops.

I nodded. "I do. I think whoever buys it will appreciate what it means." I crossed my arms over my chest. "So, what happened with Waterview? Anything?"

"Oh. Well, they weren't thrilled when they heard through the grapevine that I might have helped you," he said.

"And?" I pressed.

"They said they would be taking their business to another firm," he said. He shoved his hands in his pockets and gave a half shrug.

"Oh, man. I'm so sorry. I know that they were your big client," I said. I shook my head. Matt had once told me that they represented some huge percentage of his business, and I couldn't imagine what losing them would do to his bottom line. "I'm so sorry," I said again.

He nodded. "Well, can I see it? The house, I mean," he said.

I stood up straight in surprise. "Well, sure." We walked from room to room, as I explained what I did to each space. He didn't say much, just nodded and looked around with his eyes wide. Abby trailed at our heels, twirling through the house and sweeping her arms around like she was Miss America walking down the runway.

When we reached the backyard, she ran down the steps of the deck and began to smell the roses around Elsie and David's maple tree. Through Elsie's kitchen window, I could see her and Corrine seated around her table, coffee cups in front of them.

"Will it be hard for you to sell it?" Matt asked.

I turned to him in surprise, but he didn't look at me. His gaze was on Abby, down on the lawn. "I hope not."

"I don't mean it like that. I mean, will it be hard for you to let it go?" He turned to me slightly, and I could see his mouth was twitching down, like it always did when he was nervous.

"Probably." I took a long, deep breath. "But it's time. It's time for its next family. For its second chance to be a home."

A wind swept through the backyard and lifted my hair off my neck and across my face. Matt reached forward to brush a strand of hair away from my cheek but stopped quickly. He put his hand in his pocket and looked down.

"Alex, I—"

The sound of my own blood rushing through my ears became nearly deafening, and my heart started to pound so hard I could see the front of my shirt moving.

"I know that I don't deserve, well, anything from you," he said, his voice shaking, "but I was wondering if you ever thought about us. If you ever thought about being together again."

Yes, I wanted to say. *Yes, I think about it all the time.*

He slowly reached out and his fingertips brushed against my right hand, on the finger where I used to wear the gold band. "You took it off," he said quietly.

"What about Julia?" I said as I pulled my hand back. I felt my face flush, and I swallowed hard, taking a quick step back from him.

He looked at me in surprise, his eyebrows raised. "We broke up a few weeks ago. It just—" He stopped and shook his head. "We were better as friends."

"Well, that's a bullshit answer. What really happened?" I said.

He gave me a knowing look. "She wasn't thrilled that I was helping you with the historical status. Gave me an ultimatum, actually. And, well, here we are." He outstretched his arms in a half shrug.

I didn't know what to say. I felt as though the last five years were compressed into one moment, a point of light in the future that I had been moving toward without knowing. Like looking through a telescope at a distant star, and finding out that it looked very different than anyone ever thought.

We had grown up together, and then away from each other. We moved toward different lights, willingly or not. And yet here he was, reaching back across the divide in an invitation.

It wasn't my choice leading us to separation, but now it was mine to come together.

He moved his hand toward me, holding his palm out, waiting. I swallowed hard before I slowly placed my fingers in his hand. His hand closed around mine, and I took a step toward him. The hair on the back of my neck pricked with the familiarity of his body. I knew exactly where to rest my head as he wrapped his arms around me. It was the same embrace that we had shared since we were teenagers, the closeness remaining the same despite all the sharp edges that life had chiseled away, despite all the things we had done to each other, and for each other. The things we had done to get away from each other.

I closed my eyes and inhaled deeply, feeling a sense of calm settle in my bones. For the first time in a long time, I knew exactly what we were supposed to be to each other.

He kissed the side of my head, and whispered something that I couldn't make out, but I knew it was his attempt at an apology. It would never take the past five years away, of course, but it was the start of a new beginning.

"Can we start over?" he said into my shoulder.

"No," I said. "We can't start over." I felt him loosen his grip. "But we can keep going." He pulled me back into him, tighter than before.

"Say it," I said to him.

"Everything will be okay, I promise," he said with a laugh.

I shook my head against his chest. "You can't promise that, neither of us can. But we can try."

We broke apart as Abby shrieked in delight across the yard.

"Mommy! Look! I found a cicada shell." She held the small, translucent shell in the air, left over from when the cicadas returned to the ground. The delicate shell nearly crumbled in her hand, but she cupped her fingers around it to protect it from the breeze.

"A cicada summer," I whispered as I intertwined my fingers with Matt's.

CHAPTER 43

Four months later

"Did you fix it?" I poked my head out the front door of my house, the icy air hitting me in the face. I squinted into the darkness, out onto the front porch. Snow was beginning to fall, blanketing the neighborhood in a sugary dusting of sparkling snowflakes. The wind picked up, whipping the snowflakes around the front yard in a gentle wave.

I pulled my black sweater tighter around my waist as I stepped out onto the porch. "Everything okay?" I called.

The white twinkle lights around the evergreen garland moved in response, snow falling off the green needles. "Yes. Just fixed it." Matt's head popped up onto the porch as he secured the Christmas decoration to the porch ledge. He dusted off his bare hands, flexing them in the cold, and then jogged up the salted front steps, careful to step in the spots where the ice had melted.

I glanced back at the garland and smiled before I followed him into the house. It looked just as I had envisioned it. I had tried to re-create the photo from 1947 of the house illuminated by the white lights and evergreen boughs, with red bows at the tip of each swoop. In the front picture window stood a Christmas tree, with multicolored lights and homemade ornaments courtesy of some flour, salt, water, and Abby's creativity.

I stood in the foyer, listening to the sounds of the holiday party throughout the house. I could hear Abby's shrieks of delight from the back room, where she played with some of the neighborhood kids. I listened to the clinks of ice falling into glasses as people poured libations from the quarter-sawn oak bar, with the background music of Bing Crosby crooning about chestnuts and an open fire. A roaring fire crackled in the wood-burning fireplace, happily licking away at two fire logs. Chris stood guard near the fireplace, proudly pointing out his rocks to anyone near, and regaling them with tales of how he helped fix the house.

It was perfect. It was home.

In the end, I couldn't let the house go. I got several offers on the house soon after it hit the MLS listings, but after Matt and I reconciled, I realized that I had been restoring the house for us. For Abby. I sold the ranch house that Abby and I lived in, and used the proceeds to pay back Jack Sullivan. Matt also sold his house in Geneva National, and we used the money to pay down the mortgage on the Maple house. His business had slowed down considerably after he lost Waterview as a client, so he moved to a smaller office, but the upside was that he wasn't working a dead man's hours like he used to.

The house's plaster walls, finally smooth after hours of patching cracks, boasted photos of our family. The built-ins carefully protected the glassware my mother had passed down to me before she moved to Florida, and the claw-foot tub was Abby's each night for her bath. One of the bedrooms was an office for me—finally, I had an office space other than my bed. The other bedroom was for storage. For now. We would see what the future brought.

I walked into the dining room, where I had set up a cheese platter, meatballs, and mini egg rolls. I lifted a finger to Eddie, who was in the corner with Janie, who was unsuccessfully trying to contain Mia. She was nine months old, and desperate to crawl all around the wood floors and chew on any stray evergreen needles.

"We start back on Monday," I called to him with a smile. The week before, I had purchased another historic house at auction, in nearby Twin Lakes. It was a three-bedroom, two-bathroom Queen Anne Victorian with lots of charm and even more cat urine.

He lifted his beer in response, and then took a long swig. "I'm gonna need about six more of these in order to make that prospect less terrifying."

"You're so dramatic," I said to him with a wave.

"Feral cat colony. Feral cat colony," he called. "You've lost your mind with this one, boss."

"You always say that." I gestured my hand around the room, not acknowledging that when I first entered the house, I nearly fell over from the smell. "And look where we are. A little faith, please."

Eddie didn't respond, but looked over my shoulder. "Matt," he said in greeting.

"Nice to see you, Eddie," Matt said evenly.

Eddie shot me a look, and I shook my head. "And you, as well," Eddie said reluctantly.

"Behave, you two," I said as I turned my back and scanned the room. I spotted Elsie and Corrine, standing in the corner, nibbling at bacon-wrapped dates that Abby had painstakingly assembled and placed a toothpick inside.

"Is the snow still coming down out there?" Corrine asked as she tried to peer out the window.

I nodded. "They're saying we're supposed to get over six inches." I smiled. "Looks like it will be a white Christmas this year."

"A cicada summer and then a snowy holiday." She laughed. "Nothing like living in the Midwest."

I noticed that as she laughed, her blue eyes crinkled around the corners in the same way that Elsie's did. The two of them had stayed in touch, and after I moved into the house, I saw her visit Elsie frequently, the two of them sitting on the front porch, slowly rocking on the glider with iced tea in front of them. As summer became fall, their short sleeves turned into sweaters, and the iced tea became cider. And since the winter had blown in, they had moved into the kitchen, steaming mugs placed in their hands.

Sometimes I would see Corrine's sons with her, dressed in T-shirts and jeans, doing odd jobs around the house. There was always activity at the house, with lights on everywhere. It was as though it had come alive again, much in the way that my house had, too.

The first night I spent in the house, with Matt next to me, and Abby across the hallway, I couldn't sleep. I stared at the white beadboard ceiling, trying to understand how I had gotten to where I was. How I had moved so quickly into forgiveness and grace. And then I realized that with every hole that I patched, with every floor that I sanded, I was working on me. On my own life.

I had saved the house, but it had rescued me right back.

"Mom, can we bring out the cookies?" Abby flew through the house, her red dress smudged with dust. She hopped up and down in front of me in her white tights, the bottom of her feet gray and black.

I glanced outside at the snow coming down, more steadily than before. "Sure. People might want to leave soon before it gets bad out there."

"Yippee!" She scampered off, a trail of kids behind her, toward the kitchen to pillage the remaining treats. Matt followed, happy to have a reason to escape Eddie's gaze. He walked past my parents and his, who were gathered around the makeshift bar on the built-in buffet and laughing a bit too loudly to chalk up to holiday cheer.

A moment later, Matt reappeared next to me. He handed me a glass of red wine. "Did you say she could eat five cookies?"

I laughed. "Not exactly." I took a sip of the wine, feeling it warm my body almost instantly.

He put an arm around my shoulders and kissed my cheek. I took a deep breath and looked around the house. Every corner was filled with laughter, conversation, and light. Finally, it was alive again.

And so was I.

ACKNOWLEDGMENTS

This book would not exist if it weren't for the wonderful encouragement of my agent, Holly Root, who gave me faith that this book might be The One. Thank you for believing in it, and in me. And thank you to my fabulous editor, Esi Sogah, who said "yes" and gave me brilliant editorial guidance along the way. Thank you to the whole team over at Kensington, for their hard work, humor, and dedication. You guys are truly an author's dream team.

To the people of Lake Geneva and the surrounding areas: Thank you for sharing your beautiful home with me. I hope I did it justice. Your towns will always have a special place in my heart, and hold some of my favorite childhood memories.

Thank you also to the television shows *This Old House* and *Rehab Addict* for informing me on all things historic-house-related. I'm not kidding when I say that learning how to reglaze old windows was a joy. Restoring an older home definitely remains a bucket list item for me.

I am forever grateful for the support of my family, the whole Kilmer-Lipinski crew and beyond. I'm thankful for each and every one of you, and for giving me endless book material (ahem, old babysitters). And thank you to the entire extended Leurck family, each of whom has been a wonderful blessing in my life. Big thanks also to all of my friends, both old and new (especially Jill Cantor, recipient of far too many panicked e-mails), who supported me through the writing of this book. Without your pep talks, excitement, and offers of child care, this book would still be half finished.

And of course, thank you to my children: Ryan, Paige, and

Jake, who napped, played together, and likely had far too much screen-time while I was writing this book. Thank you for always keeping me humble, making me laugh, and reminding me that the small things in life are truly the best things. Finally, thank you to my husband, Kevin, for always supporting my dreams, encouraging me in my darkest moments, and for always believing that I could.

Keep reading for a
behind-the-book essay
and reader discussion questions
from Maureen Leurck.

A Peek Behind the Book

The inspiration behind *Cicada Summer* began with the setting. The Lake Geneva area is very dear to my heart, and this book is my love letter to the lake. The sparkling water, whitewashed piers, and brightly colored sailboats that dot the lakeshore in the summer are all images that are sewn into the fabric of my childhood.

From before I could remember, my family rented a charmingly "rustic" cottage in the Lake Geneva area, in nearby Powers Lake, for one week a year. By rustic, I mean air-conditioning was a pipe dream, spiders shared every corner, and a trip to the water meant a dangerous trek down a comically steep flight of rickety wooden stairs. One year, I slept on a box spring because the previous renter had burned down the mattress. The only television we had was a small black-and-white model without any volume control, so nights were spent catching lightning bugs and falling asleep to the white noise of the late summer cicadas. The summer of the famous seventeen-year cicadas was even less comfortable, by all standards. While all of this might seem less than picture perfect, as a child, it was my favorite week of the year.

The moment we would arrive at the cottage, I would sprint out of the car toward the water, and I would rarely return inside before dusk. Long summer days were spent lying on the pier and hunting for minnows with a net bought at the local drugstore, as the sound of boats and WaveRunners hummed in the distance. Being a small lake, it was affected by yearly rainfall, so some years it was shallow, some years it was deep. As my own preteen awkwardness turned into teenage petulance, the lake still rose and fell with the rain, and froze every winter just after the piers were taken out and stacked by the water's edge.

When I was thirteen, the owner chose to stop renting. By then, I was in high school and relieved to move on from the cottage that I didn't find quite as charming anymore. It was only when I became an adult that I realized how much I missed it, spiders and all. I'm sure if we went back today, my experiences wouldn't be quite so rose-colored, and for that I am thankful. My summers spent at the lake lie preserved and tucked away in the most secure of memory blankets, safe from the scrutinizing light of the present.

A major theme of *Cicada Summer* is second chances, and the opportunity for renewal. Even though I never got a second chance to go back to the cottage, I bring my kids to the area often. They have fallen in love with the lakes as I did. To see a piece of my childhood through their eyes, to watch and hear their delighted screams as they jump (arms outstretched like a starfish) into the water, is a glimpse of my past. And a wonderful second chance to experience a perfect piece of my childhood.

CICADA SUMMER

Maureen Leurck

ABOUT THIS GUIDE

The suggested questions are included to enhance
your group's reading of Maureen Leurck's
Cicada Summer.

DISCUSSION QUESTIONS

1. A major theme in the book is the idea of second chances and renewal. What characters have the opportunity for a second chance by the end of the book?

2. How would you describe Elsie? How would you describe the relationship between Alex and Elsie?

3. Do you think that Alex made the right decision in divorcing Matt over his flirtation with a coworker, or do you feel that she overreacted?

4. Since her divorce, Alex has been unable to fully let go of Matt. In what ways did her lingering feelings present themselves? What clues did Matt give that he was also feeling the same way?

5. Why do you think that Alex is drawn to old houses? What do they represent to her?

6. Do you view Alex as a strong character? Why or why not?

7. What does the relationship with Elsie bring to Alex's life? How does it change her?

8. When Alex begins to date Gavin, it is the first time that she feels romantic about someone after her divorce. Do you feel that she made the right choice in breaking up with Gavin?

9. Why do you think that Elsie asked Alex for help? What did she see in Alex that made her believe she was the person to help?

10. Alex has a very strong connection to her hometown of Lake Geneva. How does this affect her decisions and choices?

11. How would you describe Alex's relationship with her parents? What about her relationship with her former in-laws? How does this inform her decisions?

12. Have you ever had your own second chance? If so, how did you handle it?

Connect with U s

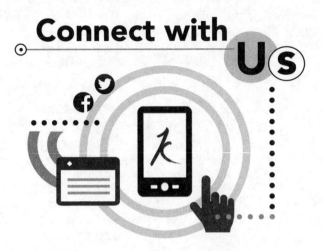

Visit us online at
KensingtonBooks.com
to read more from your favorite authors, see books
by series, view reading group guides, and more.

for sneak peeks, chances to win books and prize packs,
and to share your thoughts with other readers.

f 🐦

facebook.com/kensingtonpublishing
twitter.com/kensingtonbooks

Tell us what you think!

To share your thoughts, submit a review,
or sign up for our eNewsletters, please visit:
KensingtonBooks.com/TellUs.